ARON BEAUREGARD'S
NIGHTMARE NIRVANA

Copyright © 2022 Aron Beauregard

All rights reserved.

ISBN: 9798609374486

Cover by Zack Dunn

Interior Illustrations by Stefan Ljumov

Cover Wrap Design by Don Noble

Edited by Patrick C. Harrison III & Laura Wilkinson

Printed in the USA

Maggot Press
Coventry, Rhode Island

WARNING:
This book contains scenes and subject matter that are disgusting and disturbing, easily offended people are not the intended audience

JOIN MY MAGGOT MAILING LIST NOW
FOR EXCLUSIVE OFFERS AND UPDATES BY EMAILING
AronBeauregardHorror@gmail.com

WWW.EVILEXAMINED.COM

Jack,

I hope you enjoy this one my friend!

DEDICATION

While this book isn't necessarily for children, it is the kind of thing I would have been drawn to as a child. With that in mind, I would like to dedicate this work to my childhood favorites; Alvin Schwartz, Stephen Gammell, R.L. Stine, Christopher Pike, Kelly O'Rourke, amongst the countless others that warped the minds of teenagers throughout the 80s & 90s. This book doesn't exist without you, I love you all.

Thank you to my lovely wife, Katie, for taking countless hours and listening to me talk about these fucked up stories, your love and guidance are infinitely appreciated.

And last but not least, Mom, for buying those creepy books for me as a kid. I know we didn't have a ton of money growing up (and still, haha) but I never would have been able to read them without you. I love you. You and Ron are responsible for any success that comes from this.

THE RED WIDOW
1

ONE NIGHT STAND
13

SPEAK NOW
22

THE CAROUSEL
29

UPPER DECKER
41

THE REWARD
59

THE JIGGLE JOINT
66

SHAFTED
75

DAD'S NEW GUN
82

BAKE SALE
88

INGROUND POOL
94

THE OLD TRUCK
99

THE LAST ILLUSION
104

HOT CAR
114

CAPTAIN HUNT
116

TIMMY'S TEETH
121

WHEN THE PHONE RINGS
130

THE RETIREMENT MATCH
144

ACKNOWLEDGMENTS

I want to give immense thanks and praise to Stefan Ljumov. Without his creativity and vision to project these ghastly and macabre images from my stories, this book doesn't exist. He was able to let himself go and tap into the abstract and nightmarish spirit of these tales. The finished products are the beautifully chilling black and white interior images that you see littered throughout this vile collection. We worked tirelessly on this project for well over a year to bring you something different. Something that, when browsed through, will transport the reader into a different world. This man has a dark gift that I'm deeply excited to share with you all.

Also, to the evil painting of Zack Dunn for allowing me to purchase his work of art, "The Red Widow," and use it as the cover for Nightmare Nirvana. It's the perfect face for what I aimed to present to my readers. His beautiful nightmare served as the inspiration for the story "The Red Widow," and the painting now hangs in my living room as a reminder of the dreadful horror we've brought forth together.

THE RED WIDOW

Tom wasn't sure what was in the middle of the street when he initially slowed his vehicle. From the far corner of his eye, he could've sworn he saw a piece of roadkill, but something inside told him to stop. As he edged in a little closer, he noticed a long-tanned strap that lay coiled on the ground like a dead snake. The beaten leather purse looked like it had been through hell, riddled with rips and portions that were on the verge of total deterioration.

As he quickly snatched up the intriguing shabby handbag, he cringed, contemplating the hordes of disgusting germs potentially encompassing it. His curiosity got the better of him, outweighing his hygienically propped-up logic by far. He pried the metallic snaps open and peered inside cautiously, half expecting some kind of mangled rodent to leap out at him. To Tom's surprise, the contents seemed quite orderly in contrast to the purse's outer appearance.

"Surprise, surprise," he mumbled to himself, still knowing that he was going to take a look inside regardless.

He reached inside and pulled out the only two items it contained—a woman's wallet and a tiny moleskin journal. He removed the elastic lace that kept it shut and spread the spine. The only writing the book contained seemed to be a meticulous list of various upcoming doctor appointments. With nothing to jostle his interest, he turned his attention to the contents of the wallet—a handful of medical cards, and mixed amongst them, a driver's license. The woman in the square photo projected a captivating, white-toothed grin. Her delight was surrounded by a vibrant red lipstick and what Tom felt was an arousing curly mane.

While he was a tad disappointed that he hadn't found any money or valuables, the gorgeous woman seemed more intriguing than making a quick buck. Elena Dragos, as the laminated identification card read, lived at 66 Carver Avenue.

That's only a few blocks over! I can just go there and give it back to her, then I can see her in the flesh! I bet her body is even more heavenly than her face, Tom imagined, becoming overstimulated by the idea.

Tom hopped back in his station wagon and tossed the old bag on the passenger seat. He took off with a purpose. Seeing the woman in the photo was the most exciting thing to happen to him in some time. The dating game hadn't been kind to him, but maybe that would change soon.

Maybe after returning her belongings, she would see what a kind man he was, and demand to see him again in the future. An invitation would be more than welcome, but worst-case scenario, he would at least get a clear gawk at her splendor.

As he pulled into the freshly-paved and winding tar driveway, his heart raced, mimicking the wheels beneath him. He appreciated that Elena's house was one of the nicer ones in the area—a multi-level, spacious structure plopped upon a mass of lively real estate. Oaks and Arborvitae bushes served as a fence of nature that bordered the grounds, butted up against the tall and sharp steel-bar barrier that encased the entire property.

Still, something was unsettling about the well-maintained colonial-style home, but he couldn't put his finger on what made him feel off about it. Tom wandered tentatively up the marble steps and shook himself free of any apprehension as he pressed the black doorbell. He fidgeted uncomfortably as he waited and waited and waited.

Having stood idle for some time already, he pressed the ringer again. Just as his finger left the button, the door came open. Standing on the other side was not at all what he expected.

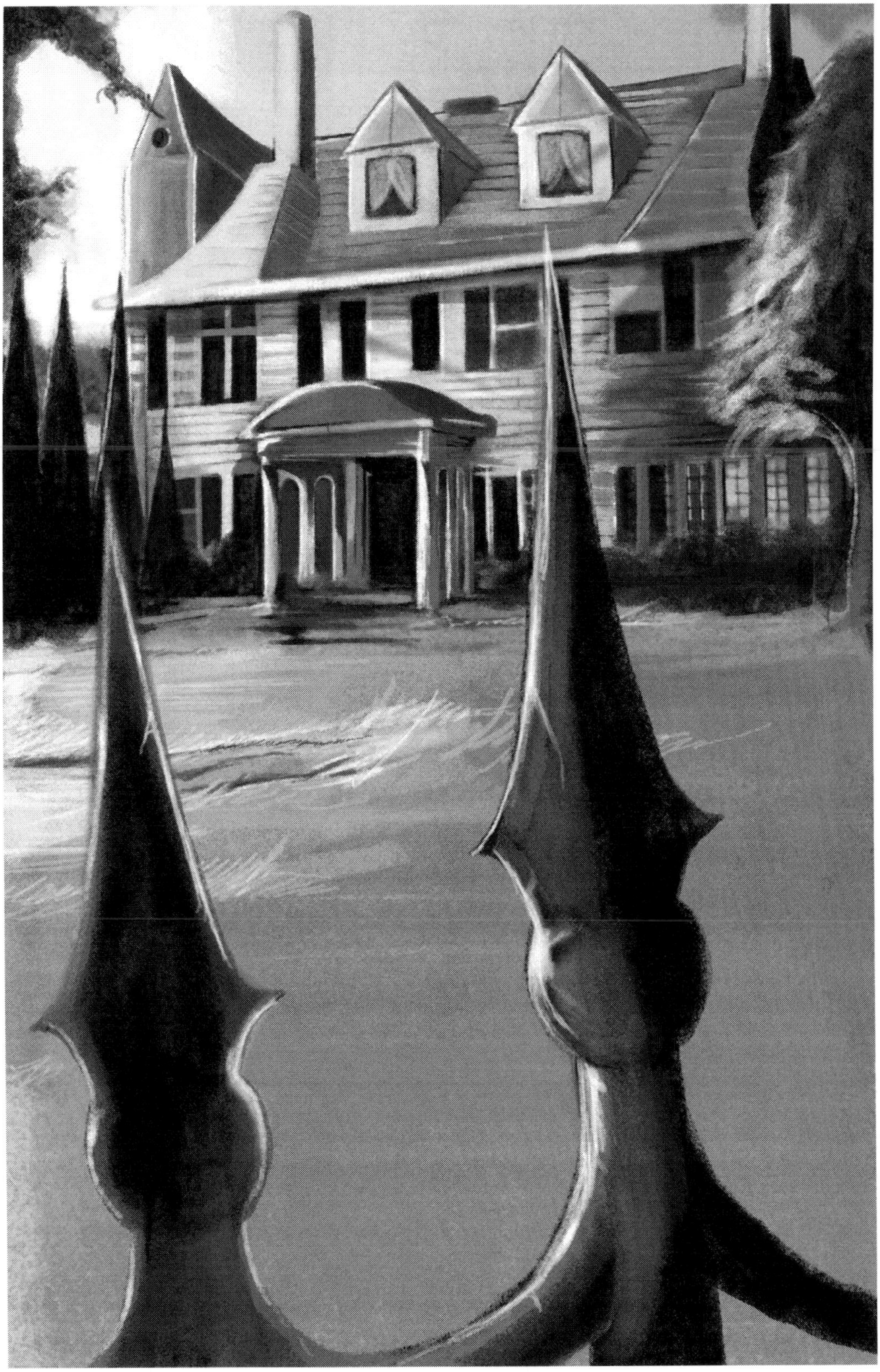

The pruned and feeble frame of a hunchbacked old woman rattled before him until it finally stabilized. She was wrapped in a red blanket, looking cold when the weather was anything but.

The woman's pale and heavily splotched skin was hideous, and her bloodshot, murky eyes disgusted him. He was seeing the exact opposite of what he had come for. The drop-dead beauty had been replaced with a vile reminder of his own mortality. While his pants weren't bursting with the eagerness he imagined any longer, he still had to say something.

"Hello, I'm hoping I... uh, I have the right place. I'm looking for Elena, does an Elena Dragos live here?"

The elder's face lit up like a sunrise, "You have her purse, oh, thank heavens! She just left a short while ago to look for it, such a kind man you are to bring it back to us."

"Oh, it's really no trouble," Tom said, extending the bag out. "I found it in the street just a few blocks away, she must've dropped it."

The woman took hold of the bag and looked inside, removing the notebook and wallet. "While it may seem like there isn't much in here, these things are all important, very important indeed. Elena cares for me now, so if we were to lose all this, it would be a significant inconvenience."

"Well, I'm glad I could help, have a nice—"

"Oh, wait! Please, won't you come in and stay a moment? I've just made some tea, the least I can do is offer you a drink in light of your kindness."

"I really can't, I have some other affairs I need to attend to," Tom lied, trying to work his way out of becoming intimate company for the seemingly senile senior.

"But Elena should be back any moment, I'm sure she'd want to thank the handsome man that found her purse. She's been looking for a good gentleman, we all are really..."

The old woman didn't wait for his reply, she wrapped her warped, arthritis-stricken digits around his wrist gently and tugged him inside.

"Alright, I suppose I can wait for a few minutes and have one cup with you. But only one. After that, I must be on my way."

Her expression crinkled with a juvenile giddiness, "You have my word, I promise, just one cup!"

Tom took a seat on the plum Chantelle sofa where he was greeted with a clattering saucer and steaming cup. "There's a little sugar, I hope that's okay with you."

After swallowing a warm sip of the British Breakfast, he nodded his head. "I'm not typically a tea person but this is good; damn good actually."

"Wonderful!"

Tom didn't care to learn about the odd old woman or prod her for any long-winded stories, but the discomfort of an awkward silence was something he preferred to break. He gazed above the fireplace mantle at an enormous oil-painted portrait of a peculiar-looking nobleman. He pointed at the magnificent artwork. "This is a striking piece, is that your husband?"

"Well, it *was* my husband. Unfortunately, he's dead."

"I'm terribly sorry," Tom said, slurping back another mouthful of the soothing infusion.

"It's quite alright, it's nice of you to offer your condolences, most people don't do that. Do you know what most people do?" She watched Tom shake his head. "The first question from most peoples' lips is 'how?' How did he die, they ask, would you believe that?"

"That's quite a callous approach."

The woman's expression became eerily cold, something frightening flickered through her eyes as she straightened up like the dead rising. "Do you want to know how my husband died?"

Tom was taken aback by the strange actions of the woman, wishing he'd never agreed to come inside. "Not particularly," Tom answered.

"He got very old, like me," she replied anyway, a giant smirk finding its way back to her face. "In all seriousness though, my poor Alfred died right on that couch you're sitting on. Almost precisely that spot."

While Tom was relieved she steered away from the more resentful tone and seemed to be in a joking mood, things were beginning to feel a little too weird for him. The morbidity of the topic was still unflattering. He hadn't the faintest idea when Elena was returning, or if she'd be as pleased to see him as the detached gray-haired woman indicated. For all he knew, Elena could be just as bizarre as her mother, or was it her grandmother?

He realized he hadn't even asked her and that he truly had no clue who the old bat was. Tom set his half-empty cup and saucer down beside the kettle and stood up.

"Apologies, it was truly a pleasure to meet you, but I won't be able to stay any longer. I have…" Tom's voice sounded like it was now somehow echoing throughout the room and bouncing off his eardrums.

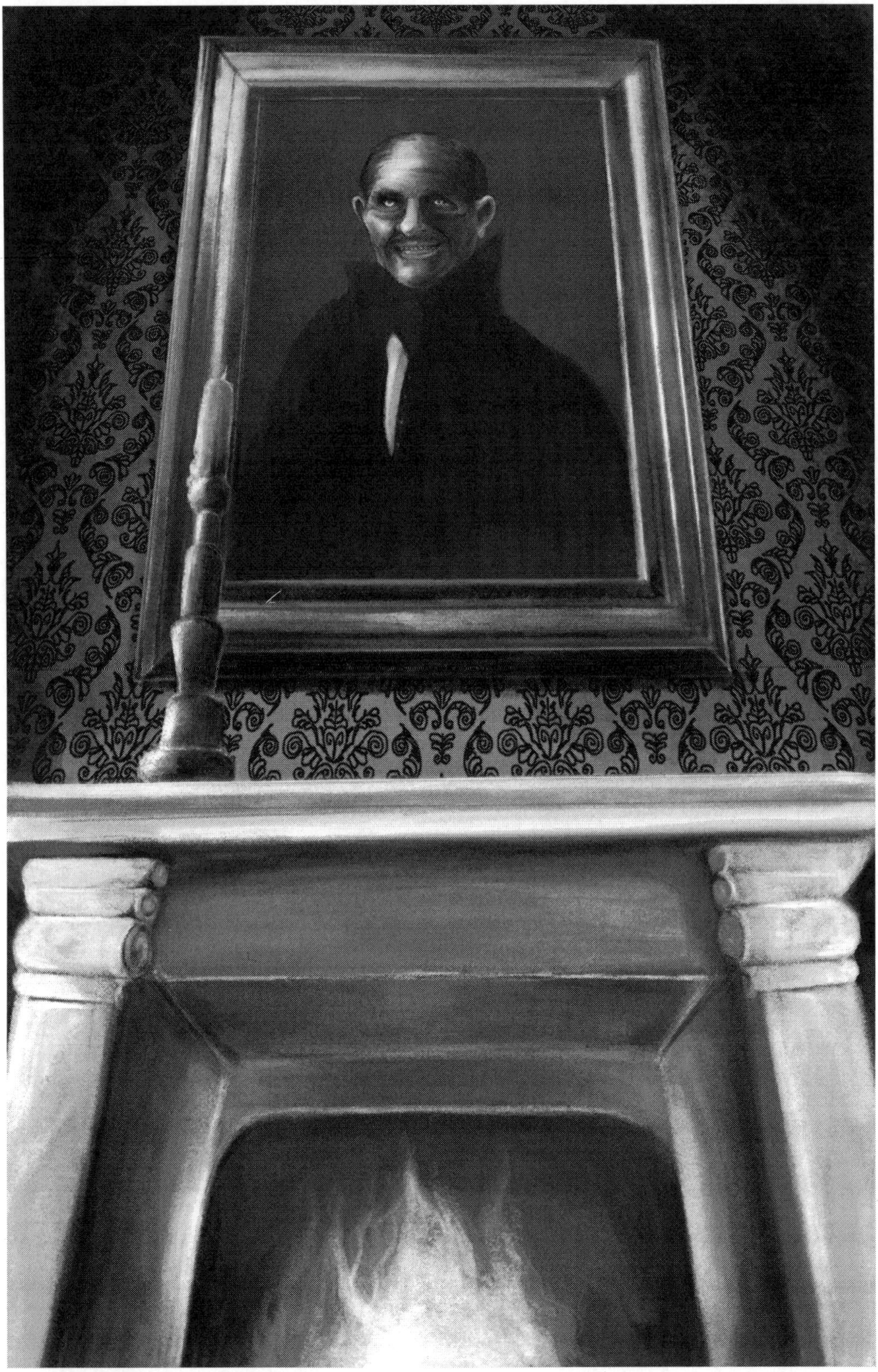

"I have an appointment..." He tried to continue, but as he took a step forward, his vocals seized up and the wrinkly features of the hag began to blur. With his vision now stripped of focus, he collapsed face-first, knocking over the tea tray and crackers before shattering through the glass coffee table.

***

When Tom awoke, he was relieved to see that he'd regained the ability to view the finer details that normally accompanied his sight. He noticed the place he was in was no longer the quaint, dapper living room that he'd been sipping his tea in before blacking out. Judging by the unforgiving cold stone walls and the amount of dirt and filth accrued on all that surrounded him, the unfamiliar atmosphere looked to resemble that of a dreary cellar.

His ears were greeted by the jingle of heavy chain and the clang of shackles. As Tom attempted to adjust his body, he noticed that his limbs had been constrained. A smashing feeling of wrongness drenched him. While his extremities had been restricted, his fear had not. He was finally concentrating enough to acknowledge the dreadful ambiance. His body was overrun with a horrible chill, and as he looked down, he understood why. There was no protection between the icy, stale air and his skin—he'd been stripped down like an animal.

He turned his head and was confronted with the difficult evidence that he wasn't the only one whose irons were chiming; another pair of men had been bound to the walls beside him.

They mumbled and drooled absentmindedly. In their eyes alone, you could tell they were shattered. Upon further observation, it was easy to see why—their mouths were dry and crusted and their casings the color of Elmer's glue. Within their food holes, a squirming, equally dehydrated, and cracked nub rumbled about impatiently; their tongues had been severed and taken.

While the duo each had unique individual characteristics, they were brothers in torture. Both absurdly overweight and harboring enormous pods of blubber beneath their surfaces. The layers of lard upon the gristle that encompassed them were obviously unnatural. The gooey, dripping vertical slits which overshadowed their esophagi were parted like a pair of labia lips stretched to capacity.

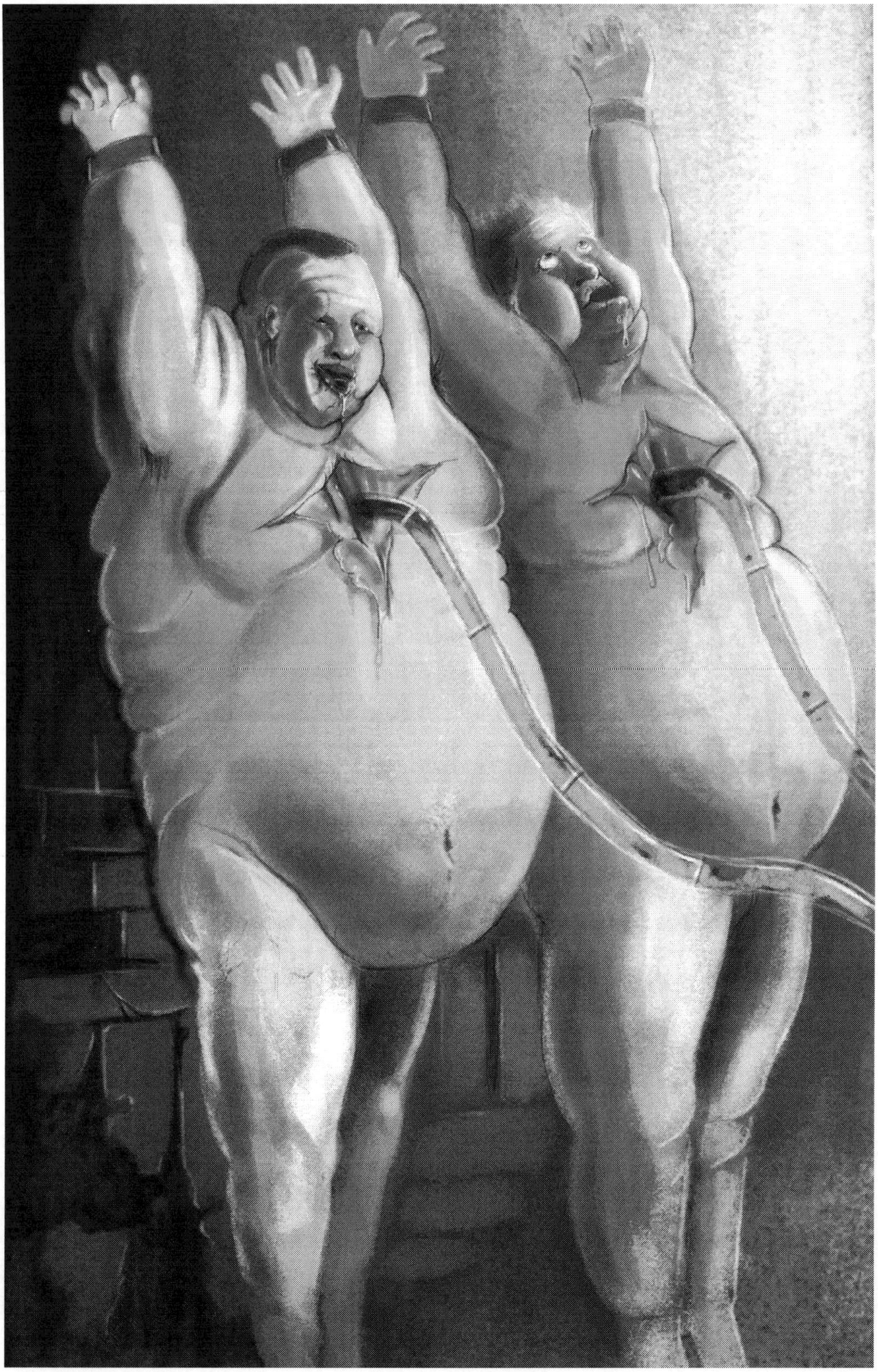

The excruciating collar cunts had long tubular plastic inserted into them, which was occupied by thick, lumpy slop. The vile muck slowly drizzled down from a pool's worth of "filler" that appeared to be fattening them to the verge of skin-ripping capacity. Tom could only imagine what the "nutrients" were comprised of.

A sight so upsetting would have been almost impossible for him to look away from had an equally unspeakable horror not been peeking out from behind the deathbed doughboys. His gaze started with the ghostly filling on the floor. It had erupted out all over the stone floor beside two other expired, morbidly obese carcasses.

Their heads were gone and their frames appeared to have been bled dry—flattened like when you're looking to squeeze that last dollop from a tube of toothpaste. Above the crumpled ones that littered the slippery stone floor sat a hexagonal, iron bathtub with pointy claw feet. And inside the tub flowed a thin stream from the warm pool of crimson which stirred within the shape unpredictably.

Tom's shock dazed him. Jaw agape, he knew not the proper words for such an occasion. They would have been of little use anyway—no words could break the rusted metal that bound him. No sentence could alter the one which had been thrust upon him. From the depths of the hemoglobin pool, a wet mass of hair slicked with copious red arose. It was challenging to tell who it was exactly until he saw the smile. The perfect pearls popped out from the maroon backdrop majestically. It was the heart-fluttering grin of Elena Dragos.

She slurped up mouthful after mouthful of the congealing essence until her belly was plump. Elena seemed a far cry from her glowing snapshot as she peered up and toward him manically, her mouth dangling down monstrously as the thirst modified her carnal form.

What she had become bordered on hallucinogenic, and she was blanketed with a vacant look of depravity. After her fill, she basked blissfully, rubbing the red deep into her pores. As she ascended to a standing position, Tom noticed her body was bare, save for the life-juice running down her so generously. If nothing else, in a sick way, Tom had gotten what he'd hoped for.

In her blasphemous form, she exited the iron pit, reaching for the pair of rusted tongs and a chipped blade that lay on a table.

As her long fingernails plucked from beneath the tools, he begged her, "Please don't, I'll do anything. I just brought your purse back! I helped you, dammit! I helped you!" As the words left him the adrenaline continued ripping through his frame.

"And you will help me more, more than you could ever know," she hissed. The tongs snatched his tongue with haste, like a cat pouncing on its prey. Then, almost as efficiently as she'd taken control of the mass of muscle, she lopped it clean off. The cherry liquid rained from his orifice as she rammed the blade into his throat, creating an opening that was just big enough to insert the feeding tube.

***

Elena drove Tom's car away from the property and abandoned it near some seldom-used train tracks. She exited the car when, suddenly, the unforgiving elements erupted out of nowhere. The fierce rainfall was heavy and couldn't be avoided.

Thankfully, she was still just a short distance from Tom's wagon when it began. She returned to the car and inspected it. With a long walk ahead, she hoped he was a well-prepared man. She opened the hatch and scanned the contents.

Wedged between a football and a fold-up chair, she spotted it. Elena quickly removed the black umbrella and pushed it open. She slammed the hatch closed and turned back in the direction she'd come from. The heavy waters dotted the fabric and beaded down around her as she strolled away from the empty vehicle, never looking back.

The walk home was about a mile or so, but once she was a few blocks away from her home, she slackened to a halt. She looked up and down the peaceful, vacant street carefully—one that she knew to be filled with kind-hearted, neighborly folks.

Only once she was sure that no one was watching, she tossed the tattered old purse back onto the concrete beside an enormous puddle of cloud spill. There it sat with the same contents it did when Tom came upon it—nothing of true value, waiting for the next good Samaritan to try and use the opportunity to balance out their karma.

Elena beamed at the sight of her placement, her smooth and gorgeous features perking up to a pinnacle. Her umbrella prevented any rain from stirring the puddle beside her handbag as she gazed down into it. The smiling reflection was different than the reality; she was wrinkly and dreary beyond repair.

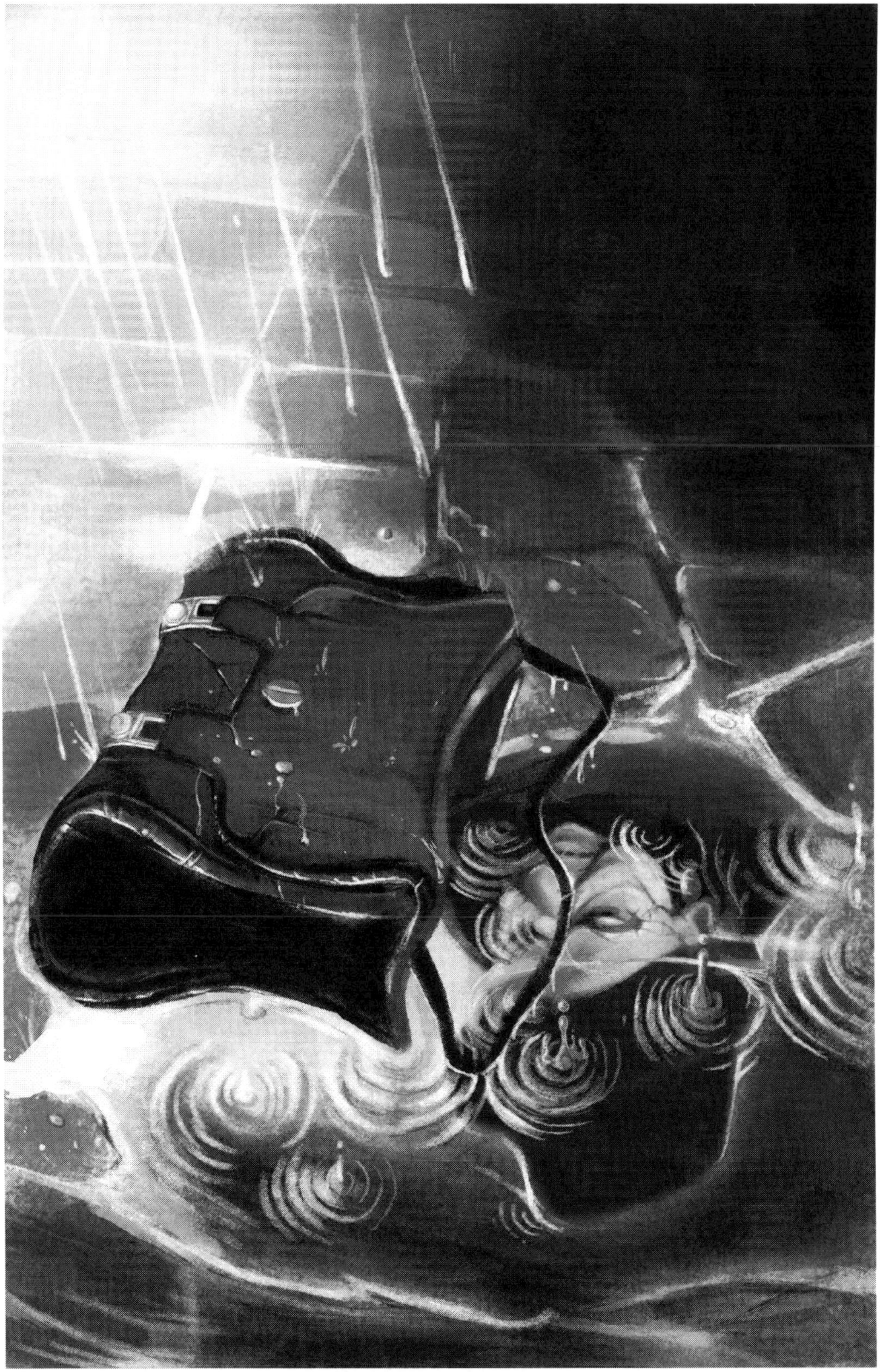

Her creased and bent fingers clung around the umbrella handle while her twisted hunchbacked and fragile frame looked like they might crumble at any moment. The deathly complexion and hazy pupils that glimmered in the pooling water were identical to that which Tom faced when he first knocked on the door of 66 Carver Avenue.

ONE NIGHT STAND

When Taylor brought the man home from the bar, she was expecting to sleep with him. She had her reasons for choosing him; they may not have been the most popular, but he had what she wanted. The man was rugged and grungy—a certain brutish almost Neanderthal aura would have been the best description to encapsulate her snap judgment.

He just seemed more masculine than the fresh-faced college boys that had been eye-fucking her all night. There was a depressing detail to his expression that showed he'd been through the wringer. That night, for some obscure instinctual reason, she needed him. She needed someone who had been through the shit, someone with experience.

She wasn't in denial; she knew exactly who she was and didn't much care if the rest of the world did too. The trashiness of her routine was amusing. She did what any young person does in their party phase—get shit-faced, zero in on a decent-looking stranger, and fuck their brains out with no strings attached. She didn't even need a first name… it was pointless in her estimation. After taking more shots than a paper target, she wouldn't remember Peter from Paul.

Taylor didn't recall much of the night. There were a few chunks of memory scattered around like toys in a child's playroom. She remembered they went to her bed immediately; clothes were stripped off, and their warm mouths connected, trading the lingering stench of their choice of alcohol. He had a bit of a nasty funk to him, but she liked that. Taylor wanted it to be dirty, that's why she chose him. Their smiles grew wide as they mimicked each other in achieving pleasure.

The next morning, the man—Ben or possibly Ken; it didn't matter—he was gone. It was just the way she'd hoped—no odd, uncomfortable awakening, no hard feelings. In fact, it went so smoothly that Taylor was already focused on the next adventure. It was while she was contemplating what the forthcoming evening of reckless debauchery would bring when she saw it.

Normally, she wouldn't have thought twice about a rubber on the floor, she would have just grabbed a tissue, scooped it up along with the goop, and disposed of it. But that wasn't an option because of a glaring problem: the latex tip was busted wide open. Hence there were no contents for her to clean.

Did he leave it inside me? Taylor wondered. She certainly hoped not. She was in the middle of what were supposed to be the best days of her life. She sure as fuck didn't have the time, patience, or financial stability to mother some drifter's baby. Being pregnant seemed like more of a buzz kill than anything, but for the first time, abortion, in an intimate sense, came into her mind.

Her initial feeling poked inside with God knew what else. There was something about it that just didn't sit right with her. While she'd never put much thought into it, her reaction was beginning to mold into what the morality of the situation meant to her. Even if it was some jobless barfly that knocked her up, the decision was on her. She rubbed her hand on her stomach as a look of discomfort swept over her.

While picturing her potential offspring made her grimace, it would still be her flesh and blood, as well as the flesh and blood of her funky fling. In her mind, she pictured a weird-ass baby with a mix of their features, then a teen version of the child bringing home a report card riddled with the letter F. Finally, a middle-aged version, unwashed, in his underwear asking for twenty dollars. Still, aborting the probable dud felt cruel.

It was probably a lot of thinking for nothing. Maybe the bum just didn't have an orgasm, or maybe he just shot his load elsewhere. Who knew, maybe his boys didn't even swim. She pushed the thought out of her mind and got ready for work. It wasn't worth it to worry about a situation ultimately out of her control.

1 Week After

The constant itch wasn't a good sign. It was a strange stinging sensation that left her feeling depressed and dirty. Taylor decided not to sleep with anyone for a while, at least until she felt normal again and any potential symptoms diminished. Paranoia was setting in, and she hated that she felt different. Regret suffocated her, and although she was still horny at times, the thought of having another one-night stand sickened her.

2 Weeks After

The fucking itch was deep and relentless. She was constantly clawing at her crotch and skin, ripping at it until it was dry, raw, and flaking off. Maybe she wasn't pregnant. Maybe that scummy man's dirty cock had given her something. She spent the better part of her days wondering if she had an STD.

3 Weeks After

Taylor's cycle should have started—she missed her period. A pain and weight came over her like she'd never felt before. She was horrified by the possibilities but knew hope alone wasn't going to change her worsening condition. There was a time when everyone had to face the music. She picked up the phone and called a gynecologist.

Days Later

Taylor didn't have a designated doctor or gynecologist. She tried to stay clear of any medical personnel unless she was deathly ill. They made her nervous. There was so much in the world that was bad for a person, and vice was the shit she was usually into—drinking, drugs, sex. She feared them… in her mind, doctors were only the evil harbingers of misfortune.

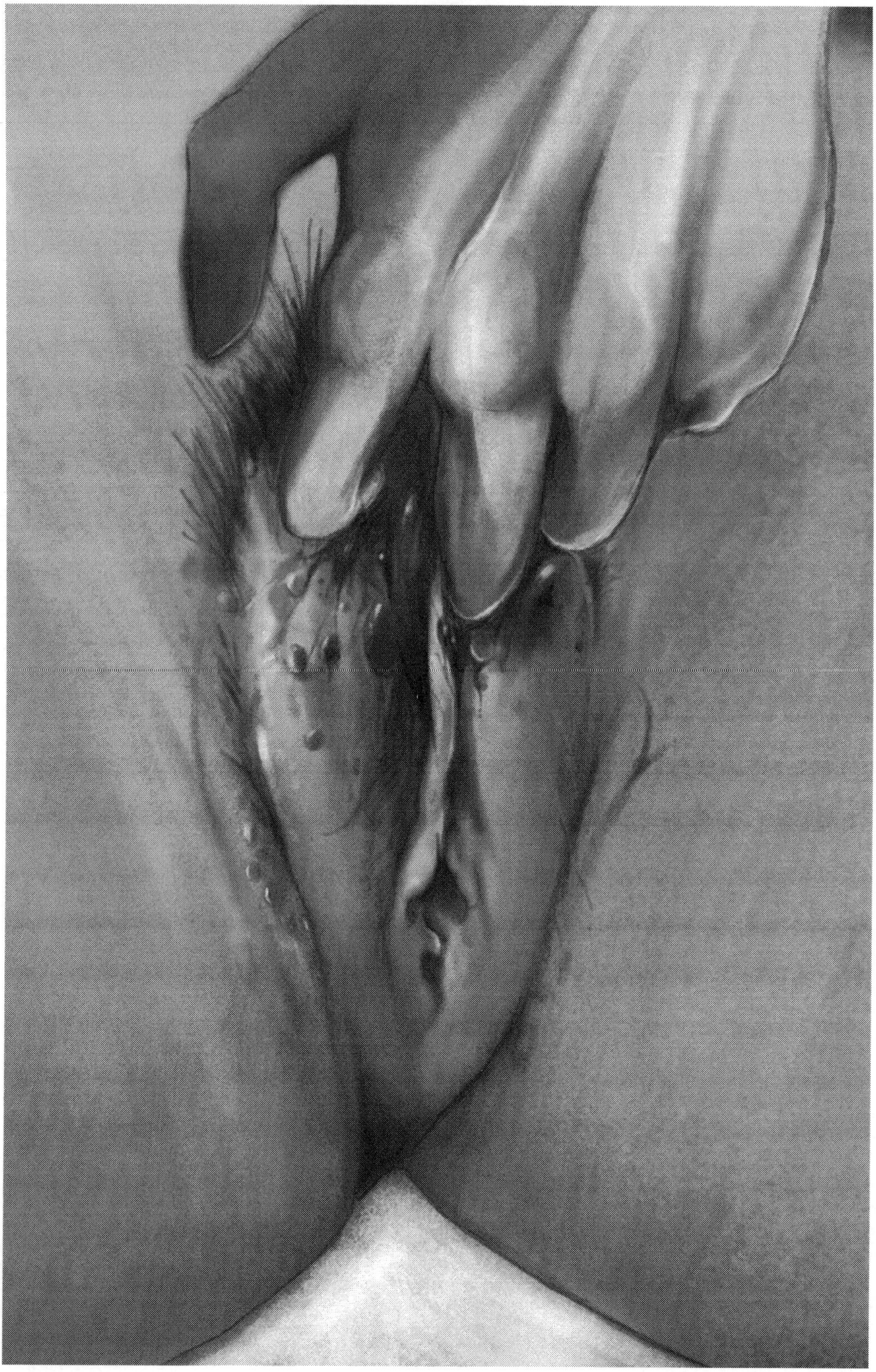

Just entering the building alone made Taylor's skin crawl. As she crept hesitantly into the office, still not wanting to go through with it, she was all nerves. She was rattling like a pile of dead tree leaves in a bone-chilling wind. The doctor's assistant, an attractive woman with a large nose, led her into the exam room. She could tell she was frightened but didn't know why. She continuously reassured Taylor that everything would be alright. After closing the door behind them, she helped Taylor to the table.

"Now, what brings you here, sweetheart?" the woman asked with a stretching smile.

"I-I slept with a man, and the next morning, I found a broken condom on the floor. I've been really itchy ever since and I feel this deep stinging pain inside. I don't know if he… if he gave me something, or if I'm pregnant, or if this is all in my head. I'm so confused."

The woman could see she was teetering on the verge of tears, "Oh, honey, it's okay, we'll figure it out. Don't worry, you're gonna be just fine."

Suddenly, Dr. Guyver pushed open the door. For reasons unsaid and unknown, his face was covered by a white sanitary mask. He didn't greet Taylor or offer words of comfort, he simply snapped his gloved fingers at his assistant, and she promptly elevated Taylor's feet up.

She secured the two steel bridges on the sides of the table and helped Taylor spread her legs nice and wide. The doctor took a seat in front of her exposed privates and plucked a steel instrument from the rectangular stand beside him. Without explaining his intent or warming her up first, he raised his latex hand and inserted both of his fingers as well as the utensil inside Taylor. She was shocked but silent as he examined her.

"Jar," Dr. Guyver commanded. As his assistant handed him a glass receptacle, his next command, "Tweezers," came out. She satisfied that request just as efficiently, handing him an enormous pair in mere seconds.

"Jesus Christ, another one," he murmured to himself. His tone was harsh and unthoughtful.

"Am I pregnant?" Taylor cried, tears running down her tight cheeks.

"Be still!" he commanded, snubbing her query.

Taylor was so stressed out and upset by the suffocating pressure of the situation that she blacked out just as her mind finished projecting the yellow, elated smirk of her disgusting last partner.

***

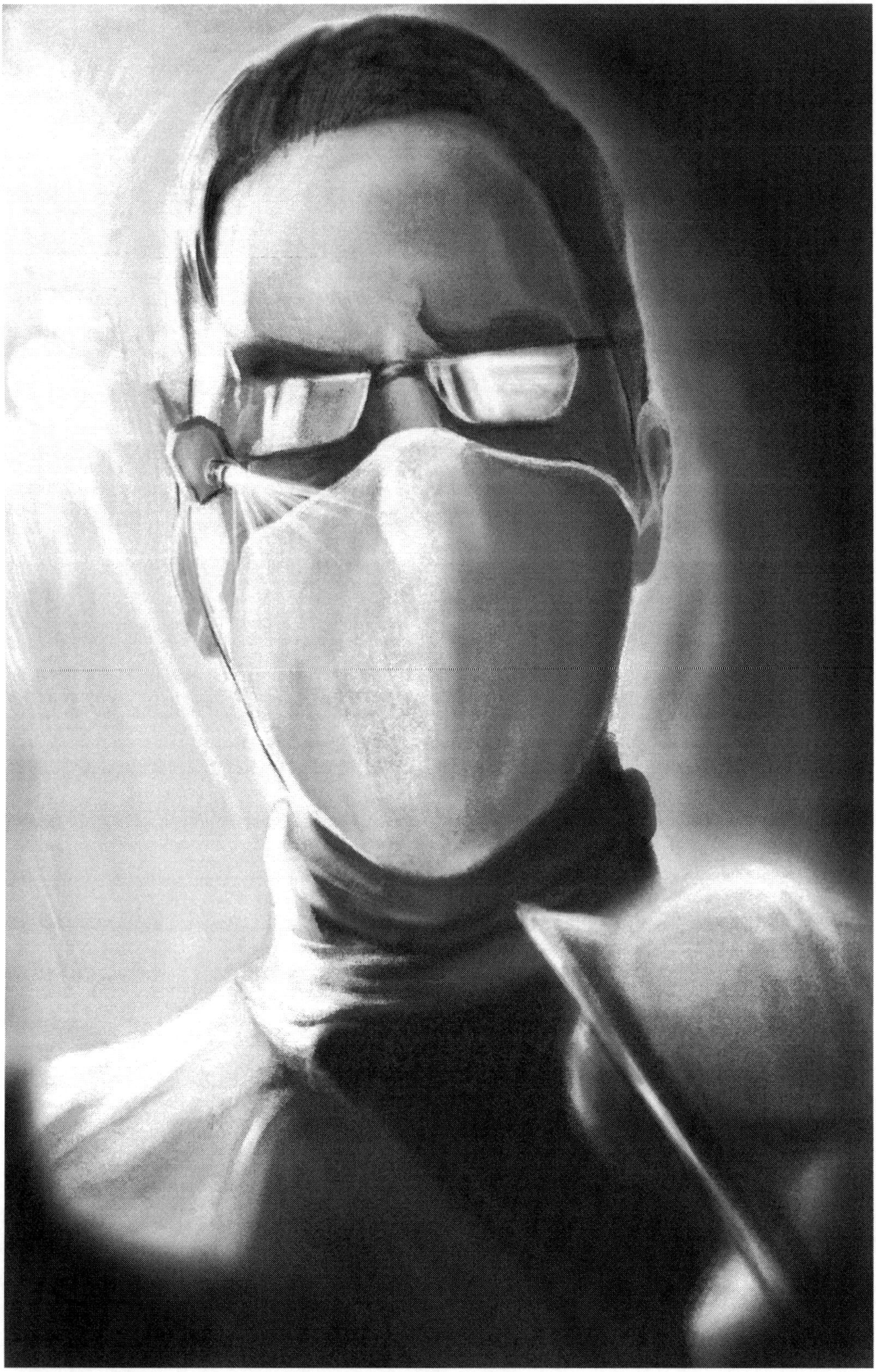

Everything was fuzzy when she finally awoke. Dr. Guyver stood over her stoically, his mask still quarantining his nose and mouth. The bright light pinned to his obscuring glasses beamed down on her. The fear was crushing.

"What's wrong with me? I have the itch and no period. Am I pregnant?"

"No."

"Then what's wrong? Tell me what the fuck is wrong with me, Doctor?!" she begged.

From the stand just outside of her vantage point, Dr. Guyver extended his arm and retrieved the glass jar he'd previously requested. Inside, amongst the blood spatter, sat a variety of plump, overfed, bedbugs. They ranged in size, but the commonality was that each one was filled to capacity. The squirming balls of blood dragged their inept bodies ever so slowly as Taylor's scream ripped through the office. The doctor didn't seem phased by her reaction. Taylor's hysterics calmed but didn't cease as he continued to explain himself.

"Young lady, your generation is one of wanderers, but what many of you fail to see is that your freedoms have a cost. As a result of your nomadic ways, these bugs—bedbugs—have evolved. They're now more resilient than ever, and spreading with the blink of an eye."

He held the glass up to the light and examined them even more closely, as if admiring them. "They have more advanced instincts now and additional knowledge about their food source—our bodies. Do you want to know something fascinating?" His question was delivered in such a nonchalant demeanor that it bordered on sociopathic. The answer seemed obvious, but Taylor still maintained a sniffling silence.

"Trust me, you're not the first woman to come in here under these circumstances. Everything I'm explaining to you is from experience. It's become so much more common now, this vile little problem. With society's ever-growing moral decay, these little devils travel well. They know us intimately, almost as good as we know each other. They know us so intimately that, in many areas around the globe, their breeding and nesting routine now aligns succinctly with a woman's menstrual cycle. They have progressed enough to understand where the blood feast lies."

Taylor's eyes bugged out of her head and the veins protruded beneath her skin. "Th-Those were inside me!" she cried, wishing he would lie or be speechless.

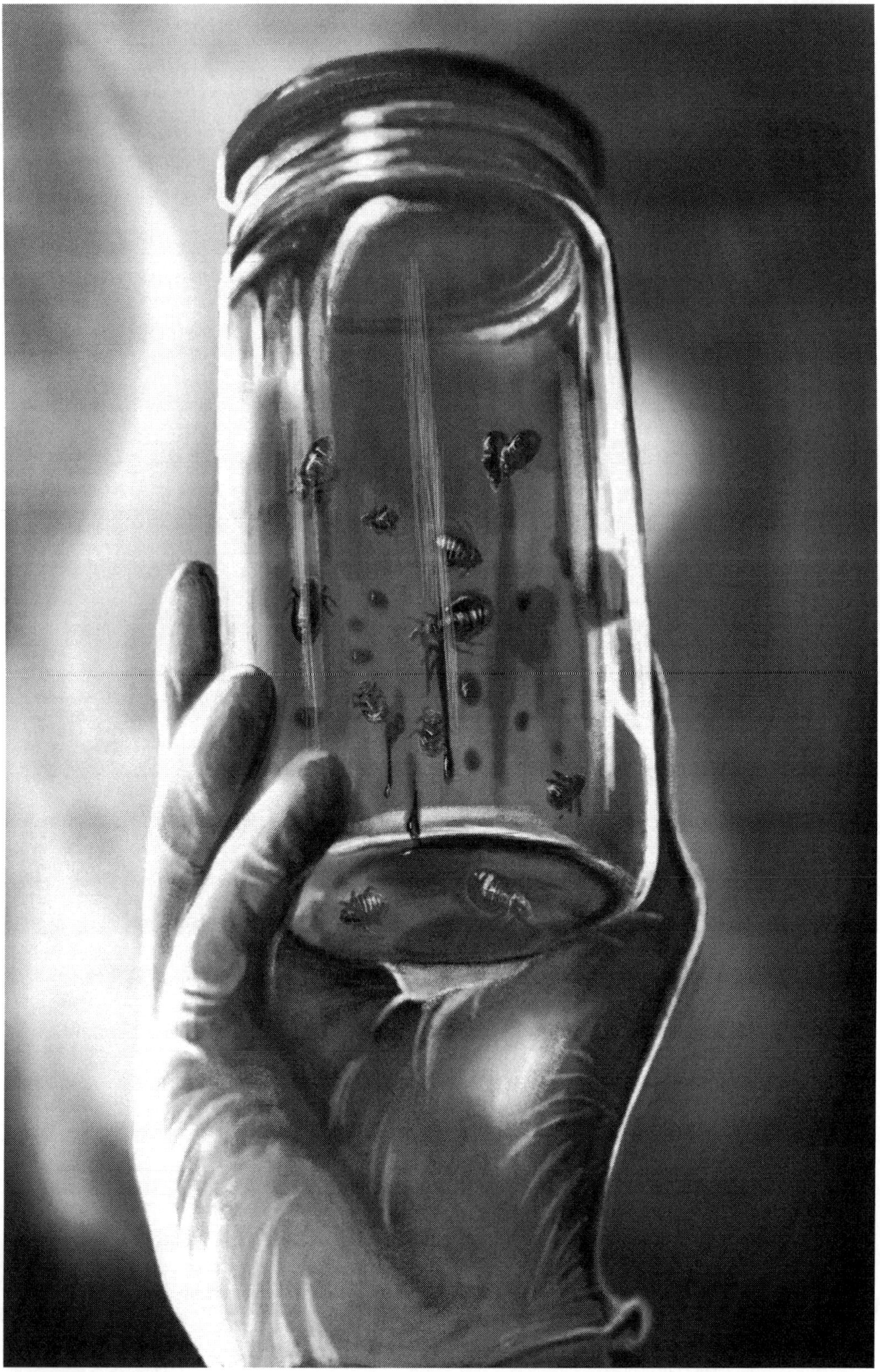

"Yes."

"But they are out now, you got all of them out, right?!"

"I believe so…"

"What do you mean you believe so! Get them all out of me right now, goddammit! Why can't you be sure!?"

The doctor let his glasses slide down his nose a bit, allowing him to make eye contact with Taylor. He held the repulsive jar of parasitic insects up one final time, "Because, bedbug eggs are typically one-twenty-fifth of an inch, and the ones that we found inside you are all large enough to be pregnant."

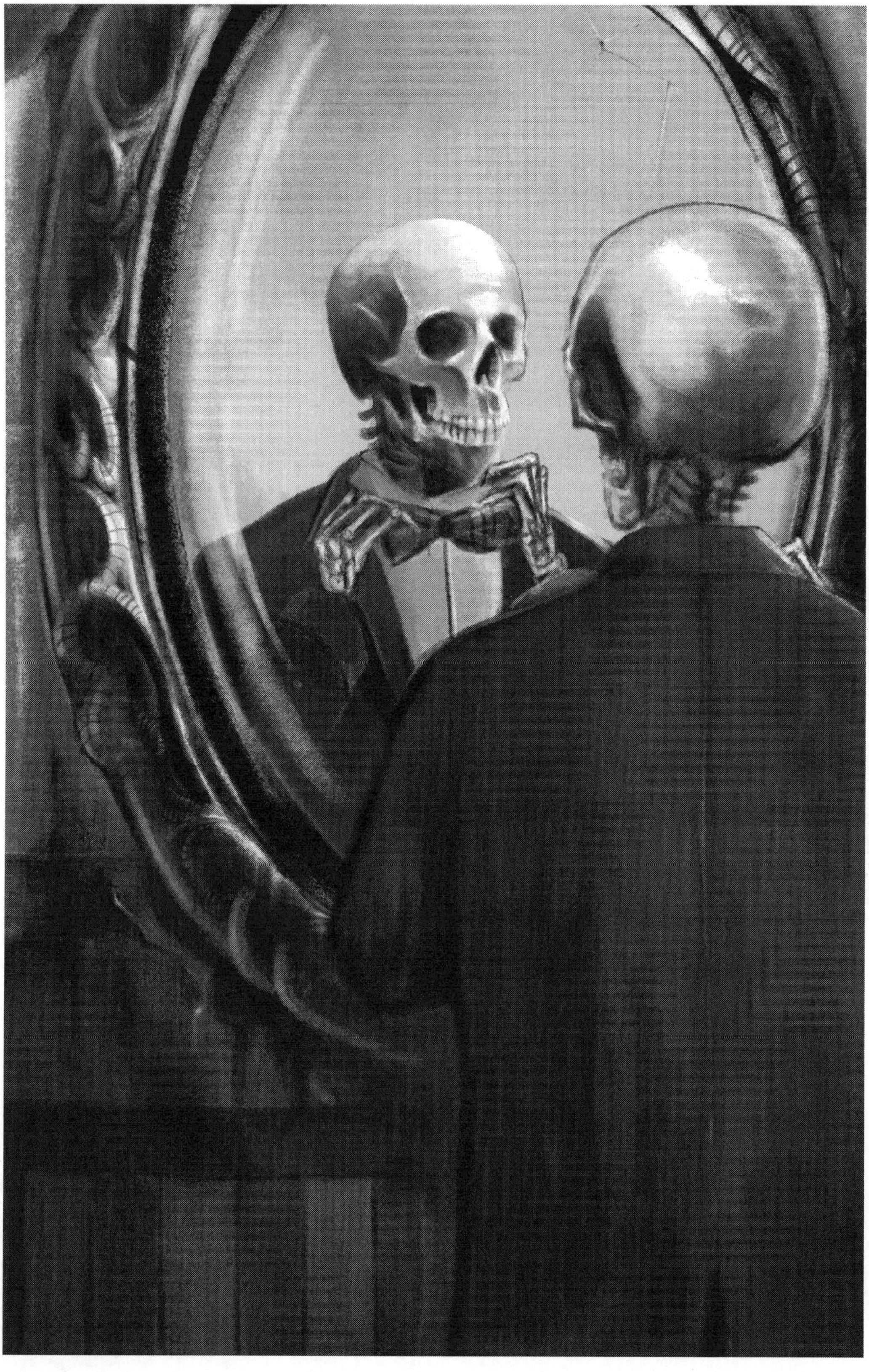

SPEAK NOW

The atmosphere was just how you'd have expected it to be—bright and brimming with emotion. A warm sense of unity stirred between the two families as they came together. Cheryl was dressed elegantly in a gorgeous white gown that dragged on for yards behind her.

David was fitted to perfection in his pressed-to-death tux. He was as clean-cut and dapper as any of their friends or family could recall. A grin of ecstasy had taken hold of his lips; she was the one.

The jubilant pair stood together with emotions running high. They were surrounded by vibrant stained-glass, white roses, and an old but dependable church organ while tears dripped from their eyes.

The ceremony was on the verge of completion as David gazed out into the crowd. Joy, excitement, and tiny hits of jealousy beamed back toward him from the sea of expressions. All the faces were in uniform, except for one—Cheryl's mother, Gale. David's eyebrow crinkled as the priest spoke, nearing the finish line.

"Now if there is anyone here who, for any reason, believes that these two should not be married, please speak now or forever hold your peace."

What the devil was on her mind, David wondered, never having seen such a look of concern cross someone's face. Gale had always been wonderful to him. The weathered woman treated him like a son and also referred to him as such. Since Cheryl's father had passed away, she seemed even closer to her mother, which could be a chore at times. It appeared Gale's mind was slipping; she was constantly telling wild stories, spinning bizarre tales of utter nonsense.

On one occasion, she'd explained how she'd be moving out soon since she'd just been elected as the dean of Harvard. In another instance, she described finishing an enjoyable luncheon with a long-dead president. It didn't seem like she was trying to lie or make trouble… more like her wits had gone limp.

Since the three of them had been living together, David noticed Cheryl had grown weary of her constant babble. She was torn on if she could even be trusted at the ceremony from the beginning.

Ultimately, she decided it would have been too selfish not to include her mother on their special day, even though she was probably too lost in her own decaying mind to notice for herself.

Considering the sweet nature of their interactions, David was baffled by the unmistakable nerves and terror she displayed. Sure, she'd said some strange things to him over time and seemed to believe them, but she'd always done so with a vacancy about her, like someone else was feeding her the words. At that moment, she looked much different. *She's going to say something,* David thought as her lips quivered.

Gale stood up, her eyes still locked onto David's as she extended her arm and pointed at Cheryl. "That's not my daughter." A collective gasp sucked the better part of the air from the room. "Dave, that's not her, you can't marry her! Please trust me, that is not my daughter!" The shouts of conviction were jarring.

"Mom, please, not now, we—"

Gale paid the alleged imposter no mind and continued her rant. "They took her away one night, right through the window. The lights shined on her and… and what came back is different! I don't know what she is, but she's not my daughter! I wish it wasn't true but she's been bewitched!"

The crowd began to grumble, feeling more awkward with each minute that lapsed. Cheryl wasn't even angry that their ceremony had been interrupted by her mother's outlandish remarks; she was more hurt than anything. "Mom, you can't—"

"She did things to me! She calls them and they do things together, sick things! They are evil!"

"Please stop," Cheryl begged.

"I know what you really want!"

Cheryl's Aunt Linda made the difficult decision for everyone and slowly sat Gale back down. She quickly whisked her away, pushing her wheelchair through the doors of the chapel and out into the lobby. As her petitions faded away behind closed doors, a mortified Cheryl and an uncomfortable David returned their attention back to each other.

"I'm sorry," she whispered as the priest regained his verbal footing. The holy man then solemnly finished his part and the bride and groom kissed deeply to echoes of traditional marriage hymns.

***

The honeymoon suite they'd picked out together was beautiful, they'd saved the better part of three years to make it happen. The weather didn't quite match what they'd envisioned, but it didn't matter as everything they had planned was indoors. As they drove down the rainy road, the striking snow-capped mountains came into view.

"Gosh, they are even more beautiful than the photos," Cheryl said thankfully.

"Yeah," David replied in a monotone fashion.

"The way they just sort of reach up and touch the sky. I've always wanted to stay this close to them. It's something else… something special," she continued on.

A thick and uncomfortable silence permeated the stale car air. David's head was still elsewhere. He wanted to listen to her but it was difficult for him to focus.

The reaction Cheryl's mother had at the wedding had now woven creepy ideas into his mind. As silly as it all sounded in his head, he kept retracing the trail of their relationship, resifting the soil, trying to analyze and recall a turning point.

The notion was too absurd to entertain but, somehow, he still was. Unjustified or not, a weirdness had set in and layered itself over what should have been strictly an atmosphere of pure love, adoration, and celebration. Instead, all he could think was that he was going to spend an evening on a secluded mountain with his new wife who wasn't who she said she was.

Cheryl could see that something was wrong, "Honey, why do you suddenly seem so distant now? We're almost there, aren't you excited?"

"I'm just thinking is all, everything's great, I can't wait to pop this bottle with you, sweetie."

"You don't think... David, you don't believe what my mother said about me, do you?"

David could tell that she sounded incredibly insulted. Her words were dipped in a disappointed tone he hadn't often heard emanating from her in their years together. At that moment, he knew the night was teetering on taking a turn for the worse, and if his response wasn't carefully crafted, he could very well sink it.

"No, of course not, honey. C'mon, how many crazy things has your mother said before? This is probably one for the record books though," he laughed, pausing awkwardly. "I'm just thinking about the roads is all, the tires seem like they're slipping a little."

The response was good, a little too good... Cheryl could tell it was unnatural but let it go, she didn't want to make things worse by pushing the topic any further. They both stayed silent until the jingle of the cans hanging from their bumper eventually ceased outside the mountain top house. David locked up the car and gathered their bags while Cheryl opened the door.

It didn't take long for them to get drunk. The alcohol helped smooth over the mini-riff that surfaced between them en route to the cabin. Their words remained brief but their love was overflowing. They had sex multiple times, immersing themselves in what they aspired to create since the first moment they fell for each other—a family.

***

In the morning, David awoke to an empty, disheveled bed. He looked around the room still regaining his bearings; the hangover pounding on his noggin was fierce. The flashes of the prior night's indecencies and the multiple satisfying climaxes slipped in and out. As he headed for the door, he prayed that Cheryl would have a big plate of breakfast ready and waiting for him on the other side. To his bottomless dismay, his prayer went unanswered.

In the spacious living room sat a form of breakfast, but not the kind he'd envisioned. An enormous, slimy egg lay propped up against the wall a short distance from Cheryl. Her eyes looked lost and her skin appeared as a scrambled static mess of digitization.

As she flickered and broke down further, the egg beside her began to crack until the top of the shell slid off. The bizarre, steaming contents mirrored what his wife was becoming—an oversized, demonic, red-eyed snarling reptile. And just as David had been envisioning his breakfast, so had they, as evidenced by the translucent drool pooling on the hardwood below their maws.

Before David could run, their sharp claws had already pierced into his surface. They plunged into his tissue and dragged him closer. Their razor-toothed chomps pulled the meat from his skeleton as he screamed helplessly. They consumed every conceivable inch of him in a sadistic and cold-blooded manner. Once the meat was gone, the pair of demons used their pulsating plum-toned-tongues to slurp up his remaining juices. The house now appeared the same way it did as when they'd first entered.

The two creatures stood beside each other and motionlessly waited. The static spawned again, flickering psychedelically upon the exterior of one of the beings. The outline of its hideous physique contorted into its prior human form. Cheryl stood calmly and turned her head as her comrade began its own metamorphosis.

The strange shell boiled chaotically before finally compressing into itself. The scaly foreign skin leveled out, coming to grips with a new façade. Cheryl's pupils jolted as she beheld her new partner, displaying a momentary glimpse of the emerald vertical slits that she'd concentrated on suppressing.

As the color transitioned back to baby blue, she grabbed hold of a familiar hand. A human hand with the same dips, grooves, and roughness as her husband, David. She pulled him in closer and they kissed.

THE CAROUSEL

The gypsies lived on the land for some time before the villagers finally decided it was time to drive them away. They were always raucous and abnormal, but their camp and tents were far enough from the pristine village to be overlooked for years. But now, the day of change had come and action was required in order to maintain their own purity and civility.

The society of filthy forest dwellers had developed and expanded with a methodical suddenness that had forced the townsfolk to take notice. To their shock, what started with a few modest camps in their once noble woods had evolved to an infestation of deranged and diseased bums.

The poorly drifters had somehow all decided to stray from their nomadic ways in unison, sewing their misguided philosophies together into a single giant eyesore.

A handful of men were dispatched by leadership to represent the village and their wishes. They arrived one gray morning at the tent city to convey their grievances in the flesh. While the band of frozen wanderers couldn't be sure why the men had come, the haggard clans seemed weary of the townsfolk as they rarely chose to interact with them unless they needed something or were readying a demand.

Usually, if they were embarking on travels west to forage or hunt, and by chance passed the gypsies, they just stared down upon them silently, like they were looking at the collective wart on the ass of society. Needless to say, when the representative from the village stepped out from his row of companions and spoke, they listened fearfully.

"Dear people, we have traveled here today to bear our objection. For many years, we have kindly left you be, but slowly, over time, you have encroached upon our village."

The speaker let his hands open up and cracked his brutish knuckles. "You have reproduced at a radical rate without forethought. You have pillaged these woods that helped feed our people. The once plentiful resources that we all shared have now become scarce. Your bottomless, parasitic approach can no longer be tolerated. Your coercive encroachment on our land will no longer be tolerated. You have brought hardship to our people, and those hardships end now."

A black-toothed elder rose from the soil and stretched his torso. The rotten man's hips cracked, echoing throughout the forestry as he approached the grim messenger. His frame was skeletal and strained of nourishment, it looked as though each word he spoke would be chosen carefully as he was easily exhausted.

The black-toothed man spat toward his corn-riddled and rough-skinned feet. "Our families are continuing to grow, our young need space to train and shelter to rest. We have not the farms nor fertile soils of your village. We have no choice but to suck from the teat of Mother Nature. We mean not to be a nuisance to you or your people, but as you know, this land is bordered by waters, there is only one direction which we can extend ourselves."

"It is not merely your encroachment that distresses us, there is considerable concern amongst our community that some of your practices attract rodents and other vermin. Our crops are being eaten and destroyed, while our homes are invaded. These ills were only brought forth to our village upon the arrival of your people. I'm afraid it has gone too far. Negotiating and bargaining are no longer an option even for a silver-tongued charlatan like yourself, old man."

"Please, I beg of you, there must be some way. We are not filled with health and vigor like your people. To uproot from our system could spell grave consequences for my brothers and sisters. These few acres of land are our home, it's all many of us know."

"And you've destroyed it!" the speaker yelled, losing patience as he pointed at the garbage and rancid waste piles with flies buzzing and squirming maggots a mere stone's throw away. He then set his gaze upon a young, mud-caked boy gnawing on a wad of undercooked rat.

As he chewed through the still strawberry-toned, gamey exterior, a few more roasted on a spit behind him. The scent of burned hair beleaguered the villagers' oxygen intake as their leader next gestured toward the child. "Look at your young, feeding on a diseased nub! The soiled ways of your people are misguided and could easily bring forth plague to our people and Lord knows who else!"

"But we don't have the resources you revel in. If you showed us your ways, maybe we could change. Maybe we can become a fruitful extension of your community. We won't know unless you afford us the chance," the elder pleaded.

The messenger and his men scoffed at the idea that the savages before them could be integrated with their own. They were lesser beings, they could not be taught nor brainwashed to defy the foulness ingrained in them. He shook his head in disbelief that the rotten elder would float an idea of such foolishness.

"You are a fool, old man. A filthy damned fool. But you shall be a filthy *dead* fool if this sinful sanctuary isn't purged soon. You have two weeks. Should you or your mess be here upon our return, you will no longer be feasting on the rats; it is they who shall be feasting upon you!"

The wrinkled thin-boned man let out an inhuman groan, his agony forcing its way from the inside out. The insects jumped off of the excrement around him at the sound of his hell-shaking their existence. The disturbed elder ripped at his pants violently until his rags were undone and his ailing procreative flesh was exposed.

His pecker had inverted from lack of use, tucking itself back into his body, but as more urine vacated his bladder, it snuck out of hiding. His alarming moaning increased as the revolting buttery torrent flushed down his legs and onto the hard ground.

The shrill screech only seemed to gain momentum and increase in the harshness of its pitch. The repulsed villagers covered their ears as it elevated. The noise was bordering on inhuman. The demonic droning was an ugliness that felt almost crippling.

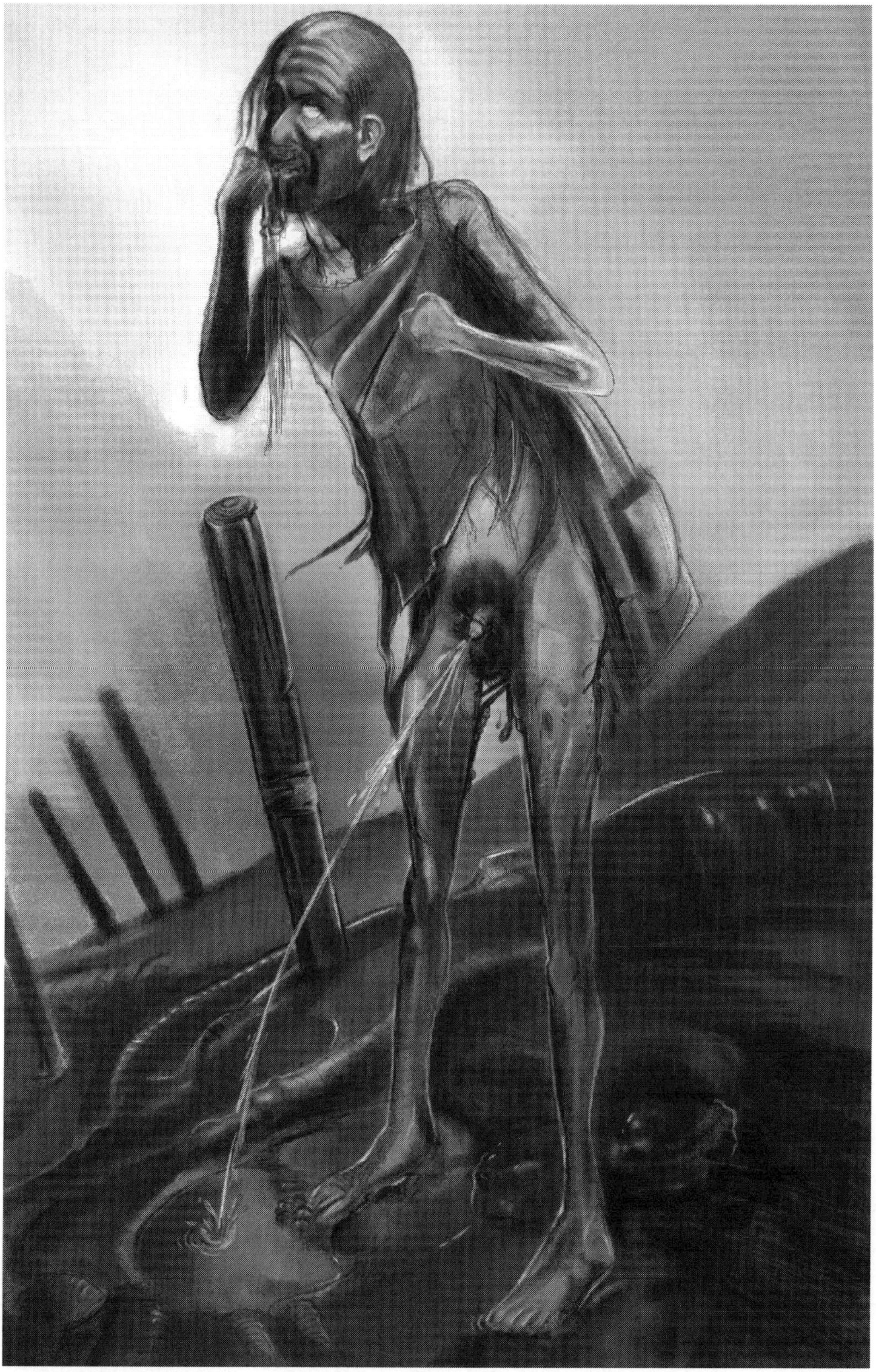

"You wretched abomination!" the messenger shouted, removing a pointed dagger and gritting his teeth.

As the blade glimmered in the cloudy light, the rest of the gypsies watched their master tremble and start speaking in tongues. They knew the battle cry, but had not a weapon to battle with aside from their own offensiveness. The human skunks emulated the rudeness of their master until the entire land was littered in the most repulsive and impoverished watery waste and defecation.

The men from the village stood, jaws cracked in awe, until the putrid smell besieged them. The potency of their sordid expulsions couldn't be missed, as it left the entire land imprisoned in a funk. The stench was so despicable that it dominated their nasal cavities.

It was a Herculean chore for the villagers to see the squatters in a more appalling light than they already did, but the gypsy populous had somehow achieved the feat. Their unhinged howls echoed through the afternoon slate sky, and while the larger portion's gibberish continued, the elder's wording shifted.

"Let he who sets foot on this land become the fallen! Let their loin be shredded by the claws untamed! Let them be opened up and feasted upon! Let their seed be stoned! Let the fragrance of our rage remain! Bring forth the suffering and let their blood flow as graciously as their wine does!"

As the vile vagabond finished his words, his many disillusioned followers also began to clear out their raunchy chambers in protest, orally projecting waves of vomitus mixtures. Within moments, the cursed grounds were heavily defiled and overrun with a collection of unhealthily tinted liquid and solid.

As shaken as the messenger was, he didn't budge from his earlier proposition. He knew any further resistance on the part of the tramps would be fatal. The scum had no leverage and would quickly be exterminated if the direction wasn't followed.

He screamed out, uncaring that the madness before them would be difficult to break through, "You must clean this now! You obscene rats! You evil pigs! Or when we return, we shall visit harms upon you ten-fold should you not obey our wishes!"

The words left his mouth on the heels of retreat, as the villagers distanced themselves from the devilish anarchy still unleashing itself in the field. They disappeared in the woods, but the wails of the ill-minded haunted them that night on every step of their journey home.

***

When the pilgrimage had concluded, the party of villagers told their leadership of the message they'd delivered and the lunacy that followed. It was decided that the wild disrespect the gypsies had aimed at them couldn't be overlooked, regardless of the mess they might be walking into. The prideful community assembled their most gritty, ruthless, and strong, then primed them for combat. They returned to the camp the following evening, only to be greeted by an improbable sight.

The acres of land appeared dark and ghostly, almost totally absent of the faintest trace of the disturbed gypsy folk. Most of the despicable mess that they'd left behind was gone, along with the majority of their shelters and their gargantuan piles of garbage.

The seemingly impossible feat was explained away by the blowhard brutes. "It only takes but one man in earshot of a campfire tale of our slayings for the cowards to retreat," the grunt swarming with scar tissue boasted to his brethren.

Upon hearing the news, the messenger and his men tried to explain to the other villagers that there was no faithful means in which the bedlam they'd witnessed could have been displaced in mere hours. Something was wrong—there had to be witchery afoot. Their words couldn't express properly to the rest of the village the wickedness that oozed into the grounds and the madness that befouled the tramps.

Still drunk off the notion of their self-professed power, the brutes saw nothing irregular. They promptly and proudly made arrangements for their new space. It wasn't so much because they needed the land or had some grand idea for the area, they just aimed to occupy it before anyone else. So, with that precautionary measure in mind, the finest woodworkers were sent off into the forest to chop down trees and gather wood. Then, the best blacksmiths would follow to help with the preparations.

What were they preparing for? They decided that the region would be used as a leisure space; an area seldom used save for extravagant celebration. The carpenters and metal workers would erect stands, stages, seating, and rides for the children. There they would host carnivals, play music, and share delicious foods together. At the center of the fantastical arrangement, all of the men focused their efforts and fashioned a beautiful carousel.

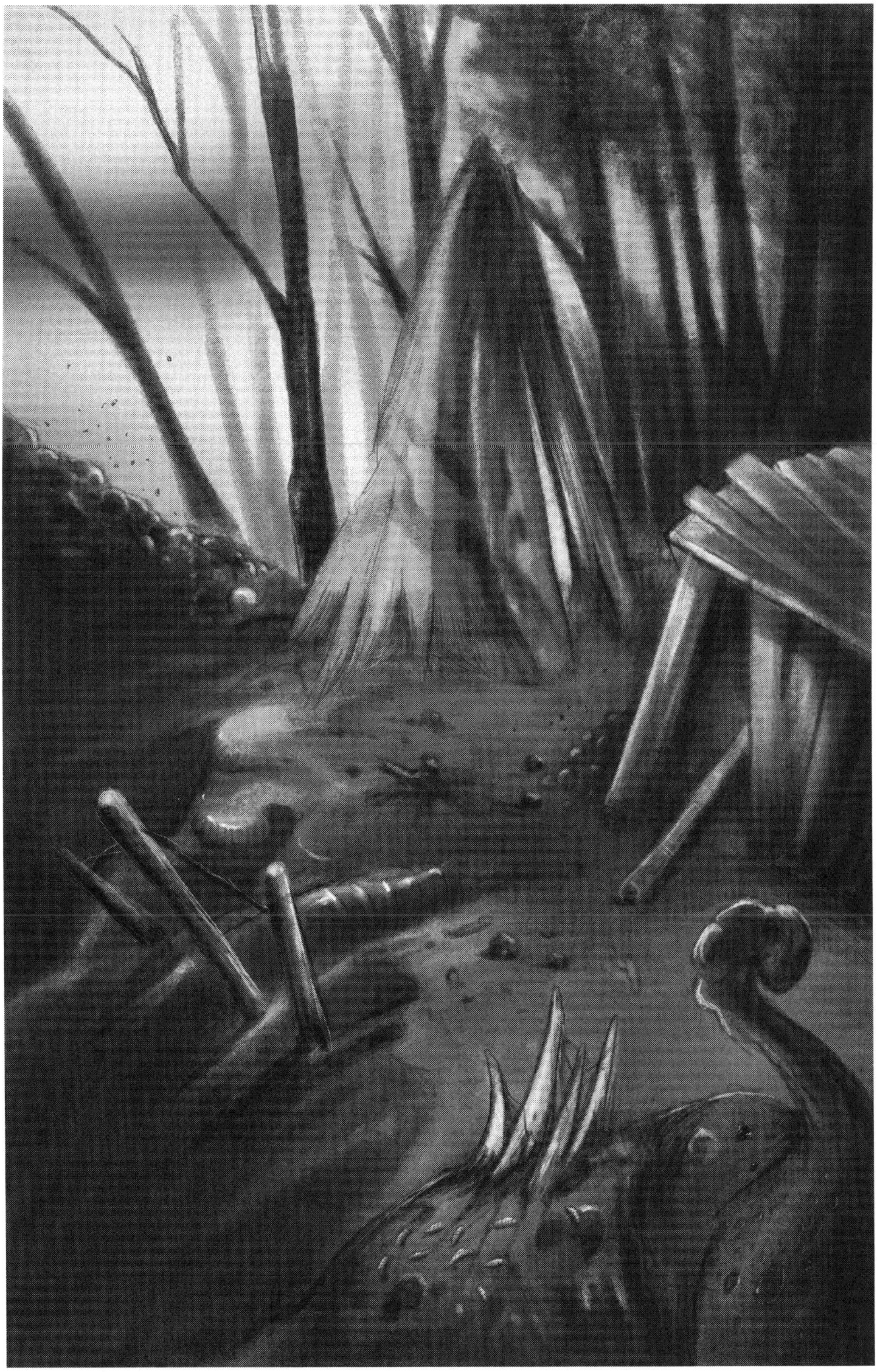

The carpenters intricately carved the detailed animals out of their finest wood and stained them for both splendor and strength. The blacksmiths molded the sturdiest metals, supporting the device and skeleton of the beast.

Once all of the pieces had been crafted, the mechanics who molded the blueprint brought the many parts together and arranged them to move as one. Lastly, before the first rides would take place, the most gifted painters slathered the showpiece in countless lively shades, bringing the towering animals to life.

With the carousel being the final cog to perfect the new festival grounds, the villagers were enamored upon completion. The surging eagerness saw children trying to climb onto the animals before the paint had even dried. They all calmed each other and paused their exhilaration. They would only need to wait one more day until the first of many festivals and cheerful times began. Just one more day…

***

The smell of roasting meat, baked sweets, and ale danced through the warm evening air. Fiddles cried a joyous melody, and the guitars followed the drums in a rhythm of perfection. Clowns and jesters juggled and played tricks on the children, while others danced merrily.

There were archery contests and wrestling matches, while onlookers gazed upon feats the likes of which they had never seen. Men swallowed excessive mouthfuls of ale, their horny eyes buried in the cleavage of the myriad of voluptuous maidens. Then, suddenly, their ears perked up and everyone paused.

A thunderous voice barked out near the carousel, "Tis time for the first run of our magnificent new ride. Let the children come forward first and tame the beasts!"

There were only thirty seats, so for the first ride, the village only allowed the most promising children of the lot to take a seat on the animals. The gifted raced onto the platform, rushing towards their animal of choice. Once the backs of the galloping horses, agile tigers, muscular lions, enormous elephants, and majestic swans had been occupied, the switch operator started the ride. The children whizzed by as their parents cheered them on, all filled with jubilation. But one person, in particular, seemed almost too happy… almost too joyful…

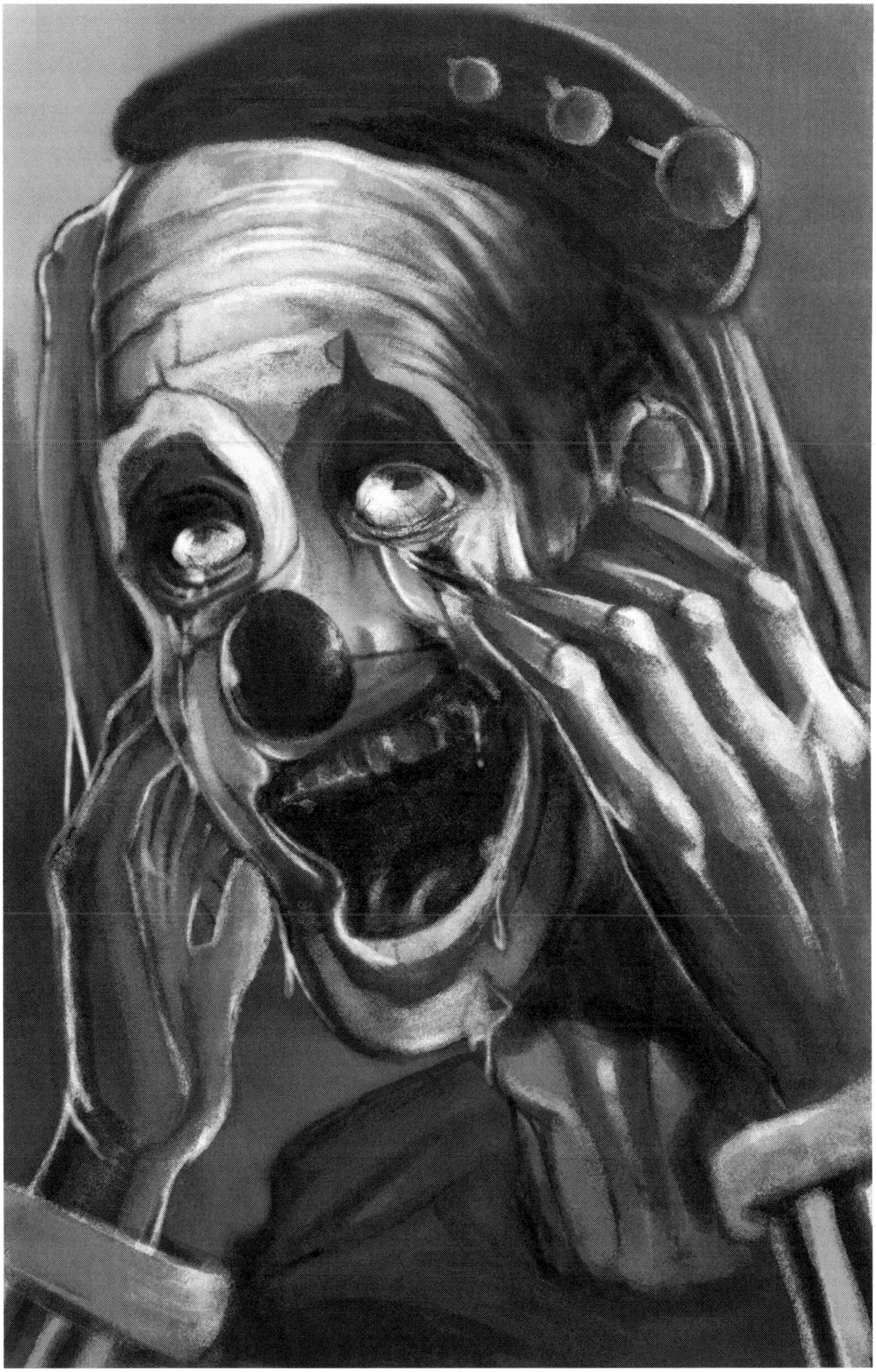

The clown who was responsible for making a fool of himself and entertaining the children so effortlessly had cracked up. He laughed and laughed until tears poured down the old fool's face.

The white greasepaint on his cheeks began to run, but his cackle never ceased. His gloved hands rubbed against his leaking face rabidly as the crowd looked on, confused by his blissful belligerence. The force of the movement appeared agonizing, and the self-destructive pattern was stunning. Suddenly, he stopped and pulled them away from his face.

The clown's inflamed swollen eyeballs were beset with bloodshot veins, and the wrinkled face of familiarity showed itself. The blackened mouth of the gypsy elder perked up as the wailing merriment escalated.

He ripped at the one-piece baggy garment that enveloped his frame until the belly had been torn. The tearing sound was ear-ripping and echoed through the night. An abominable wave of odorous excrement and lemon liquid raced out onto the ground to the cries and concern of the disturbed crowd. The soup of sacrilege continued to push out, even when it seemed there was no more that could physically be held inside.

The flood of filth had done more than prickle their nostrils and make for an unpleasant sight. It seemed, for those who could still focus outside of the mayhem, that everything around them was changing. The plentiful piles of succulent meat were no longer juicy and appetizing. They had transitioned into slop that was dehydrated and rife with maggot and worm.

The fiddler's instrument was no longer comprised of wood. Now, the mortified musician held an elongated slimy, hissing snake. Every mug that had been filled with refreshing ale was instead replaced with a muddle of hot blood and pus.

The carousel began to speed up to an eye-blurring pace until the shrieks of the children overcame the horrific prayers of their guardians. The messenger stepped up to the disgusting gypsy, trying to look past his demonic clown-like appearance, attempting to find the saner version of the man that once tried to reason with him.

"Sir, please! We beg of you to stop this witchery, spare our children! Please, halt the carousel!"

The wretched elder was still in hysterics as he extended his browed fingers and pointed toward the haunted structure. Each revolution that the carousel took got progressively slower until it finally stopped. The sick gypsy's laughter ended, and the stunned crowd watched speechlessly as his gross frame melted into the mess he'd left for them.

Their attention turned immediately back to their children whose screams had ceased, but it was not because the ride had done the same. Their tiny bodies sat clung to the countless poles, frozen in time. No longer were they warm and fleshy, they were now cold and solid, and each of the stone children had a permanent accent of terror methodically chiseled into them.

Even more threatening and disturbing than their children, were their former seats. No longer were they a detailed representation of the fearsome animals which they revered. The horses now huffed in frenzy, the lions roared with rage, the tigers drooled with depravity, the elephants stampeded toward sin, and the swans spread their wicked wings.

Violence erupted and was fixed upon the villagers. The massive swan pecked viciously at the messenger's head until it pulled it off. Then the sturdy beak crushed down on the skull, cracking it open like a carnal acorn before swallowing it entirely.

The razor-hooves of a frantic horse found a terrified lady's skull. The rear kick landed flush and dug in, kicking off a sizable chunk of bone and half of her face. The damsel fell limp and head-first, she faded away twitching and drowning in the pile of excrement.

The elephants ran over crumpled bodies, pulverizing them into a wet river of gore and fecal matter. The sound of skeletons cracking out into the chilly night would have been frightening if the villagers had time to process the dastardly details.

But others were busy trying to evade the lions and tigers. It was a futile task, the malicious cats pounced on the fittest and most physically capable, making short work of them. The unforgiving claws shredded their legs and Achilles, sending them screaming to the ground before putting fang to throat.

***

When the gypsies returned to the grounds the next day, the animals had slaughtered and chewed every villager without discrimination. It was a massacre for the ages, the remnants of those who had enjoyed the carnival were all but unrecognizable.

There was an entire village below the forest, now vacant and ready for the taking. It was all just a short hike away. The gypsies stood within the mess of death and defilement, looking off in the distance at the impressive township. While the modern conveniences and luxuries of the village were theirs for the taking, they didn't take another step. They were already standing on the only land they ever wanted.

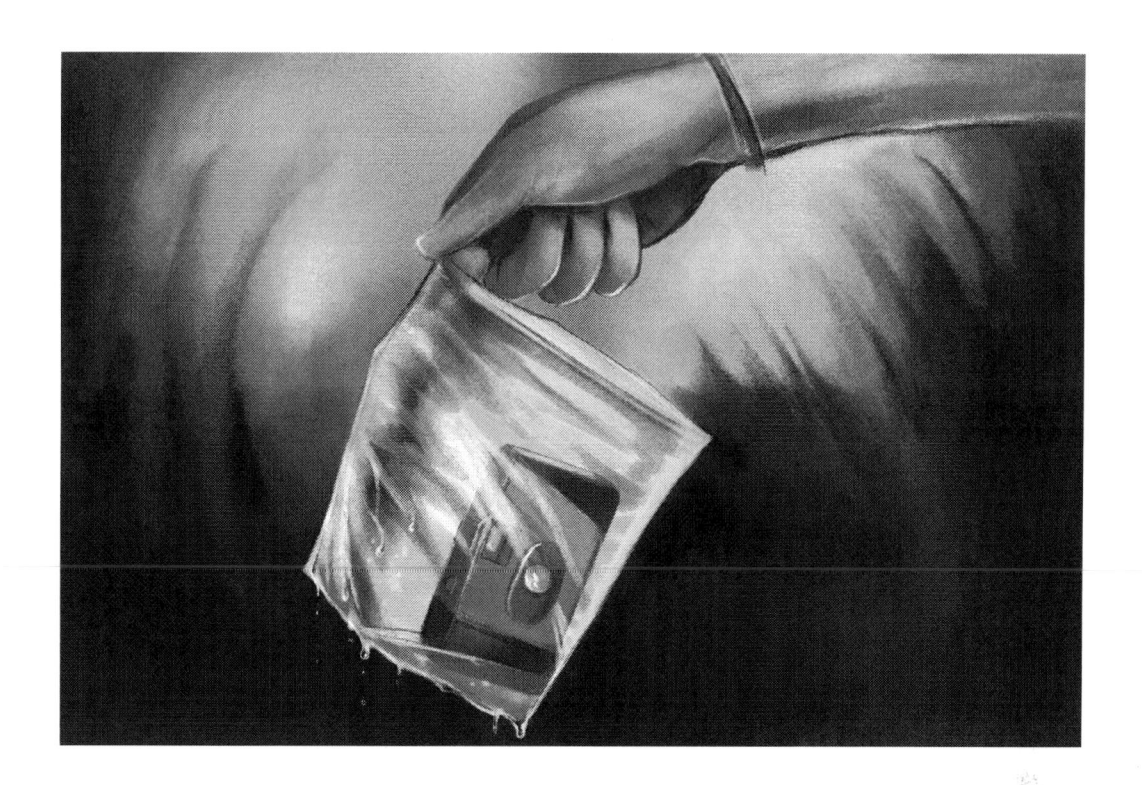

UPPER DECKER

"You ain't never done one before?" The surprise in Brad's voice bordered on disgust.

"Is that weird?" Ronnie asked, feeling some shame creep up.

"It's sad, not weird. Sad is what it is."

"C'mon, is it that rewarding?"

"What kind of a question is that? Of course it's rewarding, dipshit, it's nearly a permanent reward if you do it just right. That perfect hint of nasty that you can never quite put your finger on, that's the key. It can't be too weak but it can't be too strong either if you want it to go the distance, but it ain't easy, it takes the perfect balance of execution and preparation."

"But what does that entail exactly?"

"Usually eating mostly pickled eggs and broccoli exclusively in advance, maybe sprinkle in some gorgonzola as well for good measure. Essentially, you're just inflating your gut with the perfect storm of potent turd. This is my personal recipe, which has taken me years to craft. If you're just sitting around on your fat ass, eating McDonald's all week, you ain't gonna get that good, good. You can leave a McDonald's cheeseburger out for like a month and it won't rot, just sits there in perfect fuckin' condition. I've done it. Did you know that?"

Ronnie shook his head at Brad before he continued. "You see, this stuff's a lot more complex than you think…"

"Well, that explains your diet instructions. Finally, everything all makes sense now."

"Of course, it makes sense, Ronnie. This ain't some fuckin' game to me. I've been perfecting my skills for some time now. I know all the ins and outs… a first-timer like you should be suckin' my dick with the type of advantage I'm setting you up with."

"That's disgusting, dude—"

"I don't mean literally, I'm not a queer, you idiot. Listen, the bottom line is that it takes something special for the stench to be just strong enough to break through the porcelain tank. Not everyone is capable, do you understand?"

"Yeah, I get it…"

"Well, sometimes I still wonder with the way that you act," Brad replied snidely.

"Okay, I'm listening. I'm all in on this thing, man, one-hundred and…" he paused for dramatic effect, "two percent."

"I see what you did there," he said with a smile. "And that's good because today we find out if your deuce can produce."

"I'm scared."

"Ain't nothing to be scared of. Have I ever let you down before?"

"Too many times to count."

"Let me rephrase… have I ever let you down when it comes to fuckin' with someone?"

"Never."

"That's exactly what I'm saying. Just trust me, you got this. Now, when we go inside, just be cool. Remember, we are simply there to hang out, so just act casual. If anything crazy happens, just let me do all the talking. Okay?"

"Right on," Ronnie replied nervously.

"Alright, so you're ready then?"

"Yeah, I've been holding it for a few hours now, if we don't get in there soon, we might have some trouble. Don't want it to get stuck, might be building up a wall inside."

"Understood, we'd better get moving then."

Brad and Ronnie made their way up to the doorstep. Brad stuck his finger out and poked the ringer, letting the annoying buzz tread water just a little longer than necessary. When the door opened, they both projected false expressions of enthusiasm and innocence. The authenticity would have been difficult to decipher, although Ronnie looked a little tight on the count of him trying to keep his human volcano from exploding.

"Hey, Mr. Smalls, is Matthew here?"

"What exactly do you want, Bradley?"

"We just rented this copy of Clay Fighter 2: Judgment Clay, and I… well, we, wanted to see if Matthew could play with us."

"Video games rot the mind, Bradley. I should've expected no less from you…" Mr. Smalls paused briefly, rethinking his direction. "But on the other hand, Matthew could use some comradery. You can see if he's up for it, but next time you come, call first, okay?"

"Yes, sir, absolutely, you have my word on that."

Mr. Smalls' eyes tightened on the boys; he knew from seeing them around the neighborhood that they could be trouble. But Matthew didn't often have people come knocking at the door looking to hang out. He wasn't so out of touch that he couldn't see that his boy was an oddball. He watched the two of them scamper up the stairs with their video game cartridge in hand, and knock on Matthew's door.

"No freakin' way, Clay Fighter 2!" Matthew seemed happier to see the game than the people who'd brought it.

Mr. Smalls disappeared back into the living room, and both Brad and Ronnie entered Matthew's bedroom. Matthew wasn't surprised to see the two—neither of them had a Super Nintendo Entertainment System but they knew Matthew did.

It wasn't out of the norm for them to rent a game and then use Matthew and his hardware as the vehicle to play it. Matthew knew that they weren't interested in his company, but he was okay with that. To him, it was an even trade-off. They all coexisted and got to play stuff they normally wouldn't.

Brad and Ronnie had both very carefully selected this title… while the Clay Fighter series wasn't a particular favorite of theirs, they knew Matthew was infatuated with part one. Renting the sequel was a no-brainer if they aimed to keep him distracted enough for Ronnie to pop his cherry and drop his first upper decker.

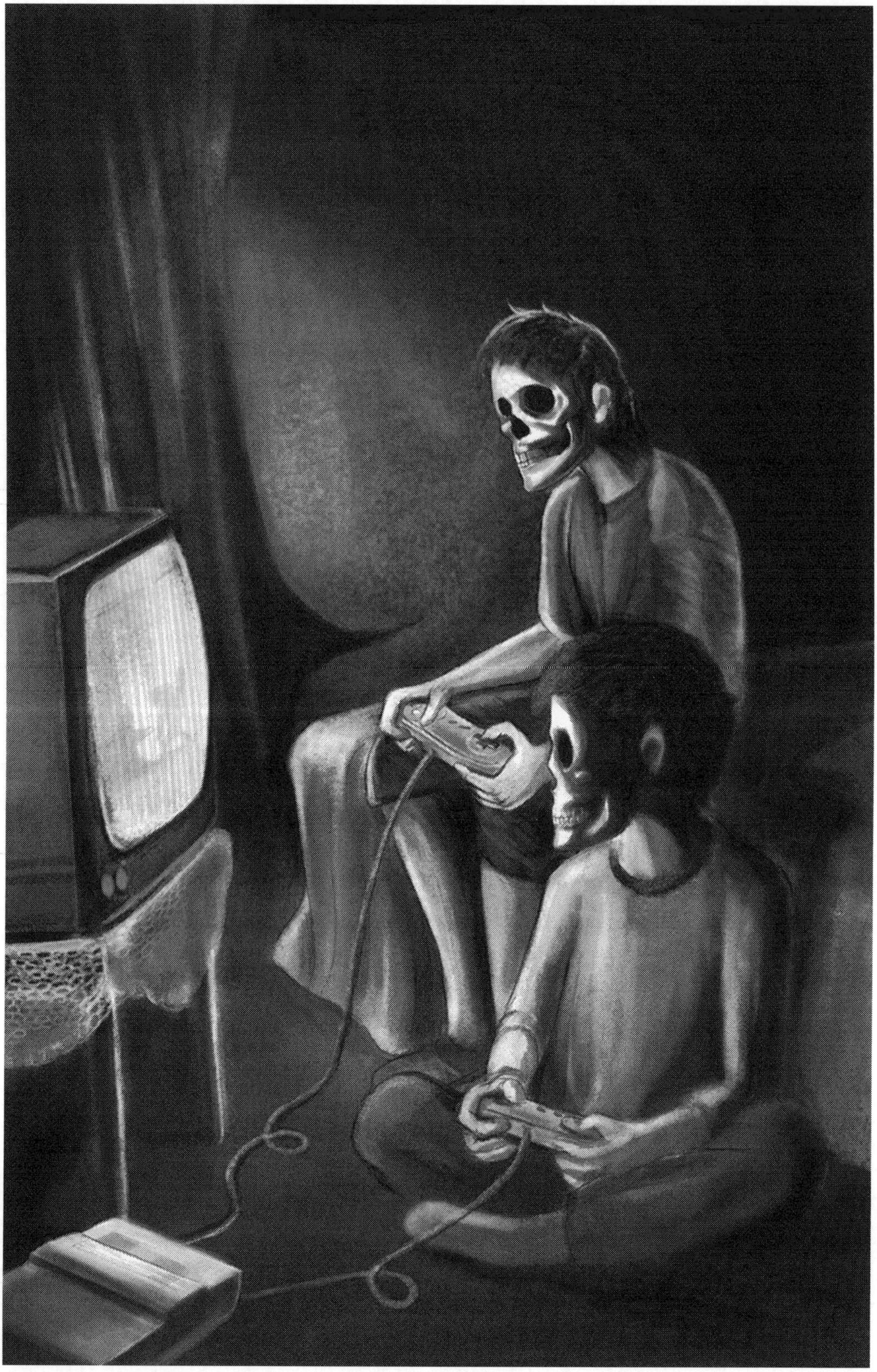

Matthew blew into the cartridge, unleashing a barrage of spit unintentionally, but when he popped the game into the console, it fired right up. The Interplay logo took over the eleven-inch tube sitting on Matthew's dresser, before the cheap Terminator 2 rendition featuring Hoppy the rabbit on his motorcycle faded in.

"Amazing," Matthew exhaled to himself. "The graphics look even better than before! Who wants to go first?" he asked immediately, letting his character selector rest with certainty on Bad Mr. Frosty, the deranged snowman.

"I can spank that ass right now if you'd like," Brad explained with the utmost confidence, picking up the second controller.

"I got winner!" Ronnie exclaimed. "But first, do you mind if I take a quick leak while you guys are fighting, Matt?"

"Sure, go now, I don't want any excuses. Are you good to go, or do you need to piss first too, hotshot? Never mind, I can just beat it right out of you and save you the trip."

Brad was stunned by his gusto. The little bastard was growing some balls, and it was time for him to kick them in. "You just signed your death warrant, turd brain!" he said while selecting Goo Goo, the massive and highly bizarre clay baby.

Ronnie quietly tiptoed out of the bedroom and gently closed the door behind him. He peeked downstairs and faintly heard the sound of the television. His chest was fluttering dramatically—he knew it was now or never. Ronnie carefully opened the bathroom door and did his best to quietly slip inside.

Just as Brad instructed, he didn't run the air vent to ensure he could hear anyone coming. And just like Brad had outlined, he carefully removed the toilet tank lid and delicately set it down on the washroom mat in front of the shower. He was sweating profusely and listening to every noise like his life depended on it while a big chocolate serpent continued to bend his bowels.

Gently, he balanced himself. Ronnie's ass hovered over the exposed water tank as his wrinkled anus began to smooth out and throb rapidly. He could barely hold it any longer, the lumpy turd pressed against his intestinal tract like a condom suffocating an erection. At that magic moment, he was in the perfect position to unload. He said a brief prayer to God that he let his first upper decker drop into the tank seamlessly, and as his beating fleshy gateway opened, the Lord granted his simple wish.

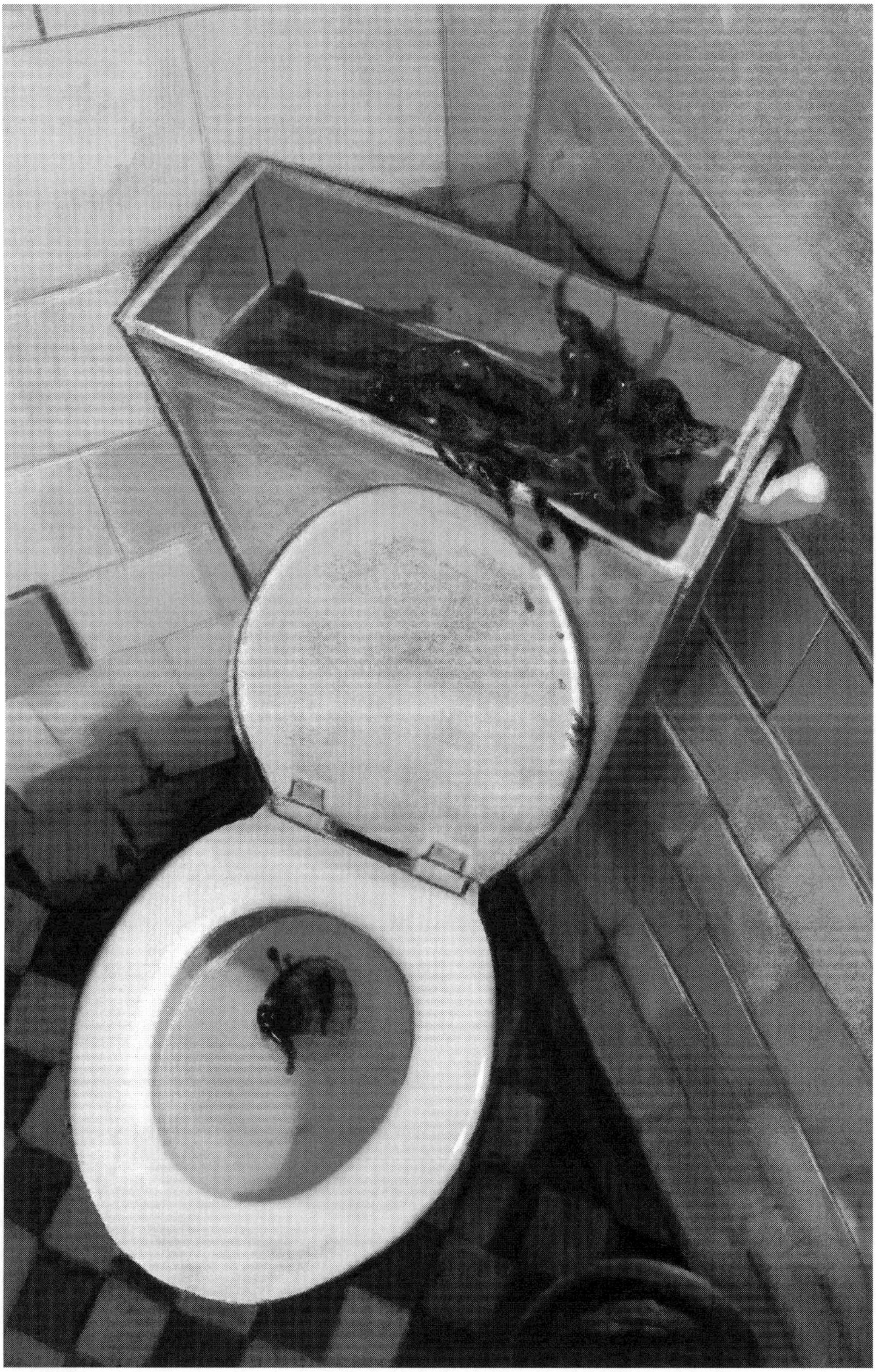

The beastly turd carried on for feet; it was probably the biggest he'd ever laid. It felt like an adult snake was coming out from hibernating in his asshole. The scent of the monster nugget was ungodly, despite being (in Ronnie's mind) delivered with his blessing. He looked down toward his feet and there was no sign of a missed target, splatter, or overflow—success was his.

Brad was right, he was truly adept in the field of sport shitting. He had effectively coached him through the birth of his first brown child. Now all that was left was to wipe his butthole, take a look at the output, cap the bitch off, and let her simmer.

Ronnie stepped down off the toilet lid and opened it up. After a few careful wipe downs, he dropped the soiled tissues into the bowl and flushed. Now he could take a quick moment and comfortably marvel at the gem he'd executed to perfection.

It looked otherworldly in length like a human couldn't have produced it. It coiled up like the cooking rings on his grandmother's stove and was probably just as hot. As beautiful as his baby was, there was something drawing his eyes off the turd. Something on the other side of the container that surely was out of place inside a toilet tank. There, in a clear plastic bag, sat a disposable camera…

Curiosity compelling him, he couldn't help but let his mind wonder what could possibly be on it. It had to be something sensitive if it was being hidden in such a funky place. It was too bizarre not to cause one to wonder, but suddenly, his wild imaginations were shattered by a dreadful sound. The sound of the doorknob turning…

Thankfully, Brad had beaten into his head that locking the door was by far the most important step of laying an upper decker. The frustrated hand outside the door moved on from twisting the handle to pounding on the door.

"Why are you taking so long in there? I need to do my business soon or there's going to be a problem." The anger in Mr. Smalls' voice was blended with irritation.

"I'm sorry, Mr. Smalls, I'm almost done!"

Trapped in the moment, Ronnie's inquisitiveness melted with his current action. He flushed the toilet again and turned on both sink faucets to create a layer of noise to operate under. If he was smart, he would have just set the lid back down, but he couldn't help himself. He had to know what was on the roll.

He pulled the bagged camera out and wiped it off with the hand towel. Once it had been cleared of any water, he slipped it into his cargo shorts. With the sink still running, he felt comfortable that the ever-lurking Mr. Smalls couldn't hear a thing, although that didn't make him any more patient.

As Ronnie grabbed hold of the toilet tank cover, the pounding started up again. The suddenness of the racket caused it to slip through his fingers, but just at the last moment, in an almost miraculous feat of phalange strength, his grasp was restored.

"Ronnie! Let's go!"

Inches away from shattering the porcelain cover, Ronnie's heart was running over time. "Just washing my hands, I'll be done in a wiz, Mr. Smalls!" he hollered back as he finished slowly setting the cover over the repugnant mess he'd left behind.

When the door came open, the stench hit Mr. Smalls in the face with force. While he desperately needed to relieve himself, he still took a step backward out of pure instinct.

"Jesus, son, what the fuck did you eat? And why the hell didn't you turn the fan on?" he asked, flipping the switch on the wall.

"I'm sorry, I didn't know you had one. I don't think I'm feeling too hot all of a sudden, must've been something I ate."

Ronnie entered Matt's room, escaping his father's hateful glare. Upon entry, he watched Matt putting the finishing touches on a nearly flawless ass-whipping on Brad. His frustration was bubbling as the shit-eating grin curled Matt's lips.

Ronnie took a seat and watched on, but his focus wasn't on the competition. Instead, he wondered if whoever put the camera inside the toilet might go looking for it. Was it Mr. Smalls that dropped it there? Did he have hot pictures of his big titty wife imposed into the film? They hadn't seen Mrs. Smalls since they arrived, but part of him hoped that the pictures were dirty.

Porn wasn't exactly easy for Ronnie to come by, so the thought of even a mildly attractive woman like Mrs. Smalls showing her pussy or sucking cock gave him a solid erection and made his blood pump. The inner pervert overrode any potential embarrassment he might face in stealing the secret pictures.

The entire time they played, Ronnie continued to think. Maybe they weren't of his wife, maybe they were of another woman, and that's why he had to hide them in such a strange place. He pictured Mr. Smalls checking the tank and bursting into the bedroom, furious about the discovery.

As they approached the two-hour mark, the nightmare scenario didn't manifest. Ronnie could only assume that if he was going to get caught, it would've already happened. Either that or Mr. Smalls didn't want to draw attention to a missing item that no one else was supposed to know about.

As Matt finished annihilating Brad for the hundredth time, he seemed to finally be ready to throw in the towel. "Okay, I'm done, fuck this stupid game!" he yelled, tossing the controller to the floor.

Brad got up and ripped the cartridge out without even turning off the system. "Let's go, Ronnie," he mumbled.

"Hey, loser! Turn it off first at least! You don't have to be such a butthead!" Matt yelled.

"Smell you later, nerd," Brad retorted.

Ronnie followed Brad from his room and down the stairs. He was glad he was moving quickly and heading straight for the front door. Ronnie couldn't get out of there fast enough, and as the entrance opened, he was alarmed to see Mr. Smalls standing outside. He deeply inhaled his cigarette, eyes burning a hole through the boys as they stepped out onto the porch.

"Oh, Mr. Smalls… I didn't know you smoked, have a good night, sir." Brad murmured, not expecting to have seen him out there at all.

"You're very observant, Bradley. I typically don't, but sometimes the stress of life and its unpleasantries can force your hand. You'll understand what I mean someday, I'm sure of it…"

Neither answered back, each anxious to end the conversation for different reasons. As they jogged down the last few steps, they heard Mr. Smalls call out to them.

"Boys, you will come back and visit Matthew again, won't you?"

They looked back at him, one nodding and the other giving the thumbs up, but they still continued walking. Once they got a safe enough distance away, they got right into the details.

"So, did you lay it in there? I heard that crazy fucker pounding on the door and I about shit myself!" Brad exclaimed.

"I did it and it was beautiful… I just wish I could see their faces when they smell it every day!"

"Me too, brother, me too."

"There was something else though, something strange in there…"

"What do you mean?"

"In the tank, I found this," Ronnie replied, slowly retrieving the bagged disposable camera from his pocket.

"Holy crap, dude! What the hell do you think is on there?"

"I don't know, but it's gotta be good. You saw how nervous Mr. Smalls looked. He's up to no good."

"I bet there's pictures of pussy on there!"

"Shit…" Ronnie muttered.

"What?"

"If they're nudes, how the hell are we gonna get them developed without getting caught?"

The smile melted off Brad's face as his friend stumped him with a painful conundrum. Teased by the thought of authentic photos of nude ladies, he racked his brain. Then suddenly, it dawned on him.

"OH, MAN! I GOT IT!" Brad bellowed.

"What?!" Ronnie shared his enthusiasm.

"Danny Vargus, my older brother's friend, works at Brooks! The guy's a total piece of shit! I'm sure if we just gave him like five bucks, he'd keep his mouth shut!"

"You're a goddamn genius!" Ronnie exclaimed.

"If we leave right now, we can make it there before closing, and by after school tomorrow, we'll be sitting pretty, with more vage on our hands than Johnathan Taylor Thomas."

The boys raced off into the night with their hearts pumping blood with fury. The excitement of the unknown, and the joy of youth, was fueled by their raging hormones and lustful desire to get their hands on something they would never forget.

***

Ronnie's foot rocked up and down anxiously as he stared at the clock. Only fifteen minutes until the bell rang, and then his curiosity would finally be quelled. One thing he found to be a bit odd was that Brad hadn't shown up for class.

That bastard, if he was gonna skip school to get an early peek at the pussy, the least he could have done was let me in on the plan, he thought to himself, a bit annoyed by the whole idea.

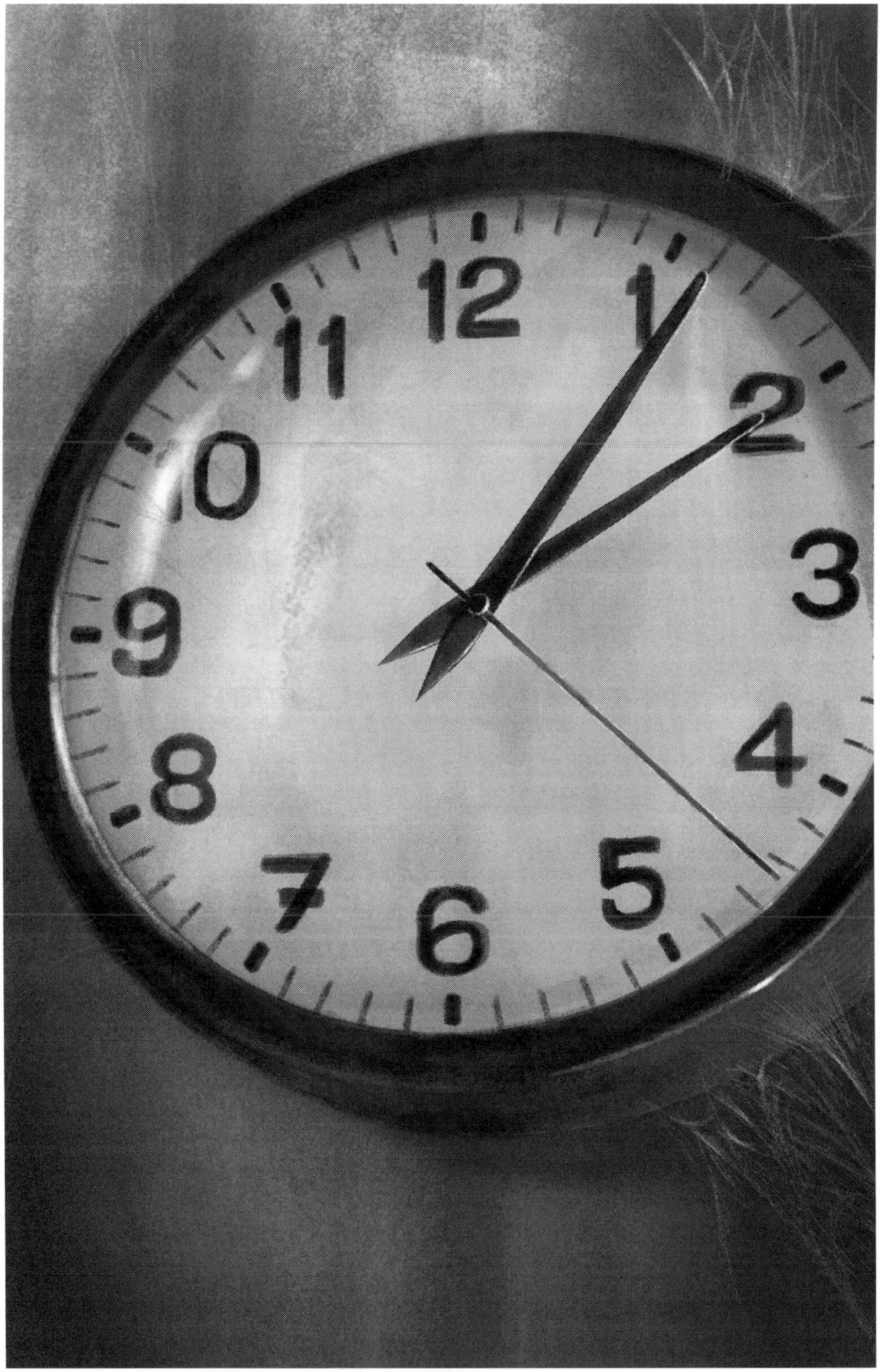

Just as the anger began to tread over his guts, a knock landed on the classroom door. Ms. Jetty pulled the handle open to reveal two large men wearing middle-of-the-line suits. They flashed a pair of police badges and one whispered into her ear. Seconds later, Ronnie's teacher lifted her arm and pointed her finger directly at him.

The men didn't have much to say to Ronnie until they got down to the station. They sat him down at a small table in a dark room and activated a desk lamp.

"What's going on?" Ronnie asked, nerves muddling his tone.

"I think that's something you're gonna need to tell us, kid. Because you're in some serious shit right now," the burly and bearded detective grumbled, lighting up a cigarette.

"What do you mean?"

"You like taking pictures, kid?" he asked while his puffy-eyed partner remained mum.

"Oh, this is about the pictures... Look, I'm sorry, I know that we shouldn't have—"

"Forget the fuckin' apologies! It ain't us you gotta apologize to, it's their families!" the burly detective yelled, letting speckles of saliva leave his mouth and find his face.

Ronnie's fear was taking hold of him. He didn't know what was wrong, but he knew it was something terrible. "What the hell are you guys talking about?!"

"I'm talking about the goddamn mess you made. I'm talking about those kids you mutilated!" he screamed, tossing an envelope with a collection of horrible gory photos onto the desk. "Man... you are one sick puppy alright..."

"SICK FUCKIN' PUPPY!" the other detective yelled, finally breaking his silence in a bizarre fashion.

His partner looked at him a bit taken aback by the strange outburst before turning his attention back to Ronnie. "Don't play stupid with me. You tried to develop the pictures with your little friend and hoped he'd keep his mouth shut. But it turns out he's not a total fuckin' ghoul like you. He called us, and voila, here we fuckin' are. That sound about right to you?"

"No! These aren't mine! I got the camera from a kid that lives down the street from me! It was at Matthew Smalls' house! The camera was in the toilet tank! I swear!"

"Christ, now I've heard it all, Richie," he said, turning to his partner. "I'm gonna need you to shoot straight with me, kid. STOP FUCKIN' AROUND WITH US! If she didn't wanna suck your little cock, and you got a little rough with her, just tell us. You'll feel a lot better once it's off your chest."

"It wasn't me! You're not listening! Where are my parents?!" Ronnie cried out, starting to sob.

"NO, YOU'RE NOT LISTENING! Your parents are the reason why you're in here alone! Who the fuck do you think gave us permission to talk to you!"

"W-Why would they do that?"

"Because, you see that dead girl in this little memento you developed?" he asked, watching Ronnie nod his head slowly. "Well, we found pieces of her in your closet. Your parents said, sure, search the house, Ronnie's got nothing to hide. Turns out they were wrong. Dead wrong."

"It can't be possible... it just can't be..."

"Well, it is, and your ass better get talking or things are only gonna get worse." The burly detective finished off his cigarette and snubbed it out in the ashtray.

"Brad! Brad was there with me! He can vouch for everything I'm saying! Just call him!" Ronnie yelled, believing he found his ray of hope.

"That weirdo down at the drug store said the two of you showed up there together. Really, he is just as much of a suspect as you at this point. But that's not the problem."

"What's the problem then?!" Ronnie's emotions were boiling over violently. He felt like his life was crashing down on him.

"The problem is, we tried askin' him already, but he never made it to school this morning. And wouldn't you know it, the last person he saw was you…"

Earlier that Morning

Mrs. Smalls had been waiting outside of Brad's house since before sunrise. When his front door finally came open and he jogged down the steps, her heart started to race. She shifted the car into drive and crept down the one-way street at a snail's pace. Once she got close enough to Brad, she tugged at the front of her top, exposing her mountainous cleavage, and rolled down the automatic window.

"Hey, Bradley, need a ride, honey?" she asked.

"Mrs. Smalls?" he replied in a voice that showed that she was about the last person he imagined seeing that morning. "Mrs. Smalls, what are you doing here?" he asked, unable to take his eyes off her enormous breasts.

She wasn't the most attractive mother, but Mrs. Smalls clearly knew how to work with what the good Lord had bestowed her with. She leaned over, further flaunting her busty top, and slid her sunglasses to the tip of her nose. "Why don't you hop inside and find out?"

Brad's heart started to smash against his ribcage. He knew she must have figured out what they'd been up to last night. He was now wondering if the disposable camera in the toilet actually belonged to Mrs. Smalls. Why else would a woman he'd only interacted with on a handful of occasions be showing up outside his house in such an accidental fashion?

While Brad remained speechless, Mrs. Smalls decided to lay it on a little bit thicker. "I know you have my pictures, Bradley. You've probably already seen my body, but do you know what can be soooo much better than pictures?"

Brad took a big gulp and tried to swallow the lump in his throat. "W-What's that?" he squeaked, almost too nervous to get the words out.

"The real thing," she replied in her most seductive voice.

The car doors unlocked, causing Brad to jump back. His mouth began to water as he further stared her down. His mind had been made up a long time ago. He'd been dreaming about getting his pecker inside of the first female that would have him for years now. It was time for the wet dreams to dry up... it was time for the real thing.

"Are you a virgin, Bradley?" she asked, biting her lower lip. His frozen lack of response was answer enough. "That's okay, we can fix that. C'mon, get in."

***

When they pulled up to the dilapidated building, Brad wasn't sure what to think. It was a private setting; the factory clearly hadn't been in use for some time now. During the awkward car ride, they'd drifted far away from the city and into surroundings of rural randomness. The factory was clearly no longer in use—overgrown vegetation blanketed the entrances.

"Where are we?" Brad asked, getting a bit anxious.

"Somewhere private. Somewhere that no one's going to bother us."

"Why here?"

"If we're gonna have fun together, we can't let anyone else know. You understand that, don't you?"

"I won't tell anyone," Brad replied, shyly trying his best to conceal his raging arousal.

"That's a good boy," Mrs. Smalls replied, pulling around and parking the car out of sight from the lonely stretch of road.

They both exited the car, and Brad followed Mrs. Smalls to the rear entrance that was wrapped in rusted chain. She extracted a key from her purse and unlocked the chains, opening the door. A dark staircase leading to the bowels of the aged building appeared.

Brad felt a strangeness simmering in his guts, but that now conflicted with his hormonal excitement. "What's down there?" he asked with a hint of embarrassment.

"A grown woman being with a young boy isn't exactly accepted, so we need to take precautions. Once we're inside, no one will be able to see us, and then we can do whatever we want, okay?"

"Okay," he replied, licking his lips in anticipation.

Upon entry, Mrs. Smalls locked the door behind them. She activated a battery-operated lantern before they worked their way to the bottom of the steel steps amid the eerie darkness. Once they reached the floor of the basement, they approached a lone chair that was surrounded by numerous rotting crates.

She set the lantern on the ground and pointed to the chair, "Have a seat and relax," she instructed him, pulling down the top half of her dress and exposing a pair of hardened perky nipples.

Mrs. Smalls approached him and rubbed his shoulders seductively. She let her pointed breasts graze his back as she guided him into the chair.

"Now, just relax," she whispered into his ear, causing his erection to throb with ecstasy. "I just want you to feel this," she told him, turning off the lantern.

"Can't we keep the light on?!" Brad yelped.

"I just want you to focus on the feeling first," Mrs. Smalls whispered, putting the boy's hand on her bare breast.

"That feels so good," he giggled.

"I have something that feels even better, but you have to trust me, okay, Bradley?"

"Okay."

Mrs. Smalls felt around in her purse until she felt the texture of the rope against her fingers. She knew the knots by heart, and in a matter of a few seconds, she had each of the boy's extremities bound to the seat.

"I don't understand, why are you tying me up? Aren't I supposed to touch you?" he asked.

Mrs. Smalls offered no answer, and all Brad could hear was a faint and unsettling rustling noise.

"Mrs. Smalls? What are you doing?"

Other odd noises continued that he couldn't quite place. One sounded like a cap unscrewing, grinding against metal.

"Mrs. Smalls, I don't think this is such a good idea anymore, can you please untie me!" he cried.

Then the smell hit him; it was one that he oddly enjoyed while sitting in the backseat of his father's station wagon every time they pulled up to refill. It was the smell of gasoline.

"Mrs. Smalls! Why the fuck does it smell like gas in here now?!" he screamed, having reached the pinnacle of discomfort and fear.

"You know, my husband thinks I'm having an affair, but really, it's something much worse than that," she finally replied, ignoring Brad's question.

"What the fuck are you talking about?!"

"I was still trying to figure out how to develop those photos. I wanted to remember what it was like so badly, that I just couldn't let them go. I would've figured it out, even if I had to learn how to develop them my goddamn self. They might be gone now, but at least I'll have a couple of fresh memories to hold me over."

"Untie me! Let me go!" Brad cried in full-on sobbing hysteria.

"I would've never even known that you boys took them if it wasn't for that god-awful smell in the bathroom. It just wouldn't go away. So, I had to take a look before anyone else got curious about it. When I saw that the camera was missing, I thanked my lucky stars that I still had some pieces of the Maynard girl down here."

"Turn on the light!"

"Alright then," Mrs. Smalls replied, flicking a match across the rough edge of the box.

When she tossed the lit stick at Brad, it took less than a second for his entire body to become engulfed in flames. He screamed as loud as he could, but there was no salvation from the charring heat. As he burned alive, more of the room was revealed by the leaping flames.

Nestled just out of sight where they'd initially come down the steps, sat the corpse of a young girl. Her mangled face and once precious features were beyond distorted. Most of her hair had been sliced off, and long gory patches of rotten skin still glistened with a relative freshness.

As Brad's runny vision angled down at his hands, he noticed the rope had burned away and he was no longer restricted. But unfortunately, he was now devoid of the strength necessary to take action. The meat on his arms blistered with an aching rawness, and then transitioned to a char.

He now understood that Mrs. Smalls was not the quaint and polite housewife he'd always believed her to be, but that revelation did him little good in his final moments. While the sick woman watching him incinerate in the shadows held the recipe for pain and death, Brad burned away holding the recipe for the perfect upper decker. One that, for him, regrettably worked just a little too good.

THE REWARD

One dark day in the city, a young girl fell out of a window. She lived so high up in the tenement, almost in the clouds of the filthy city smog. By all accounts of those who saw it, the little girl was dead without a doubt. There was nothing between her and the cold, unflinching concrete that laid below.

Then, suddenly, in almost magical fashion, a man appeared out of nowhere. The city commuters were shocked when he ran into the picture with a super-human stride. He selflessly snatched the doomed girl out of the air mere moments before she would have splattered all over the dingy city sidewalk.

Everyone cheered. It was as if they'd arrived at the conclusion of a concert or pep rally. The stressed onlookers felt a deep sense of relief to have avoided bearing witness to a terrible tragedy. It wasn't every day that people had the opportunity to witness an act of heroism like the man demonstrated for the neighborhood that gloomy afternoon.

The story quickly got out and made the news. The cameras posted up everywhere in the bustling city. They didn't have to look far to speak with the many residents waiting to sing their praises of the man. Each individual that saw the miracle was more than happy to tell the story of the little girl who was rescued after tumbling out of the window.

"He's a hero," one said, singing his praise.

"I've never seen anything like it," a woman explained, wiping tears from her shaken eyes.

"That man came out of nowhere. That poor little girl would have been dead if it wasn't for him!" another shouted.

The man got a brief fifteen minutes of fame, a snippet or two on the local TV news, and a small column of print in the back of the weekend newspaper. But after that, the incident faded away with all the other news stories. Most everyone forgot about it… except the little girl.

As the girl grew older, she started to realize that the man had never been properly rewarded for his actions. She thought about him for a great deal of her existence, never letting the memory slip away from her.

When she was younger, she never had a way of contacting him since the incident had occurred. But years later, she had at last matured and blossomed into a more resourceful young adult. She still felt the same burning urge within her to find the man that saved her.

The feeling flourished inside even more with each day that passed. It became an obsession for her. Until it reached a point where she couldn't eat or sleep. All she could think about was the mysterious man who had altered her existence and saved her life.

It didn't take long for her to go through the archives and find the write-up about the incident. She studied the old newspaper clippings and engaged with the smeared photo of him staring back at her. Her fingers ran back and forth over the ink like she was touching him.

After a bit more digging, she found out that, like her, he still lived in the area. They weren't in the same neighborhood anymore, but he wasn't too far from where she currently resided. The man deserved so much more than just the handful of minutes in the spotlight years ago.

The next day when the sun rose, she set out to meet with him. It was that day that she would finally come face to face with her savior. It didn't take her long to arrive in the morning. The dreary sky was almost at full dimness with just a few slivers of light cutting through the city pollution again. It was just like her vivid memory of that fateful day.

She ascended the stairs to the high-rise complex until she stood before the man's door. She knocked gingerly three times and waited.

After a short time, the door creaked open dramatically. Her heart was thudding wildly. The anticipation had been killing her. Would he be how she remembered him? Would he bear the same kind and glowing eyes that wanted to make a difference? The eyes that sought to preserve life no matter what the cost?

When she got a look at the other side of the door, she was a bit surprised. The man had changed. He was quite old and gray now. He was a far different version than the one she remembered stealing her out of the air all those years ago. His skin was riddled with liver spots and wrinkles, but his caring smile still hadn't faded.

"Hello there, young lady, to what do I owe the pleasure?" the old man asked curiously.

"You might not remember me. The last time I saw you, I was only six years old," the girl replied.

The elderly man continued to ponder who exactly the pretty young one before him could be. After wracking his aged brain a bit more, a look of enlightenment seemed to set in.

"It can't be," he whispered under his breath.

"You saved my life," she added promptly, dispelling any doubt about who he was speaking to.

"For God's sake, it's… it's you," he replied in disbelief.

"Yes, it's me."

"Come in, please come in." The man's astonishment was evident as he cleared a path for her to enter. He offered her a seat on the couch and then he slumped down into his favorite chair.

"I never thought I'd see you again," he said.

"Well, I never thought I'd see you period," the girl replied.

"What brings you my way after all these years?" he wondered aloud.

The girl still stood before him, not accepting the seat he'd offered. Instead of readying herself for friendly conversation, she began removing her clothes. First, her shirt came off, and then her pants, socks, and shoes.

"What are you doing?" the man asked, stark confusion setting in.

The girl continued removing her garments one article at a time. She placed all of them neatly on the far end of the couch until she stood before him completely naked.

"I never had a chance to reward you for what you did for me."

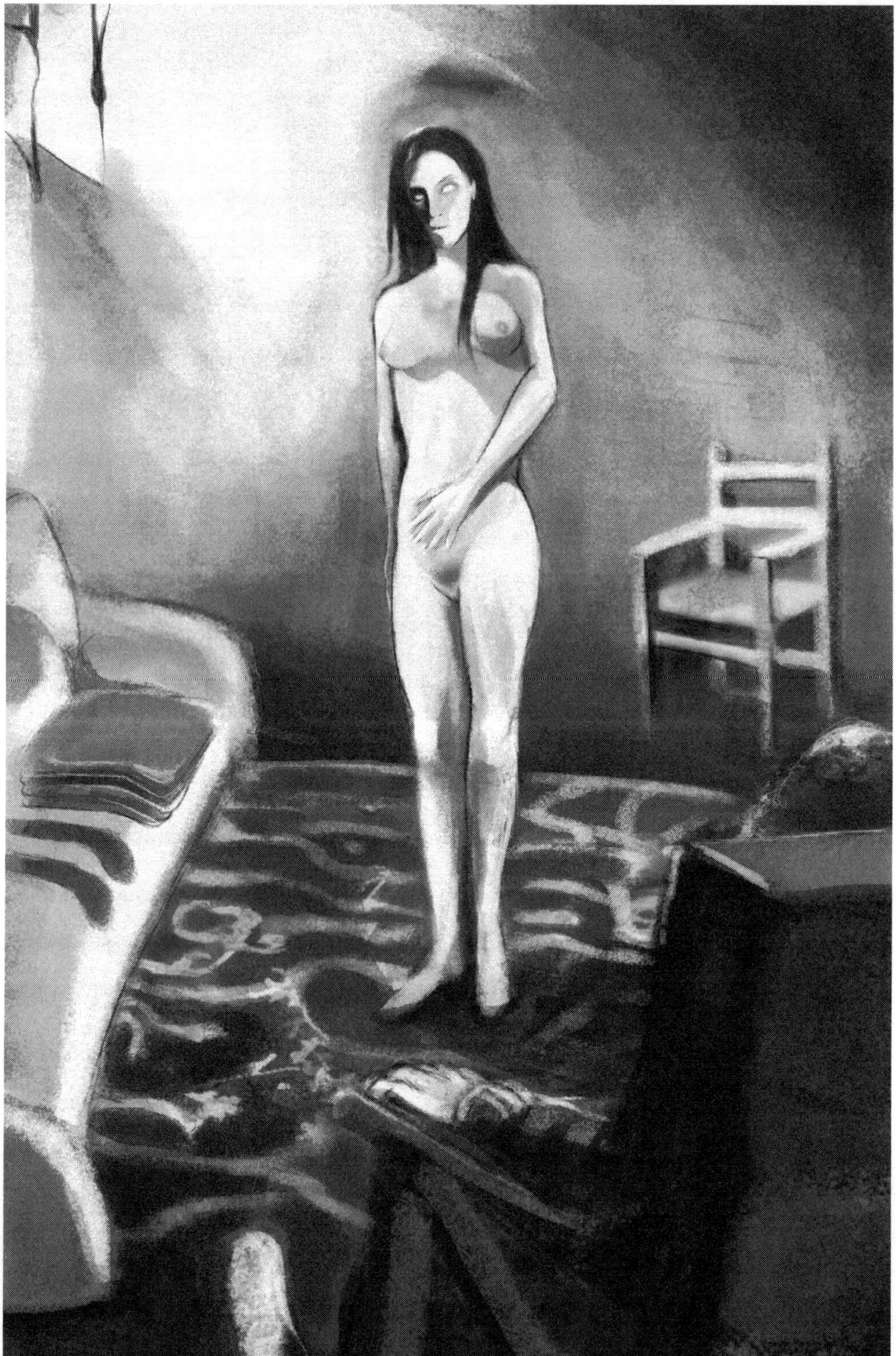

The old man sat dumbfounded, unsure of what to say. The idea of taking advantage of the girl felt evil and dirty to him. There was no way he would be able to do what she wanted him to.

"Do you like what you see?" she asked the man.

The man didn't feel comfortable looking at her body. He still remembered the young girl that needed help. The tiny body that was too innocent to touch.

"You're very beautiful but—"

"But what?"

"But you're just a young girl, this isn't right. It isn't right for me to look at you like this," he replied, shifting his wrinkled brow out of her alignment and focusing on the clothing on the couch.

"Maybe you shouldn't look then. Maybe you should just touch me instead," the girl replied, taking a step forward.

The man was overwhelmed and paralyzed with fear. He couldn't seem to find the appropriate words to respond to her. His wrinkled brain remained frozen in limbo, unsure what to do next.

The girl stood over him with certainty and took hold of his spotted hands. Slowly, she lifted them and dragged them over her tight stomach, and finally left them to rest on her pointy nipples.

The old man's heart began to beat furiously in his chest. The mixture of excitement and stress created a bizarre sensation and pressure inside him. The aged member in the old man's pants that hadn't found solidity in ages was now as hard as calculus.

The girl spread her legs and dipped her fingers down, letting them slide over her clit. She rubbed it side to side vigorously.

The man's eyes couldn't help but drift down to the intense flicking action that was occurring just below his slumped eye level. He hadn't seen such a ripe and ready piece of woman since he could recall.

"Do you like it? Do you want it?" she whispered.

Finally, the state of shock that the old man was immersed in wore off. He quickly removed his hands from her breasts and was able to formulate a few words. "You don't have to... we don't have to do anything. You don't owe me anything," the old man explained.

"But I do, nothing could be further from the truth," the girl replied.

As the girl reached behind her back, the old man began to hear the sound of tape peeling off of flesh. When her small bony hand reappeared, it was clenching a long and pointed knife.

Before the oblivious old man could understand what was happening, the unforgiving steel was already inside him. It jammed through his shell and plunged deep through his frail and tender torso. The blade sliced into the old man's meat before skewering a pair of his vital organs.

She'd pounced on him animalistically, stunning him with ruthless violence before he was able to rise from his recliner. The stabbing repeated as the old man threw up a mixture of puke and blood all over himself.

She left the blade half lodged inside his sternum and retreated to the bathroom to shower. Blood swirled down the drain, mingling in with the warm water. Once she'd cleaned herself thoroughly, she dried off and made her way back to the living room. The man was wheezing in his last breaths as he watched the girl get dressed. With the look of betrayal and confusion still carved into his expression, he was able to muster one final query regarding the incomprehensible turn of events.

"Why did you stab me? I was... I was the one that saved you... I saved you, damn it," he cried, coughing violently as hot blood erupted all over his chest. "I saved you when you fell out the window..." he managed.

The girl looked at him the same way he looked at her, they mirrored each other's pain to a tee. "You don't understand, mister. You never did. What you, and the news, and all those other people never understood was... I didn't fall out of that window... I jumped."

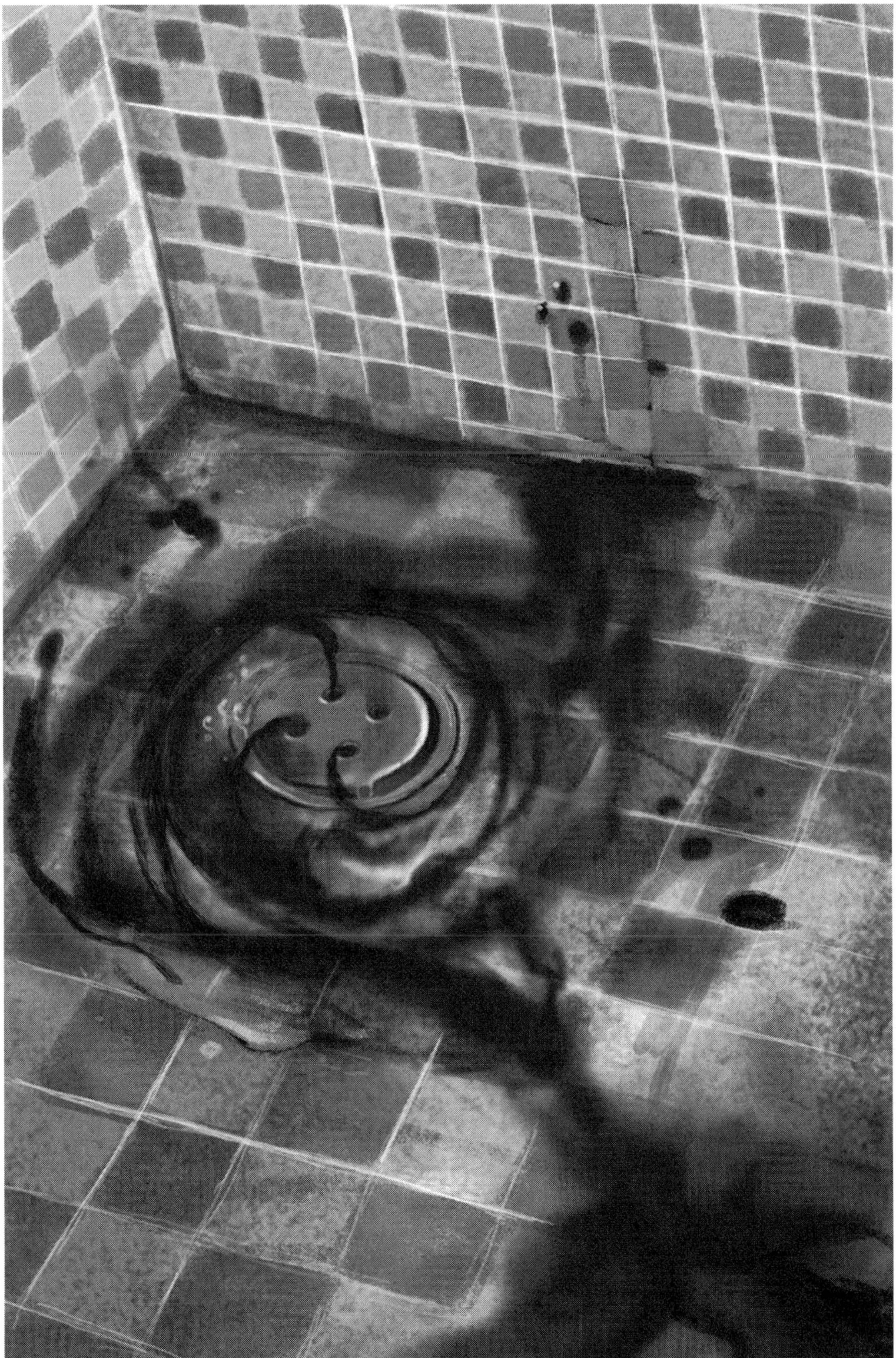

THE JIGGLE JOINT

Cali applied a thick coat of bronzer to her already orangey complexion in preparation for her next encounter. Alex was a client that had proven to be highly lucrative, and in turn, he was her top priority. The man treasured watching Cali grind her bolt-pierced clit against the chrome pole and shake her thick ass like an earthquake was in the works.

In her industry, you had to be aware of the prospects with deep pockets. It wasn't her first time around the block, she understood all too well how much the right man could bring in. She understood that it was a lifeline. Like fish in a barrel, once the hook was set, Cali jerked it deep and far, ensuring that there would never be room for escape. Ensuring that she would be privy to a lavish rock and roll lifestyle.

Her movements were hypnotic and the vibes she emitted at times seemed otherworldly. Cali held a crippling control over her men—they acted like well-trained dogs for her. They sat where she told them to sit, they stayed quiet when she hushed them, and they always kept their eyes on her and no one else.

The human horndogs found themselves gripped by an unforeseen devotion—slimy men that didn't have a shred of devoutness to their own families magically found loyalty in a whore. They all obeyed, but more importantly, they paid.

She'd woven a sticky web, one that her admirers often found themselves entangled within helplessly as she sucked them dry. Cali offered the party flocks and regulars fleeting moments of ecstasy in exchange for their prosperity. She'd become so adept at applying the squeeze, that she had no qualms about boasting her yield amongst the other dancers.

The ladies weren't immune to her charms either; she mesmerized both sexes and even the inbetweeners. As she swung about the pipe like some strange half-breed—part athletic humanoid, part slithery arachnid—they all salivated, oozing susceptibility.

"Damn, Cali, that ass looks better by the day, sugar. I know it's against Leon's stupid fucking policy but… would you… would you wanna get a drink with me sometime?" Bambi asked nervously.

Bambi was the new girl. She'd only been there a few weeks, but already she'd become less concerned with making money, and unable to unglue her focus from her gorgeous peer. She stared at her chest like the construction worker that had just gotten out of work and was ready to get ripped. True to her name, she was a deer in headlights.

"You're so cute, honey," she turned to the scrawny rookie that seemed like she might've had a little bit of a heroin problem. She used her arms to press her breasts together and arch her back. "But why would a sweet little thing like you wanna get a drink with me?"

"Because you're breathtaking…" she replied, cheeks blushing a shade deeper than what she'd artificially applied to herself at the start of her shift. "You probably know that already, but I just wanted to tell you, you're perfect to me."

The girl was clearly head over hooker-heels for her. That sort of confessional style love admission was uncommon in the filthy trade they'd decided to invade. But around Cali, the special moods wormed their way into the hearts of the unsuspecting with regularity. She didn't have to do much except be herself for the golden opportunities to zero in on her. She was more than magnetic.

"While that does sound lovely, I have a client to attend to. ATM Alex should be here shortly."

"Oh, I didn't realize he'd be here today," she replied, still too green to pick up on the regular's schedules. There was a tiny hint of jealousy that accompanied her response, an emotion that Cali heard ad nauseam in nearly everyone that she spoke to.

"Maybe you can take me out and buy me a drink… and dinner sometime though?" If she was going to chill with a low-level stripper, there needed to be a reasonable payoff that was more valuable than a myriad of mushy compliments and a cheap orgasm. She could get some from just about any damn direction she turned in.

"I would love that," Bambi chirped excitedly.

There was no way Cali was blowing off her best client for the new girl. There was a good reason she'd branded him with the backstage nickname of ATM Alex. He'd earned the label on account of spitting out dollars with a religious negligence, faster than a cash machine. Every Tuesday night, same place, same time.

The income Cali pulled in from his lust was something that she counted on like clockwork. Alex always sat discreetly in the darkest corner of The Jiggle Joint. She'd seen to it that it was reserved for him, and him only. She couldn't have anything or anyone interfering with their appointment.

They usually started there with some conversation about general bullshit, and after a few forced laughs and drinks, they made their way into the back. He got whatever he wanted but it didn't come cheap. Alex wasn't a bad-looking man, so Cali looked forward to fucking him. Every time he busted a nut, it was accompanied by the sound of a cash register opening in her mind.

"Well, if you can't see me yet, you wanna at least do a quick line with me before you go?" Bambi asked sheepishly.

"Sure," Cali said, never being one to turn down a high.

Bambi pulled the credit card out from the slot in her phone, and then pulled her panties aside. She pushed her long fingernails inside herself and extracted an 8-ball from her pussy.

Cali did a camel-sized bump and chased it with a small collection of pills that she'd been hiding inside her bra. She felt the shit kick in immediately and then looked down at her phone screen. It read 7:00 PM.

It was time to rub her silicone stuffed tits in Alex's face for a few hours and then collect the BMW payment. But when she peeked up at their table, for the first time her strung-out skull could recall, Alex wasn't there.

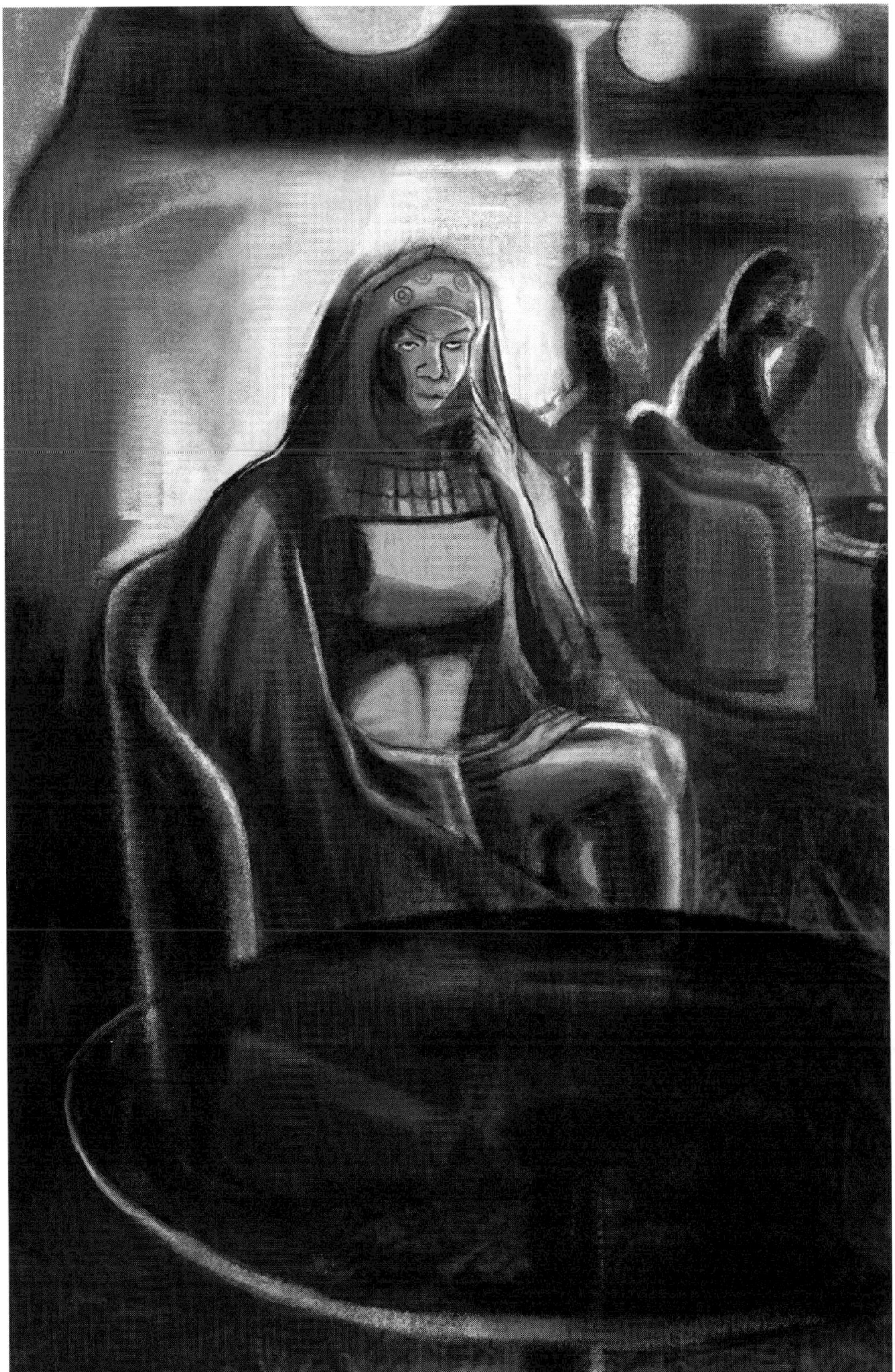

Panic and confusion set in without reservation—her meal ticket, her elevated status, her entire life all hung in the balance. The drugs only served to amplify her warped emotions. Even more alarming, their table was occupied by an unfamiliar woman…

Her face looked like she'd ordered a can of Coke and someone had spiked it with soy sauce. A combination of shock, anger, and repulsion took hold of Cali as she flipped her hair into Bambi's face.

Bambi took notice of Cali's sudden attitude shift. She might not have known Alex's exact schedule, but she knew where his table was and what he looked like. He most certainly did not look like the sinister woman that was currently occupying his seat.

"WHO THE FUCK… is that third-world looking bitch that's sitting in Alex's seat?!" Cali barked, locking eyes with the woman who she noticed had been keyed in on her from the moment she'd entered her line of vision.

"She's been here for a while now, hasn't said a peep to anyone, had a drink, nothing. Looks like she's just been waiting for someone," Bambi replied.

"You saw that dumb skank sitting in Alex's seat and didn't say anything?!" Cali was looking to vent her frustration and venom upon whoever was accessible.

"I didn't know he was coming tonight, I swear!" she replied, now nervous because of her crush's misdirected outburst.

"It doesn't matter what night it is! It could be Mongo the fucking janitor wiping it down and it would still be a problem because nobody, and I mean NOBODY, touches Alex's seat."

"I'm sor—"

"Hush, I'm gonna let it slide this time, only because you're new, but you'd be wise not to let it happen again."

"It definitely won't, I promise, Cali," she replied, achieving a new level of embarrassment.

Feeling wronged and increasingly savage, Cali strutted her ass in the direction of the glaring woman in the cushy chair. The woman was draped in a mix of wine and ebony-colored cloth. A spotted headband sat atop her furrowed brow and slithered under her dark veil.

Contrary to the overdose of skin that was on show in the crooked establishment, the mysterious woman was nearly covered entirely save for her face and forearms.

She approached the eerie woman without a drop of fear in her system. Cali advanced to the table until she was looming over the out-of-place patron. The stripper stood tall and comfortably in her thong and skimpy top, confident and cocky as always.

Their eyes remained bitterly entangled; like the first one to blink lost their soul. The staring contest started with no end in sight, a natural hatred manifesting amid the smoky, polluted air of The Jiggle Joint. Cali had figured the odd woman would be the first to say something but, still, she remained mute.

Cali's perfect body trembled with rage—she'd held her tongue for as long as her hot-headed state would allow her. "This seat is reserved, bitch. So, get lost, or else," Cali sneered at the stranger with a territorial defense mechanism that bordered on animalistic. The Jiggle Joint was her turf, she wouldn't permit people to just stroll in and serve up the disrespect without repercussion.

"Cali?" The woman seemed immobilized by the gravity of her thoughts.

"Who the fuck wants to know?" The charm that she so often used to her advantage was left by the wayside.

"You have a way with people, but you have much to learn, child," she replied in an eerie islander accent, ignoring the question.

Her response was enough confirmation for the enigmatic woman. As she opened her hand, Cali's gaze drifted to the sparkle of her wedding band—the symbol of her love, the symbol of her rage. Without warning, she blew a cloud of fine snowy dust from her palm directly into the stubborn stripper's attractive face.

The woman watched carefully as the particles got sucked up Cali's nostrils before she even realized they'd been sent. It wasn't uncommon for powder to find its way into her sinuses, but this wasn't anything like the yayo she normally inhaled.

A sense of aloofness seized her. The always in control, running the show nature vanished from her expression. Suddenly, the leer of vindictiveness and wrath melted off her entirely. Her shoulders slacked and the screws loosened. She'd become a ball of slutty putty.

"This is the end," the woman whispered. "There's no more money left for you to steal. You're going to have to earn it like you did before. The hard way. Now, take it off. Take it all off. And don't you let up until every inch is stripped away," the woman ordered.

She set down an extended cruel-looking straight razor on the table in front of her. The woman watched as Cali reached for the blade absentmindedly like she was picking up a dollar bill on any other day.

***

When a new track hit, Cali stormed the stage. She'd already cut off her underwear and stood completely nude and blank-faced. The men were initially thrilled in seeing her flesh upfront, but by her song's end, the club had virtually cleared out. The froth-mouthed whistling men quickly realized that although she wasn't wearing any clothing, she still planned on stripping.

As the thumping and sleazy electronic instrumental dug in, so did the straight razor. First, she cut around the skin on her forearm, just deep enough that she could dig her fingers in underneath. Once she had a grip on the sheet of skin, Cali ripped it back toward her.

The horrifying noise was so distinct that it cut through the music. The few straggling horrified patrons sat in a state of stupor that couldn't be cured. Discounted bar snacks were coming up with the liters of alcohol they'd been washed down with. Chunky puddles of undigested gruel plopped down on the already stained rugs.

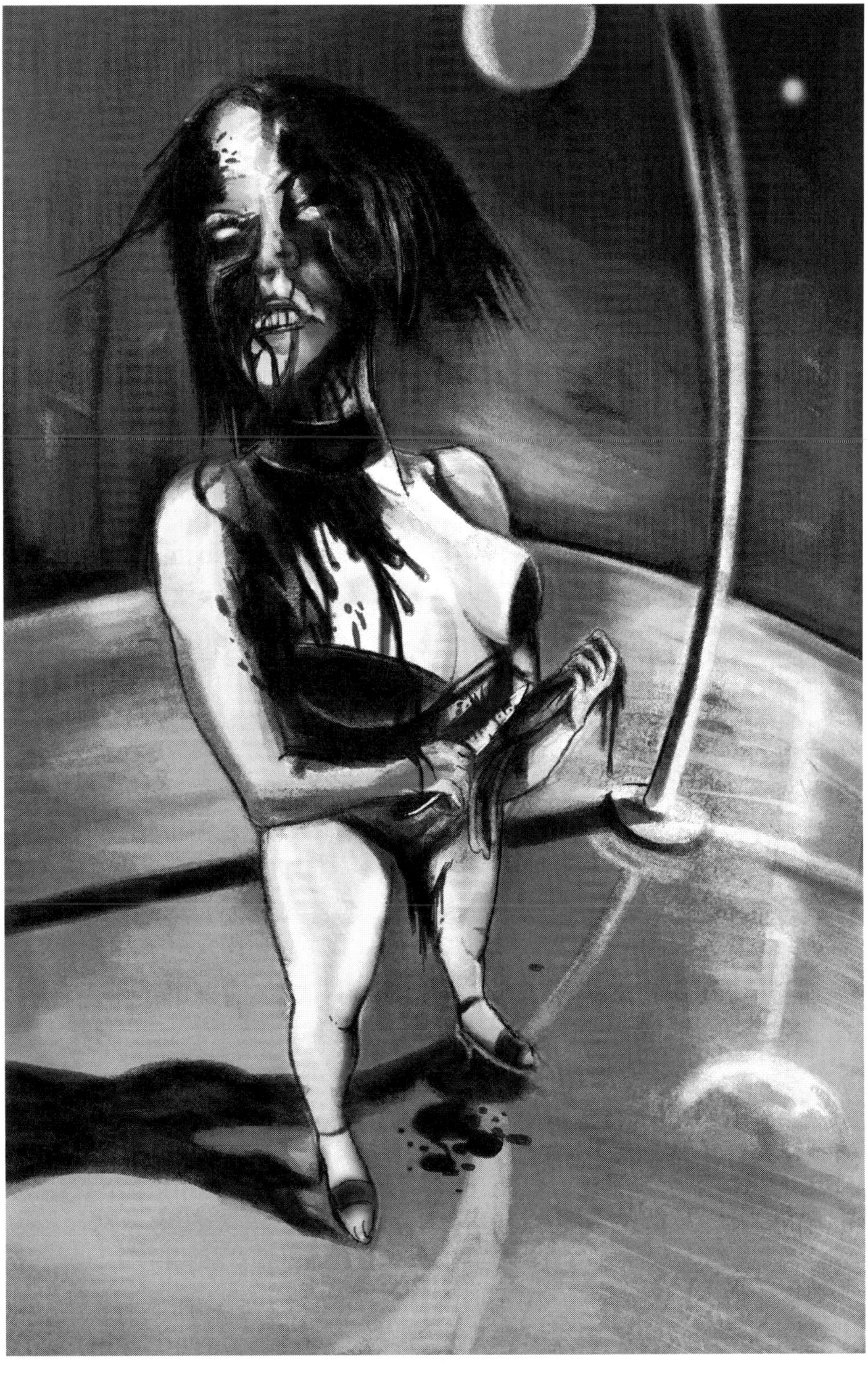

Cali continued on, merely exposing the slimy muscle beneath. But it still wasn't good enough. She stabbed into her flesh heartlessly, like it was her sworn enemy's car tire, until she'd carved out a route that led down to the bone. She let out an ear-splitting scream as she took off the meatloaf-sized hunk of her essence and dropped it down on the stage.

Despite the cries and morbid groans, there was no pause in her performance. The blade found her throat flesh next. The half-foot incision allowed her to stick her free hand under the skin that covered her collarbone and shoulder.

She yanked down violently like a dentist pulling a tooth and used the blade in her other hand to cut through the tight tissue until she'd exposed herself all the way down to her belly. Her blood-speckled right implant dropped out onto the growing mess on the stage beneath her.

Cali was beyond the point of no return. The look in her crazed eyes said that she wasn't done yet. The gore that gunked up the steel was far from the last. While blood continued to flow, and skin continued to tear, the wicked woman sat watching, her grin widening with each new bone uncovered.

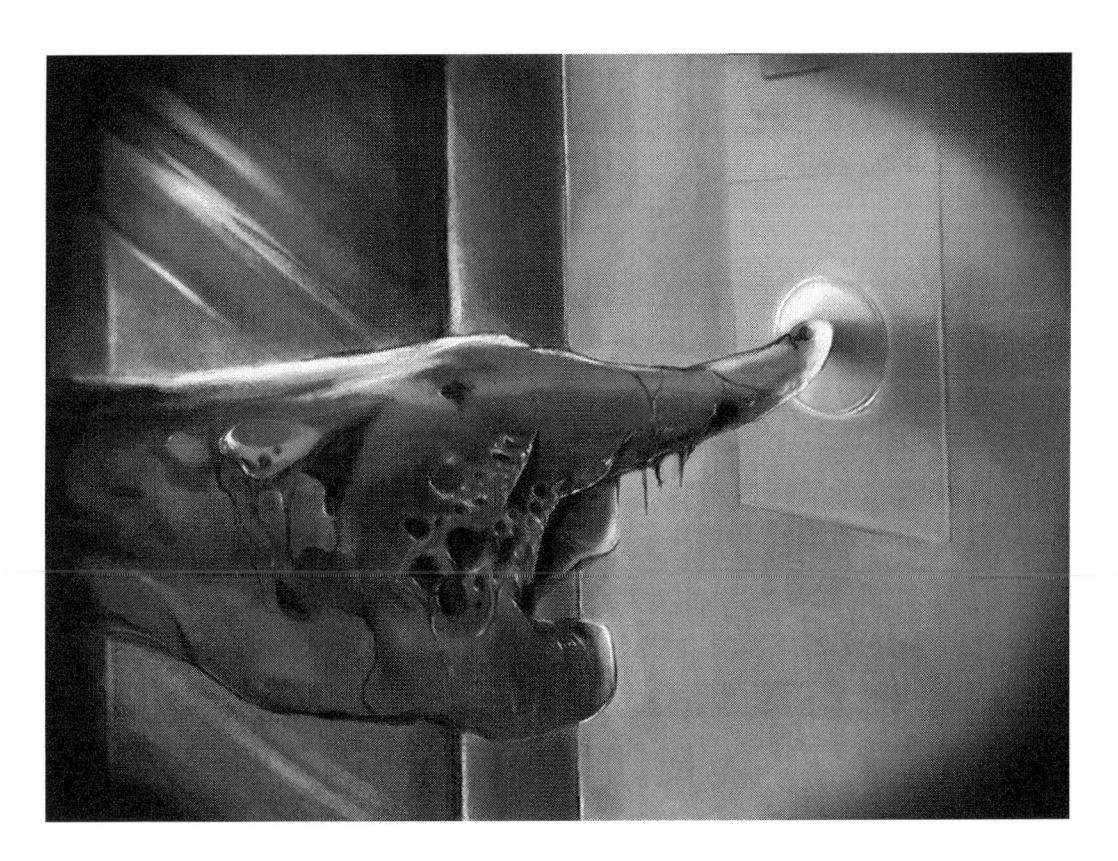

SHAFTED

There were a handful of renovations going on at the old hotel. The stagnant halls were filled with peeling wallpaper and moldy scents. Some folks in the city claimed the soon-to-be reopened establishment was haunted. If nothing else, it certainly *looked* haunted. There was no urgency behind the task at hand, the building wasn't expected to be reopened for six months. It surely wouldn't be an overnight effort based on the gargantuan face-lift the nasty building needed, but the timeframe was more than generous.

The first team to arrive was a pair of mechanics; their job was of a more complex nature than the rest of the work that would take place elsewhere in the hotel. The older of the pair was a weary veteran, a ripened man who knew all the tricks of the trade. His final job sounded like a routine one, the only challenging aspect would be simultaneously training his replacement. They were set to review an issue with the main elevator, which had fallen out of compliance and at minimum required updates.

The grizzly mechanic confidently crept up to the control box with his protégé and called the elevator. He inspected the numeric indicator with a wrinkled brow, and as the massive steel rectangle traveled down to the midpoint of the twenty-third floor, he pressed the stop button and opened up the doors.

"Eh, the cylinder's beat to shit, she can move now but that won't be the case for long if we don't get this thing replaced. Follow me," he commanded the trainee.

"Where are we going?" the baby-faced youth inquired.

"We're finished for the moment."

"Finished? Already?"

"Yeah, they don't just have elevator cylinders hanging around at the corner store, kid."

They made their way out from the side entry and approached a payphone outside. The old-timer fished a few coins out of his pocket and fed them to the outdated device.

He punched in a number he knew by heart, and while he dialed out, his counterpart waited. He noted how the old man spoke with authority and confidence during his initial greeting, but wasn't afraid to cut through the bullshit with the parts warehouse.

"A month? For a cylinder? You'd think we were waiting for the second coming of Christ!" He slammed the historically abused payphone down on the receiver and looked at the kid, "These people just don't have the same sense of urgency anymore. I hope you're not like that, I hope you have more class than those clowns."

"Yes, sir," replied the boy firmly. "Now what do we do?"

"Now? Now, we wait, son. Not much else we can do. They've got us by the balls. I'm just glad this is a slow job. Next time, if that ain't the case, you might need to shake them up a little. Sometimes you gotta light a fire under their ass, you got it?"

"Yes, sir, I'm willing to do whatever it takes."

"You better, otherwise, it'll be your ass." As he turned his back to the youngster, he offered the closest thing to a goodbye that he could muster. "See you in a month, kid."

"Wait, before you go, can I ask you something?"

"Spit it out," he replied, twisting toward him again.

"Do you ever get scared coming into an old building like this? A building folks say is haunted? Usually, you're alone, right?"

"Don't believe in that nonsense. Things like that'll only scare you if you let 'em. I don't let nothing scare me. Remember, you're in control of your thoughts. You ever seen a ghost, boy?"

"No…"

"Well, there's your answer."

"Yeah, you're right, it's stupid. Hopefully, I can think just like you do one day."

"You'll get there," the old man concurred while sending him a final friendly wink.

***

The mechanics eventually returned the following month. The two of them wheeled the wide cylinder through the eerie lobby in unison until they finally reached the maintenance shaft. The doors were still propped open just as they'd left them and in severe need of a polishing. Their stained reflections appeared distorted just like the rest of the building.

"We got a long day ahead of us, kid; this install is no amateur job. But at least it'll be a damn good piece of experience for you," the seasoned senior explained.

"I can't wait," the young man replied, eager to get his feet wet.

After about three hours, they finally paused, and the old man fished a drink out of the lunch bag in the corridor. He leaned up against the grimy decaying wall like he was getting ready to take a load off.

"We'll have a quick drink, and then we'll fire this son-of-a-bitch off and see if we did as good as we think we did." As he took a big swig of his soda, the young man opened his own and looked up at him reluctantly. "What? I can tell you wanna say something, kid. Why don't you sack up and just go ahead and say it?"

"I know you said you don't really get scared, but don't you think it's a bit creepy about those painters? Everyone in town has been telling ghost stories about this place since I can remember, and then mysteriously, the only other people working on the building just disappear," the young man inquired, pepping up but still sheepish.

"I suppose it's odd that they just vanished. I mean, I'm not spooked by it though, not one bit. Don't let those tall tales get in your head, son. Usually, there's a more human explanation when people go missing. Not the hogwash you hear makin' the rounds."

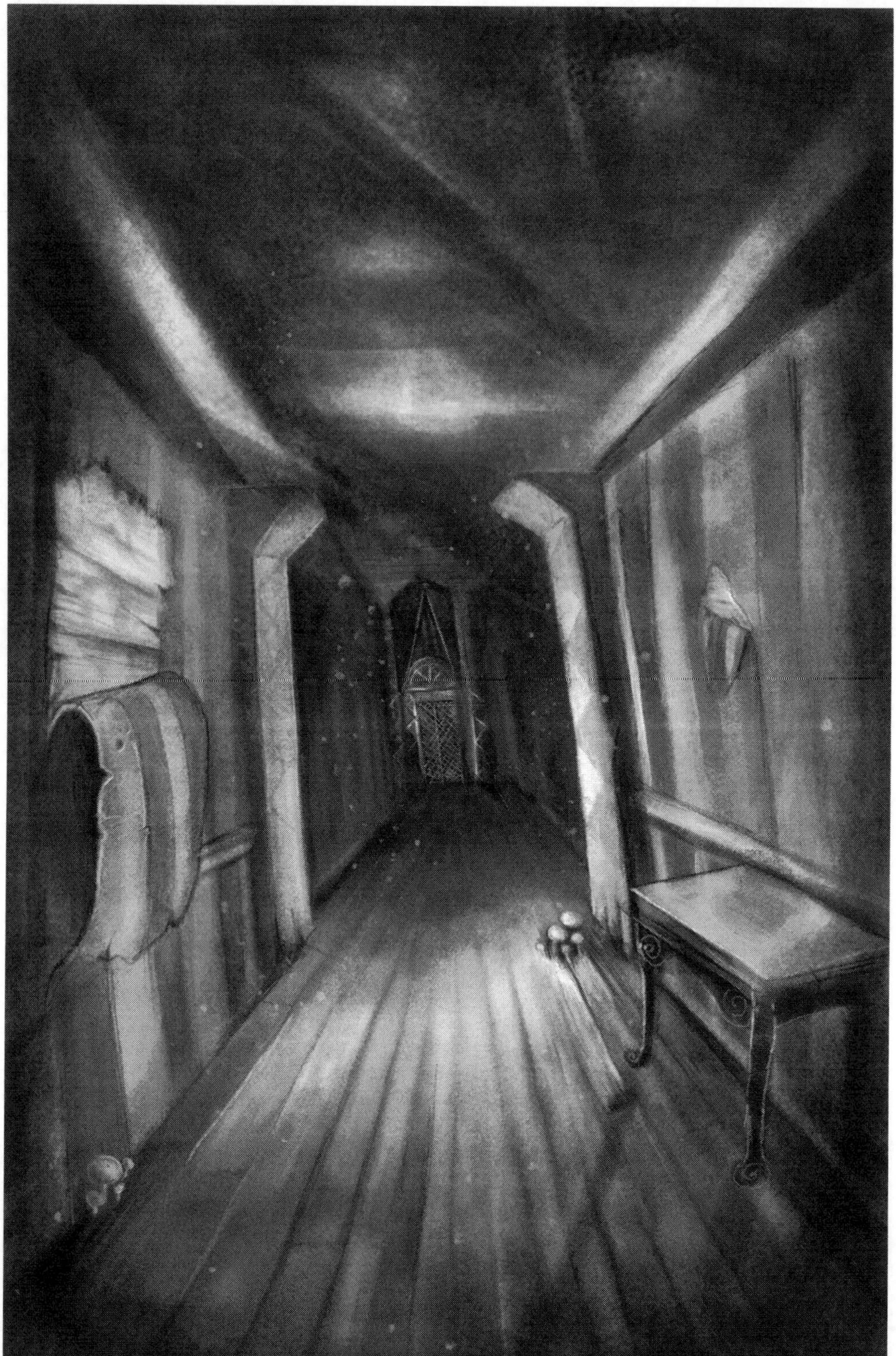

"The police said the security camera across the street caught them coming inside, but they never came out. They covered every inch of this place and found nothing. How do you explain that?"

"I don't, I just do my job and move on. If you're so damn worried about it, then let's fire off the elevator now and get the hell out of here."

"Fine, I don't wanna spend one extra minute in this hotel if I don't have to. The place just gives me the creeps."

A shiver ran down the young man's spine as he approached the elevator, looking over to his teacher as he nodded. "Go ahead, kid, I'll let you do the honors."

The young man pressed the button, and the elevator started up flawlessly. They looked at each other in delight over a job well done. The young man's delight was more jubilation at the thought of them making their exit in mere moments.

The kid wondered what it felt like for him. The old man didn't get excited about much, and he was officially retired after the job. In his mind, he knew that there was probably a part of him that was sad. The working phase of his life was shutting down, like an old fire that had run out of wood. The flames had stopped jumping and the ash was no longer red and vibrant, he was getting closer to being cold and extinguished.

As the elevator doors came open, he studied his face. He wasn't exactly sure what he was looking for, but the reaction he witnessed was anything but what he'd expected. The kid watched, shocked, as the stone-pulsed professional's jaw dropped.

His eyes now suddenly held a bottomless fear and his skin color turned ghostly in a matter of seconds. The youngster's concern grew leaps and bounds as the old man grabbed the area of his chest where his ticker was located. He looked like he was having a heart attack as he collapsed to his knees, hyperventilating.

The young man was terrified to ask and unsure if he could answer, but he did so anyway, "What's wrong?!" he cried. Saliva spat out from his dying superior's lips and his movement stilled. He didn't have to wonder what had caused the episode for long, the smell crept up from behind and hit him like a golden-glove boxer.

As he turned around, there sat the painters on the floor in their speckled overalls with their paint cans and brushes strewn below them. Maggots and flies covered their juicy, dripping flesh. They had gobbled up sizable portions of their now green and gray exteriors.

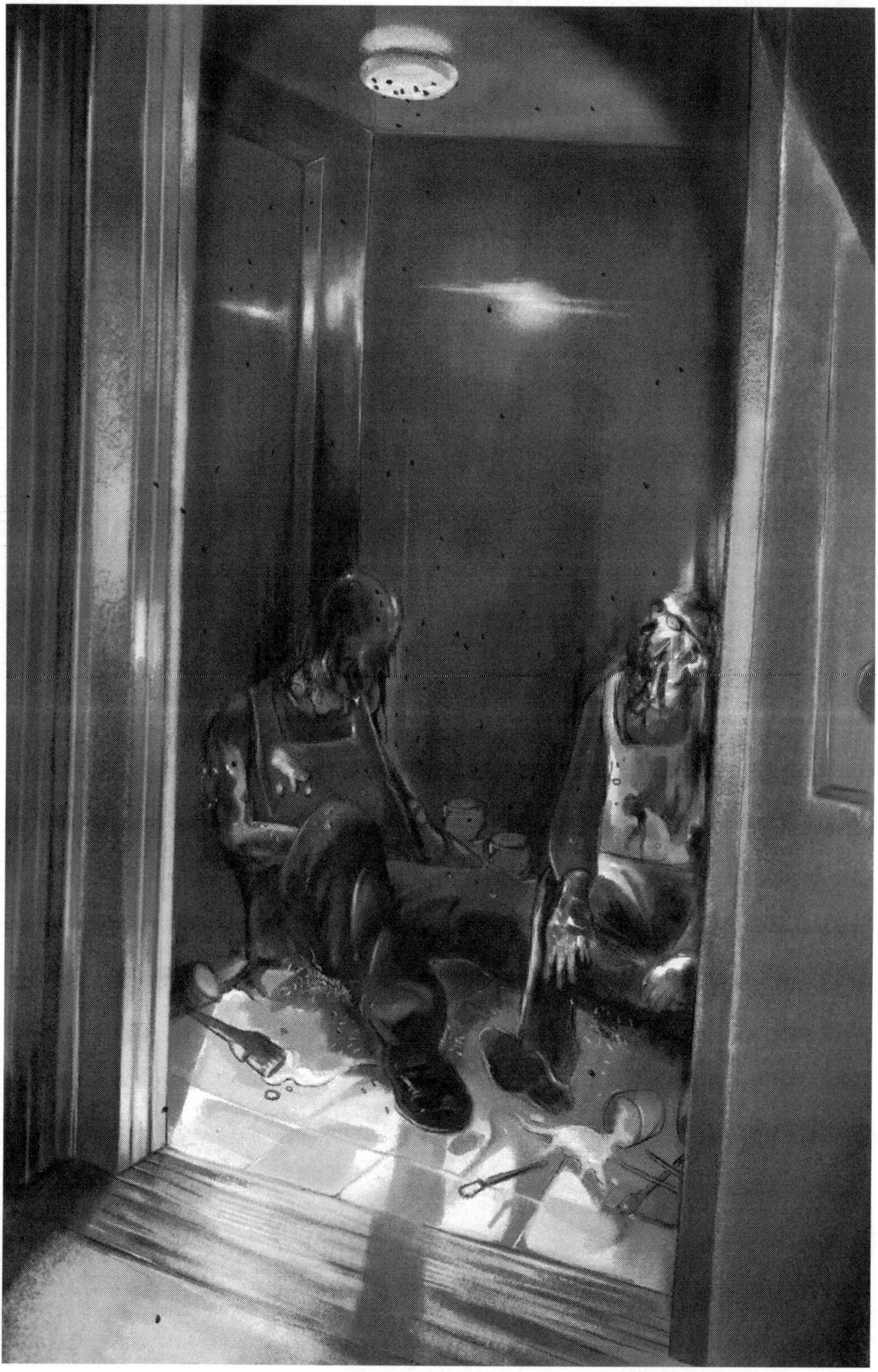

Some of their bones were left exposed, and the vermin nested within their mouths, guts, and other self-made orifices. They were no longer alive yet still harbored some life, but not in the way anyone would ever want if they had a say in the matter.

The painters had arrived to start their work before expected. Just like the old mechanic, they were go-getters, anxious to get their job knocked out ahead of schedule. Still, it turned out the old man was right, there was a very human explanation for their disappearance.

DAD'S NEW GUN

Andrew's parents had no idea just how easy it was for him to hear what they were saying in their bedroom at night. It was probably obvious if they'd taken the time to think about it, but the thought never really seemed necessary.

There was a vent that connected the two rooms, which sat right beside his bed. Oftentimes, on nights of extreme boredom, he liked to snoop. He leaned right up against the duct passage and opened his innocent ears.

Their chatter was usually a little muffled, but everything could be heard clearly. He often heard them talking about his future, or their marriage issues and financial problems. It wasn't often that he found their banter interesting; it was usually depressing… until one rainy night…

"I want the gun for protection, okay? There was another burglary just a few streets over. They roughed up the family pretty bad. I want to be ready." Andrew could tell by the way his father spoke that the decision was final.

"But what about Andrew? What if he finds it or thinks it's a toy?" His mother's voice sounded defeated, but she was still willing to argue.

"He's not even going to know we have it. It's going to be locked up in the closet."

"Well, what's the code?"

"What would you need the code for?"

"For times when you're not here. I may need to protect us."

"It's six, six, six."

"Why would you make it that?"

"Because he would never think it was that."

Andrew started to reason that it might be a good idea for him to learn how to use the gun too. Just in case his mom and dad weren't around and the bad men tried to come in the house and hurt them, or worse...

Then, one day, not too far after he'd eavesdropped and gained the intel, while his parents were making dinner, he snuck upstairs into their bedroom. He figured it would probably be on the top shelf of their closet, where they usually hid his birthday and Christmas gifts. He pulled the chair away from the desk and dragged it to the front of the closet.

There it was, a single steel box with a three-digit combination lock. He turned each number to six, and it popped open just as he'd imagined it would. His father's gun filled half of the tin, and the other half was filled with boxes of bullets.

Mom and Dad were topping the last layer of the lasagna with a variety of cheese shreds when they heard it: BANG! The noise was so brash that it startled them both enough to jump. "What in God's name was that?" Andrew's mother asked.

His father didn't want to assume anything, but the sickening look in his twitching eye showed he already had a theory. "Andrew!" he cried.

When his parents found him, he was slumped over in their bed, lying lifelessly in a pool of runny red destroyed flesh. The majority of his cranium was missing. The lone shot had traveled through his forehead and sprayed the contents of his skull all over the velvet Jesus painting that hung over their bed.

His head looked like a ruined pile of slop, similar to the ground beef mixture with the bright tomato sauce used in the lasagna. Andrew's tiny dead body was still convulsing violently while his father cradled him. His mother looked on in horror, her windpipes releasing a nasty series of blood-curdling shrieks that wouldn't stop for hours.

***

The house felt like an eerily quiet and cold chamber without Andrew joyfully playing around inside. Those days were over now, and the morbid reality made it hard for his parents to even be around each other anymore. The boy's absence was a nagging and painful sore that hung on his parents' hearts with no intent or possibility of healing.

Their relationship was rapidly rotting, the same as Andrew's cold dead body was under the fresh soil. It had become much worse than the arguments Andrew had heard through his vent when he was still alive. They didn't even speak to each other anymore. They lived in their own minds, sinking into guilt and hatred.

Neither could bear to sleep in the place where it happened, so they decided to swap rooms. They moved all of Andrew's old toys and furniture into their room and bought a new bed set. They laid in silence beside each other trying to sleep but neither could. Instead, their eyeballs just slowly cracked and dried out in the chilly evening air until it happened for the first time.

BANG!

The exact same disturbing, ear-ringing noise they'd heard on Andrew's last night alive. The sound was alarming—they didn't want to believe it, but deep inside they succinctly knew exactly what the racket was.

It had come racing through the metallic vent like a bullet from a gun. There was no confusing it, the frightening audio had come right from the room where it happened. They both looked at each other, prepared to speak for the first time in weeks.

"What was that?" she inquired.

They both got off the mattress and slowly crept into the bedroom. There was nothing there. Andrew's father gazed into the partially open closet door, and on the top shelf, the locked steel box sat untouched. Andrew's mother began to cry before his father led her back to bed. They didn't know what else to do besides try to ignore it.

BANG!

Again, the noise shot through the vent, alarming them and also reminding them of what they'd let happen. They returned to the room to find the same results—nothing. They both cried in bed the rest of the evening, not attaining a wink of sleep.

The next night, they were so exhausted that they both passed out before sundown. As darkness fell, the hands of the clock pushed deeper into the night. It was the only time they'd found peace since Andrew's death. The dreams could resurrect him, at least temporarily, until…

BANG!

The noise was back. Andrew's father launched upward but found himself alone in bed. He wasn't sure if the banging had come from his dream or through the vent again. He wondered where his wife had gone as his feet found the cold carpet. He didn't want to, but he knew he had to check the room.

As he entered, and his eyes adjusted to the black, he was greeted with a mortifying sight. His wife laid slumped over in almost the same position as their son. The top of her scalp dangled partially detached—the inner warm red and hunks of gore sprayed everywhere.

Just like with Andrew, the entry wound started in her forehead, before pushing everything inside it out the back. Andrew's father took his new gun from the blood-drenched hand of his twitching wife, and sat down beside her destroyed skull. He wondered where things went from there… until he didn't.

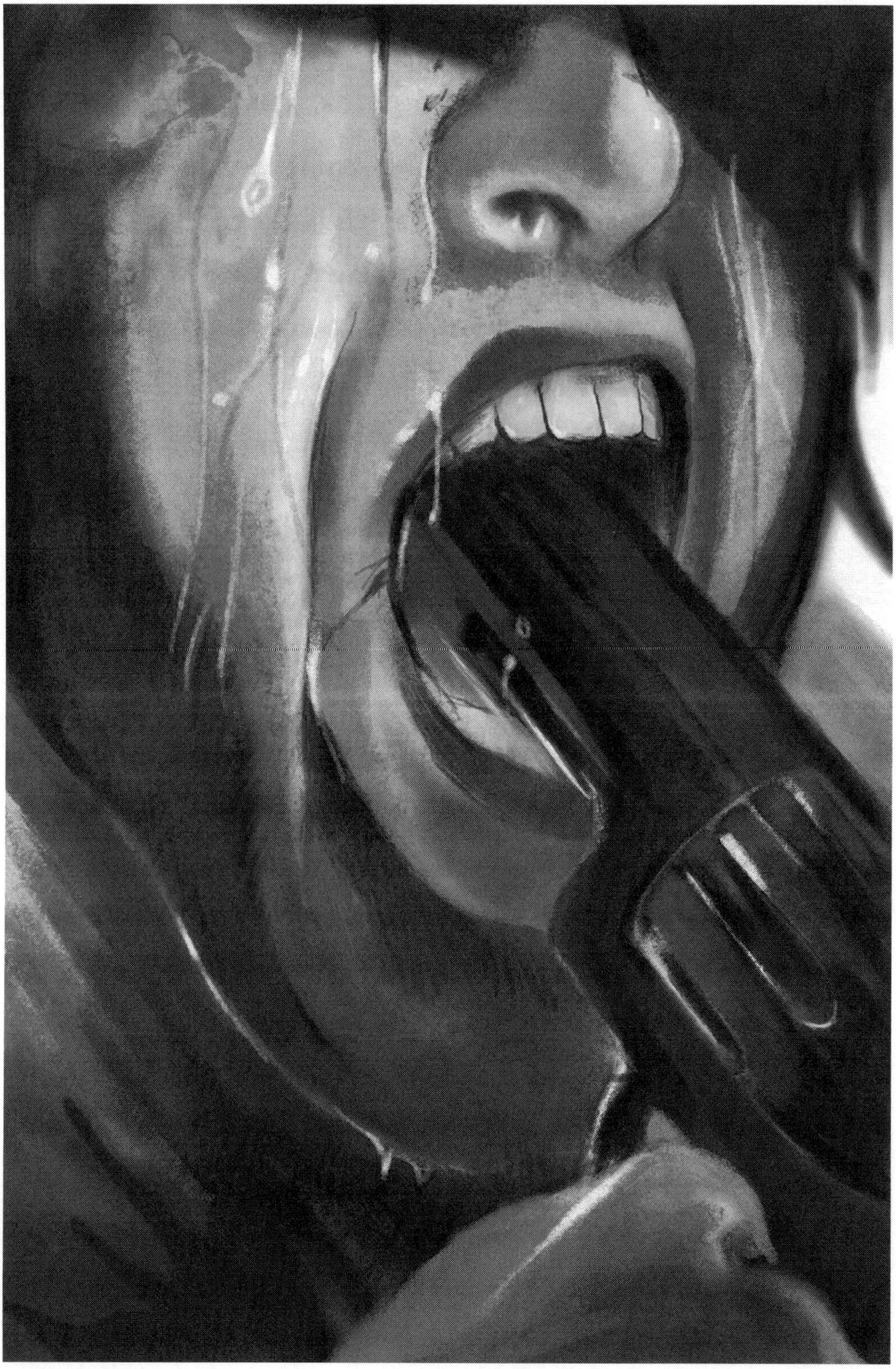

BANG!

BAKE SALE

Being the fattest girl in Calcutt Middle School turned Patty into a magnet for mockery. There wasn't a day that went by when the voices didn't creep up from behind her. The relentless potshots and stinging jabs left her with a profound sense of dread each morning she awoke.

She'd been branded with so many cruel nicknames over the years that it was difficult to remember them all. Her classmates never seemed to run out of ideas for her, but Fatty Patty was the one they used most often. It just kind of rolled off the tongue and was fun to chant in unison. She was constantly serenaded with the mean-spirited songs, the shrill voices of her fellow students drilled into her massive head: FAT-TY PAT-TY, FAT-TY PAT-TY, FAT-TY PAT-TY!

If Patty ignored them, their horrible hymns would never cease until a teacher or occasional parent noticed and intervened. In the rare instance that she felt froggy enough to defend herself from their unprovoked ridicule, they would simply change their lyric and call her Crabby Patty instead. She was damned if she did, damned if she didn't.

Patty was morbidly obese, spools of lard clinging to her every which way; her broad roundness towering. Her lower body was particularly puffy, earning her another name that she detested the most: Horse's Ass.

Her classmates could be so evil and heartless, there was no moment of consideration or the slightest pity. She always felt discomfort and harsh judging eyes falling on her during lunch—a period that everyone else looked forward to. When she ate, they stared and snickered, pointing fingers, and belting out callous laughter. The language they were using had gotten to a point where she was unable to eat in the lunchroom.

Each day, Patty found herself discreetly exiting with her lunch box and chomping down her meal quickly in the girls' bathroom. She smelled the vile shit that her peers were comprised of lingering in the bowl. She stared at their bloody boogers clinging to the lavatory stall while she wolfed down her peanut butter and jelly like a savage. She was away from their malice, but she still heard their voices:

"Go ahead, have another bite, you fat cunt! You look like you're about to explode! I want to see you explode all over the fucking room, pig! I can see the lard inside you splattering everywhere!" Justin Weiner's voice echoed in her cranium.

"You could NEVER get a boyfriend. Oh my God, you'd be bigger than him! You look like a man! Who would ever want to kiss a nasty fatso like you!?" Sara Benton blabbed.

"Hey, I bet you ten bucks that Horse's Ass dies from a heart attack before we graduate," Danny Vargas hollered.

There were some students who felt bad for her, but not a single one of them was willing to be her friend. They knew any relationship with Fatty Patty would instantly turn them into a secondary target—guilty by association. So, even the scarce handful with a conscience who could sympathize with her situation were just as malicious as their cold-blooded counterparts.

Maybe internally they wanted to help but that civility remained buried, their graciousness would never see the light of day. It would be replaced by a fearfully manufactured disdain. It was the fuel that distracted them from her bottomless persecution.

Patty tapped even deeper into the appetite that had opened the door to her derision. She loved chocolates, pastries, pies, cake, and candy. So much so that any sweet treats around her (those belonging to her or otherwise) would be quickly devoured.

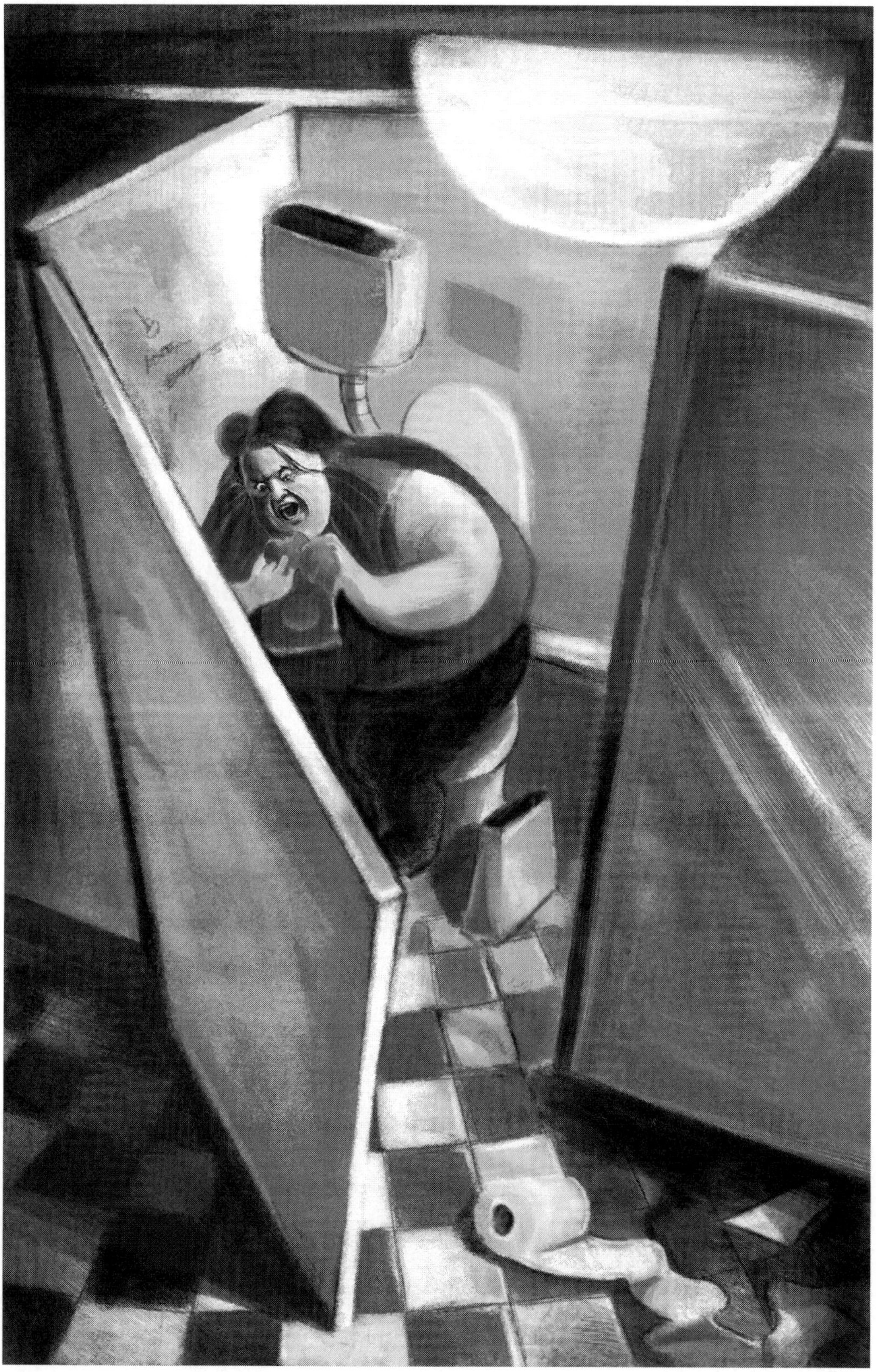

Her singular strength was baking, and that was in large part because she got to eat the outcome. All the work wasn't for nothing. When you drew or painted a picture, you couldn't swallow it afterwards, but baking was different.

The school bake sale was a unique time of year for Patty. It was highly uncommon, being that it was one of the few times a year that her sneering peers seemed to lay off. It was a rare period each year where she was given a stage to shine. People didn't call her names or heckle her. They didn't tease her about the jelly rolls lining her body. Instead, they lined up in front of her table to try her delicious creations.

For a few days, the other children all still had the sugary taste of her pastries upon their pallets and remembered Patty in a good light. But all good things must come to an end, and eventually, the taste wore off. The foulness sprang from their mouths again and twisted her existence back into a sour one.

The gym at school was massive, and all the other girls who baked had their own tables set up not too far away from Patty. But Patty's table was the place that everyone lined up at first. It didn't matter who you were—kids, parents, even the girls who manned the other seller tables.

They knew that Patty's treats would dry up quickly, and if they were going to get a taste, they'd need to see her before they started to sell their own. Even the horrible voices of her constant torment changed their tune during this rarified atmosphere.

Justin Weiner, Sara Benton, and Danny Vargas were the absolute scum of the schoolyard. A trio that didn't speak to each other often, or have much in common, outside of the fact that they all derived a twisted pleasure in crushing Patty's self-esteem into a fine dust. Still, just like the rest, their faces blended into the crowded line that snaked around the gymnasium. They each found her table and politely purchased Patty's delicious creations like there was no animosity to speak of between them.

When the bake sale officially began, the room was full of chatter and excitement. Most of the event-goers' eyes were predictably locked on Patty's table. The golden-brown crust was tanned to perfection. The delicious dough that surrounded the blueberry, cherry, and peach pies that Patty had spread across her table looked irresistible. A sense of deep pride hung on her flabby face.

The large knife plunged into the pastries as she cut them up and handed out piece after piece. The oozing, gory pie innards dripped down, staining the white paper plates with an overflow of sugar-soaked filling.

After all of the fifty or so people in the gym had inhaled at least one of the sweets, the traffic began to disperse somewhat. Sara Benton approached Patty with a little fruity filling still smeared about her lips and nicely asked, "What's the secret ingredient?"

Patty stared back at Sara's shimmering golden hair and hazel eyes blankly and void of emotion.

"Like how'd you get it to taste soooo perfect? I mean, it doesn't take a rocket scientist to figure out why you'd be good at it…" She waited for an answer that never came before continuing. "But it's a little different this year, not quite as sweet."

Patty found the tone Sara used to be comical. It was so friendly, and at the same time oblivious; like they'd been the best of friends for their entire lives. It was all a lie.

It was as if she'd forgotten all the torment she'd been responsible for, all the sickening stress and hell that she'd shoveled so mercilessly. Sara may have, but Patty hadn't. She just stood there, obese as ever, with a giant grin on her face. She wasn't about to give up her secret to anyone… they'd find out soon enough.

It was just minutes later when everyone in the gym started to convulse and throw up. A warm, lumpy multi-colored vomit splashed and puddled all over the hardwoods beneath them. Patty watched, tickled, as each and every one of the partakers in the bake sale churned out an enormous pile of partly digested pie, blood, and bile.

Their eyes were red and pulsating. Their throats were like spouts, launching forward a stream of sickness. A disgusting sickness that was almost as abhorrent as the years of torture they'd put Patty through. But that was all over now. The previously deafening chatter at the start of the sale had died, along with everyone else in the room.

INGROUND POOL

Fred never had friends before he decided to build an inground pool in his backyard. But all these "friends" seemed to come out of the woodwork when he finally opened the massive rectangular swim space. He had never been partial to the beach. The traffic, the people, and the lack of personal space were all points of discomfort for him.

Finding reprieve in isolation, he lived in the woods, so it was a lengthy drive for these friends to reach him. They never cared to make the drive before. But now, with the burning sun bearing down on them, somehow, at least one of these friends seemed to find their way over every other day.

It was like magic how their formerly busy days suddenly birthed massive stretches of time, which they chose to spend in Fred's pool. It was only a matter of time before they started to bring *their* friends next—the people they truly enjoyed the company of.

After that, they brought their wives, who looked at Fred with disgust. But those looks of hatred quickly transitioned to delight when they saw the smiles on the faces of others paddling around in the clear cool-blue human aquarium.

Then, they brought their kids. Their wild, obnoxious, booger-eating seeds. They jumped about yelling utter nonsense and ran all over. They disrespected Fred, his pool, and his property altogether. They ran inside to use the bathroom soaking wet, leaving puddles of water on the hardwood floors. They ate all of his food without asking. They ripped up the plants in his garden and teased his dog without fail. And the parents did NOTHING.

They sat enjoying his pool selfishly, while he was constantly trying to corral the little hellions. These attempts often concluded with the children swearing at him and spitting on his shoes. They called him a dummy and pushed his buttons like he was a beloved arcade machine.

Fred's peace and tranquility had been shattered. When he looked into the mirror, he saw a coward, and was met with a constant shame and embarrassment hot on his face. They'd taken over his life, stolen his dream, and made it a nightmare, and he'd sat by idly, allowing them to do it. They would never change. It was solely up to him to break the cycle.

The next day, Fred explained to all of his friends that he would be doing some safety renovations on the pool and deck. He felt bad about no one being able to stop by for the next few days, but he planned to make it up to them. At the end of the week, he would throw a wonderful party, the biggest bash they'd ever seen.

The day of the party arrived before they knew it, and Fred's friends arrived in droves—his driveway was overwhelmed with traffic. He watched each person that entered, making a careful mental note. Just as he had hoped, everyone he'd invited had come to the celebration. He was happy. The day just wouldn't have been right unless *everyone* attended.

Many inquired about the tall locking fence surrounding the pool and the pyramid of big blue drums that had been laid down beside it. Fred took the opportunity to recite the morbid story about the local boy that drowned in his neighbor's pool a week or so ago. He made all of the drastic changes in an effort to avoid a similar incident.

"It's purely precaution, safety first," he explained in a caring tone.

The barrels were merely some high-quality pool chemicals. He'd pumped them into the water a few nights ago to keep all of his guests swimming in the most hygienic of waters.

"You'll know the difference once you're in," he explained with a wink.

Once everyone had digested their healthy fill of corndogs and cheeseburgers, they happily hopped into the water. There were so many people, it was almost a little crowded inside. With Fred's pool being so large, it was quite a sight to register.

Someone from inside the pool yelled over to Fred, wondering why he wasn't wearing his bathing suit. "What's the matter, Fred? The water's not that cold, you big chicken! Buck, buck, buquawk!" the man screeched, emulating a scared chicken as best as he could.

The laughter from the pool was deafening. They found great comic relief in Fred's cowardice. A small boy close to Fred looked up and pointed at him. "Chicken, chicken, chicken!" Without warning, Fred slammed the fence shut. He retrieved a lock from his pants and snapped it onto the crude-looking gating, trapping everyone inside.

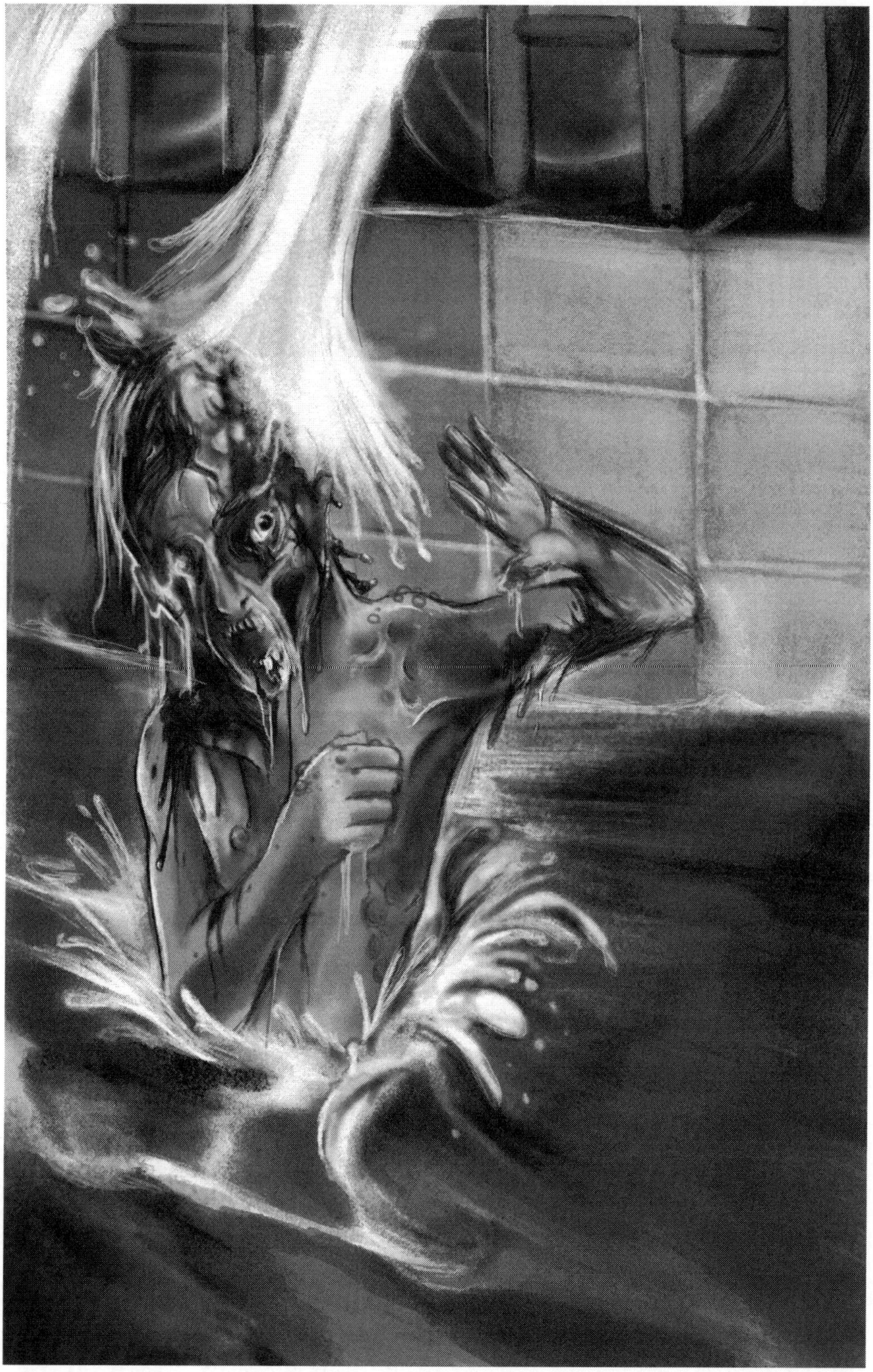

He twisted a knob on the top of the barrel, and immediately, a strange scent of a chemical nature wormed its way into the nostrils of the many swimmers. The noxious steaming liquid began to spurt through the fence and taint the beautiful blue that they'd all come to enjoy with regularity at Fred's expense.

The water wasn't the only thing that the unforgiving acid connected with. The burning fluid dropped directly onto the head of the sniveling young boy who'd enjoyed mocking him. Within seconds, the powerful chemical burned all the hair and flesh off of his skull.

The child's boney white skeletal frame was no longer hidden. The meat curtain had been pulled back, and the process happened so rapidly that he was still moving in skeleton form as he faded out. The boy's shrieks and cries may have died, but all the others grew louder as the steaming scarlet water floated towards the other swimmers.

All of Fred's friends began to scramble, attempting to scale up the fence and escape the approaching acid. Fred drew his pistol from his pocket and shot those friends. He watched holes blow through their bodies as they fell back into the corrosive liquid. Their faces were no longer crinkled with judgment, they were melting off.

He watched the entire process, taking great pleasure until the inground pool was just a lifeless soup of blood, skin, organs, and bone. The water was still steaming and red when the last one let out their final gurgle. No more friends, or their friends, or their wives, or their children any longer. Just quiet. Fred knew that he had quite a mess to clean, but that was of little consequence. His serenity had finally returned.

THE OLD TRUCK

A sign that read 'FOR SALE' had been propped up on the hazy smeared windshield of the old truck only for a few days when the gray-haired man came knocking. The farmer had recently decided he should sell the old truck in spite of her always having been a reliable vehicle. He'd been through the best and worst of times with her, but of late, the bad was overshadowing their entire history.

Too many rotten memories were resurfacing each time he looked at the old truck or sat inside her. Too much mystery and misery. Too much rage and heartache. It felt like a spear was being pushed into his ribcage each time he gazed upon her; the pointed steel slowly pushing his way into his pumping heart and twisting. An amplified version of the stabbing pain he endured daily is what he imagined his child felt last.

The seats were saturated with sin, and the steering wheel would only drive him toward torment, no matter what direction it was aimed. The tires remained tired from his daughter's final ride.

The farmer's daughter was the last one to drive the old truck. On the night she took it out, they later found it with the doors sprung open, and abandoned in a ditch on the shoulder of Old Furnace Road.

Sadly, his daughter was nowhere to be found. It wasn't until months later that she was finally located. It took some curious children taking a seldom-used shortcut into the bush to discover her corpse floating in a lake a few miles north of where the old truck was recovered.

Due to the advanced stage of decomposition, it should have been difficult to determine the cause of death, but fortunately for the police (and unfortunately for her), the signs were all too obvious. They noted on account of her ruthlessly crushed hyoid bone and splintered larynx, that strangulation was the definitive kill method.

Maybe the most gruesome detail of all was that the killer had also taken her face. They detected deep incisions at the borders of her skull, the distorted slab of flesh had been peeled back and transposed with a slimy patch of rotten tissue. The last memory that the farmer had of his baby girl was when the authorities called him in to identify her. All that was left was a dissolving and bloated carcass that looked closer to a monster movie villain than the child he recalled so fondly.

After the funeral, he knew he needed to sell the old truck. Otherwise, he'd never erase that image of his butchered daughter from his mind— the horrendous involuntary grin that only existed on account of her expression having literally been skinned. The exposed pink gums haunted his slumber and daydreams. Her foul and milky lost eyes burrowed through him. His nostrils still puckered from her rancid scent.

As much as the vulgar myriad of lingering thoughts about his baby's desecrated body repulsed him, knowing that the unhinged psycho who'd defiled her still had never been caught was eating him alive inside. The leads went as cold as the leftovers in his refrigerator. Not that he'd expected the tips to come pouring in… they lived in America's heartland, not some big city. Witnesses were far and few in the remote country.

So, when the farmer answered the knock at his door on that dark lonesome afternoon and came face to face with the gray-haired man, he was mostly grateful. A strange comfort found him as the man held his hat in his hands at his doorstep and inquired about the old truck. He found himself torn—filled with both agony and excitement. The farmer led him out to the front yard where the old truck sat forlorn.

"Do you mind if I start her up and maybe just drive it around your lot?" the gray-haired man asked.

"Please, go right ahead." The farmer tossed him a pair of keys with a pale rabbit's foot dangling from them.

The gray-haired man started her up and she purred. She still had a mechanical soundness that one wouldn't expect for a truck priced so affordably. He pulled the truck away from the lonely road at the front of the farm and back over to the rear of the barn.

Once he parked it and his boots hit the ground, he reached back inside and ran his hand over the old raggedy seat cushion. He closed his eyes for a moment and took a deep breath. It seemed like, somehow, he felt a comfort from the old truck. He took his attention from the interior cab and looked back toward the farmer.

"Why would you sell a fine truck like this for almost nothing?" the gray-haired man asked.

The farmer didn't want to lie, but he also didn't want to talk about the nasty memories that the old truck always brought to his mind. "I just don't want it anymore," he replied, not lying but also not really answering the question. The farmer hoped that he wouldn't be persistent, just wanting to complete the transaction as quickly as possible.

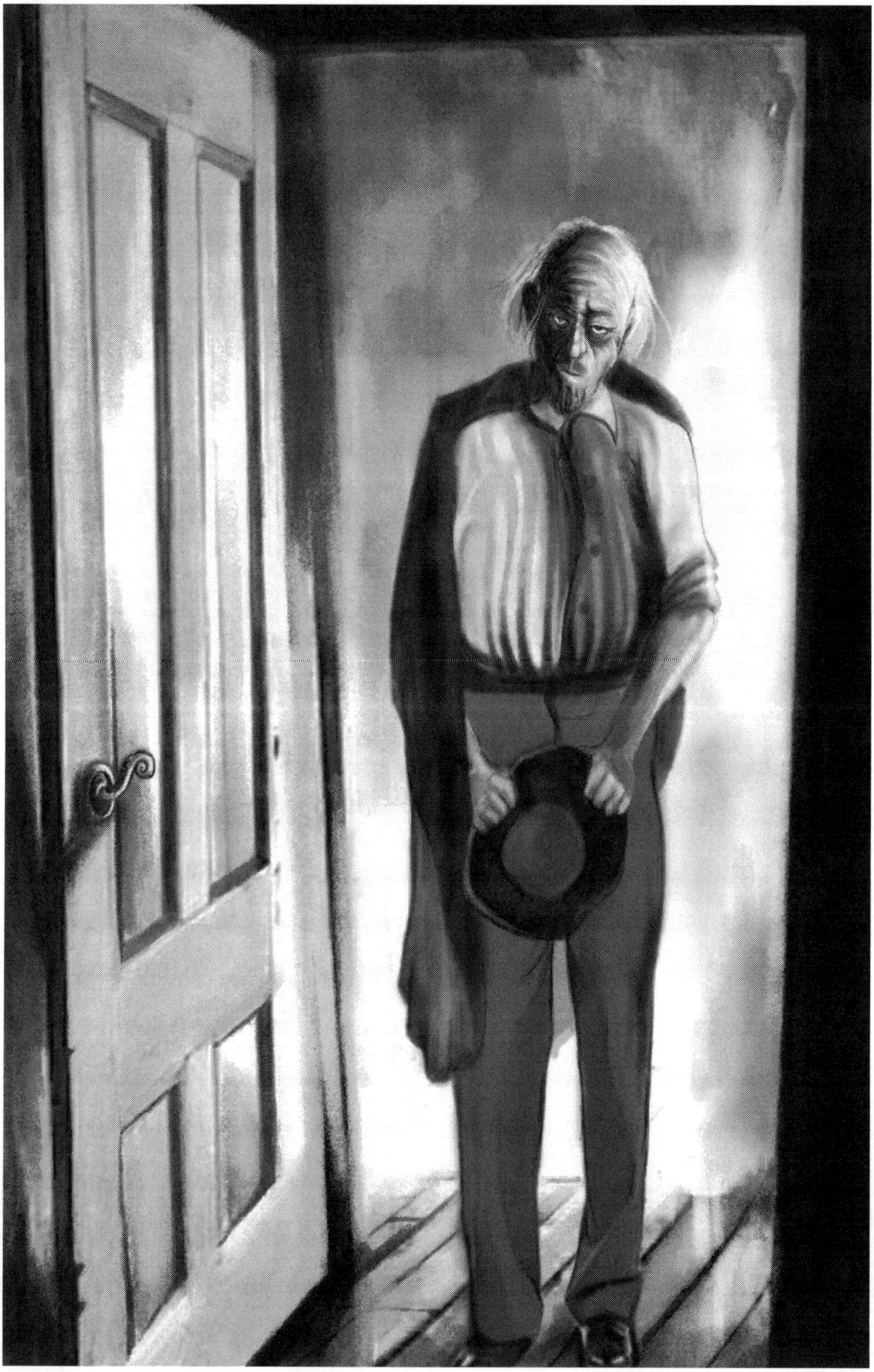

"Don't you have a daughter… or a son maybe that you can give it to?" the gray-haired man asked.

When the farmer heard the word daughter, it felt like a nail driving into his heart. He hadn't really stopped to consider that questions of such a personal nature might come up while he was selling the vehicle. The gray-haired man's meddlesomeness was beginning to irritate him. In light of his swelling fury, he decided to give a sterner response.

"Do you want the truck or not?" he asked.

"No, I don't want the truck," the gray-haired man replied.

"Why not?" the farmer wondered aloud.

The gray-haired man removed a big, sharp knife from the inside of his jacket and stared into the farmer's suddenly fear-filled eyes. A look of imbalance took hold of him, and an absurd mania boiled violently within his withered long-standing frame. He'd been resisting a sinister urge for the length of their interaction.

"BECAUSE I WANT YOUR FACE!" he screamed as he drove the blade into the farmer's cheek tissue and began to carve.

THE LAST ILLUSION

Calypso the Cunning was something of a maverick in the niche that was live performance magic. Most magicians or illusionists liked clean tricks that dazzled, meticulous preparation, and organization. They presented their acts like masterful artists with very deliberate and calculated strokes. Everything had to be perfect before they unveiled the everlasting "wow moment" that would keep a buzz about them humming until they circled back to town again.

Calypso's renegade version of the ancient stage show art was quite the opposite of respected tradition. Instead of clean cuts and phantom separations, he used extreme violence and gore. His imagery was comparable to hi-tech, cinema-grade quality special effects.

The nasty tricks looked entirely authentic to a point where some patrons even fell ill during his act. Eruptions of blood blasting out from a sawed through neck or limb was a regular occurrence. The gore geysers blanketed the stage area and sometimes even splattered all over members of the audience.

Being faced with the macabre realism of Calypso's illusions, they were delighted and always relieved when it was proven to be just a convincing trick. He believed that euphoric relief was the reason they bought tickets. The rollercoaster of emotion arriving at a satisfying and thankful finish made for an experience like no other.

Many of Calypso's peers scoffed at what they labeled as "amateur antics." They claimed the violence covered up an unpolished routine, but all the people that paid their hard-earned dollars to see Calypso's twisted entertainment had a far different opinion.

Asses were filling the seats, and while he didn't reel in enormous crowds, he had a stable consistency that most magicians could only dream of. Calypso believed that petty jealousy was the reason his fellow performers referred to him as a hack.

In spite of the smear's venomous intent, he actually enjoyed the reference. The irony as it related to the subject matter of his performance was marvelous, as it was more than linguistically appropriate.

The majority of magicians also acted as the face of their franchise. Typically, a well-groomed, fit, and sleek appearance held the crowd's attention and could take the focus off the spots within illusions that required audience distraction.

Calypso the Cunning disregarded that common ideology and operated under a mask that projected a black and white swirl, which he called the mask of madness. Patrons didn't just stare at him, they stared into him. It was as if he was hypnotizing the masses that chose to gaze upon him with the slow churn of his skull twisting back and forth.

Veterans in the performance industry crooned about his disrespect toward the business. The extreme nature of the shows was desensitizing potential customers to traditional wholesome magic. In their eyes, he was corrupting the crowds.

It wasn't uncommon for his jealous peers to approach him backstage, offering friendly advice. It was always the same thing: if he wanted to be taken seriously and stop damaging the genre, he would need to reveal his face and cast away the cheesy side effects.

The problem with the advice was that Calypso the Cunning was much more successful than those posing instruction to him. It seemed rather foolish to accept advice from the less fruitful. Unlike many of them, he was monetizing outside of performances. The very things they claimed were bad for business and would hold him back were inflating his pockets.

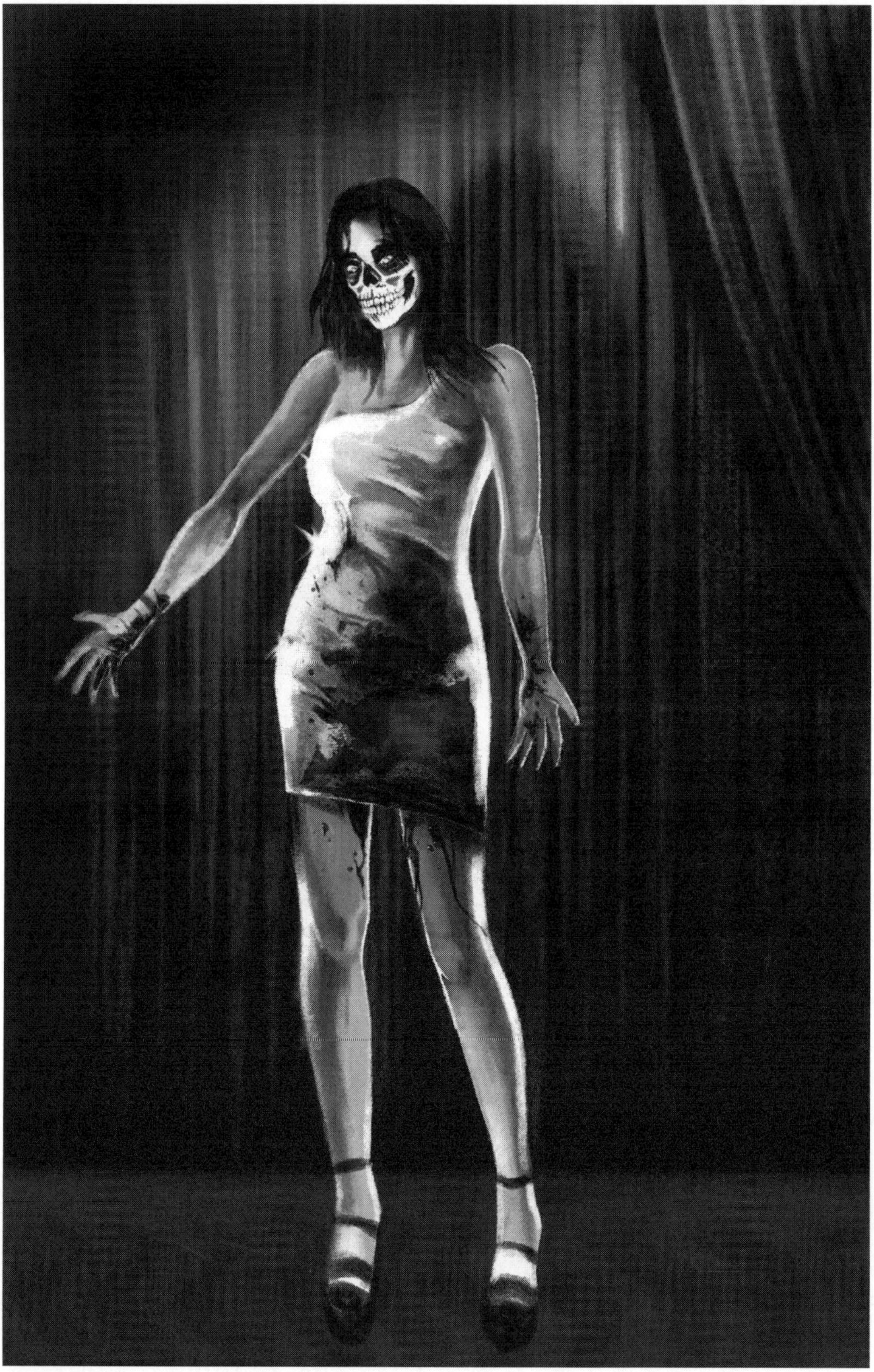

The deranged magician sold off replicas of his mask of madness and tee shirts of gory tricks involving his beloved assistant, Dead Betty. The merchandise was selling as fast as the blood squirted—just like death and sex would anywhere.

Calypso the Cunning, always the cordial one, thanked them for their foresight, but continued his act, defiant and unflinching. It seemed like he'd made the correct choice, or at the very least, the most lucrative one. After all, he'd gotten into the business to make money, not friends. And make money they did, hand over fist, force-feeding their creative violence to the masses.

Both Calypso and Dead Betty began to rake in thousands of dollars for mere hours of work. By the end of their first year as a mainstream act, they reached a tier that was inching closer to celebrity by the day. They were such a relevant sensation that The Grand Royale Casino in Las Vegas granted them a trial show, an opportunity that was unheard of for a pair of raunchy rookies.

If they were successful in captivating the audience, they had the potential to become a permanent fixture in Sin City. They were on the verge of not just any magician's dream, but any performer's dream. Once they displayed their torture at the trial show, they both knew that their ghastly displays of death would leave them set for life.

The duo set off to a city where it felt like night was day exactly one week in advance of their tryout. They readied themselves and allotted extra time to practice and prepare relentlessly for their lone stab at the big time. Their only focus would be executing a single marvelous performance. Their finest yet, and one that would be remembered forever.

But when they arrived at their luxury suite at The Grand Royale Casino, strange things started to happen. Fresh off the hypnotic glow and wicked temptation of the enticing strip, before they could even unpack in their room, the telephone rang.

A befuddled look found its way into Calypso's brow. They had just arrived. Who could that possibly be?

Dead Betty watched him wander slowly to the phone and lift it off the receiver. "Hello?" he said, curiosity at a pinnacle.

"Just saw you come into town, hack, if you had any kind of head on your shoulders, you and the pair of tits would go back the way you came. If not, I can promise you that you won't walk across that stage again," the sick-sounding man remarked with a phlegmy cackle.

"Who the hell is this? I have just as much of a right to be here as anyone!" Calypso barked.

"The who isn't important. There are many of us, and we all feel the same. We've been watching you tarnish the trade long enough. This call is long overdue, and the appropriate repercussions are long overdue. It's time to wipe away the slime that you perverts have left on us for good."

"The spotlight chooses you, not the other way around. We didn't come this far to let some two-bit prank caller who doesn't have the sack to name himself stop us. If you wanna stop the show, you're gonna have to buy a ticket, just like everyone else."

"We'll see about that…"

When the caller disconnected, they thought that would be the last of it. One of the many nameless bitter rivals had taken their shot at giving them the jitters. They'd gotten their rocks off standing in the shadows of jealousy, and creating an unnerving aura, instead of focusing on what they might do to develop their craft and potentially please a crowd. Now that they'd stated their pathetic piece, they could go back to crying in the mirror. They were wrong…

The bizarre communications continued. The raspy bastard on the line reminded them multiple times that their fate would be altered should they proceed. If they found success come their trial show, they should turn their backs on it. If the performers didn't heed their warnings, the sick croaky voice claimed they would bring Dead Betty's character to life, dismember her and violate the parts they'd separated from her core.

They'd break every bone in her skeleton until mobility was no longer an option. They would drive Calypso to insanity, then cut up his body until each piece was small enough to grind into a puree. Like the corkscrew on his mask, he would be shredded and twisted into a pulpy concoction that looked like something he'd use on stage.

It was hard to tell if the intimidation tactics were merely hollow jokes from a place of hate or if they held a far more malicious intent. Either way, Calypso and Dead Betty decided they weren't willing to gamble or call bluff—they promptly reported the violent promises to the authorities. All the calls were tied back to a series of random payphones in the city; they were untraceable.

Whoever was responsible for the morbid assurances had concealed their identity. It wasn't surprising considering that Calypso believed envious magicians were at the root of it. It wasn't likely an illusionist was going to leave evidence behind.

They must have been even more pissed off than before, since now a pair of "hack" rookies were potentially being offered a job that was reserved for legends. It was clear that in cutting that line, they'd, in turn, made people want to cut their throats, or at the very least, inject that thought into their minds.

Regardless of the true intentions behind the harassment, both Calypso and Dead Betty were rattled. But as frightened as they were, they were even more afraid of blowing the gig. They were willing to die for their opportunity. They stuck together with a keen eye out each day leading up to the night of the show. The way they saw it, if the show made a splash, their worries would vanish like a bird in an open cage. They would be able to pay for an elite security team for the rest of their days.

***

There was not a single free seat in the arena when Calypso the Cunning's odd music began to play through the speakers. The kill-hungry crowd salivated, wondering how many horrible ends Dead Betty would see that night. The deep purple curtains finally parted, giving way to a cheer from the onlookers—the mystery of the first trick had been solved.

Dead Betty was knelt over with her head trapped inside a wooden block above a monstrous weighty blade. The intimidating steel glimmered as she struggled with her arms chained behind her back. The layer of duct tape over her luscious black lips only added more realism to a presentation that never came up short in that department. Calypso side-stepped out from behind the gaudy guillotine, miming his actions as usual.

He gently tapped the side of his head. Something was missing, but what? Suddenly, he remembered and rushed back behind the contraption. He returned, clenching a sizable oval basket with a white lining inside.

He set it down below Dead Betty's head and waited. The thick fraying rope beside the guillotine appeared to be the trigger that Calypso was reaching for. But he suddenly pulled back and reverted to his profound thought antics until it came to him.

He pointed out toward the audience and a bright spotlight illuminated just about where his finger was aimed. A young lady with a lustrous expression stood up at once. "You want *me* to kill Dead Betty!" she screeched with delight.

She raced up to the stage, nearly tripping from the thrill of participation. Calypso helped hoist her up and then gently placed the rope into her hands. Dead Betty was squirming and squealing just like she always did, the participant standing in awe of her credibility.

Calypso walked to the other side of the stage while holding up a trio of fingers. Much of the audience seemed familiar with the routine and were happy to play along. "THREE!" they shouted all together. As the show-goers looked on in anticipation, one of the three fingers dropped and only two remained. "TWO!" they continued. The young participant's hand was shaking now as she held the rope and the next finger fell, "ONE!" they screamed much louder than before.

As the final finger collapsed, the crowd was silent. The young lady triggered the device, and it seemed like hours before the cruel steel cut into Dead Betty's spine, swiftly severing her pretty head. The red expelled with the ferocity of a cannon and shot out into the audience as the crowd gasped in unison.

Many had seen it all before, but Calypso's tricks were so convincing that, until they revealed themselves, there was always that small amount of doubt left festering. The doubt that you hear about around campfires and in urban legends. The doubt that something might have gone horribly wrong.

Just like many shows before, the participant rejoiced in Dead Betty's demise. It was always exciting to see the kill in all its gory glory with a realism that defied the physical realm. Seeing the deep red was like nothing else. The head-turning and stomach-quaking visuals left almost nothing to the imagination.

The young girl lifted Dead Betty's cranium up out of the crimson-coated wicker basket, and held it up for the crowd as they cheered. She shook the detached leaking sphere all around as blood splattered onto members of the audience. After a few moments of excitement, she looked back to Calypso for direction. Surely there was only so much time to celebrate before moving on to the next trick.

When her eyes came upon where he'd been standing, they found a space absent of matter—he'd somehow just disappeared. This wasn't uncommon. Oftentimes, once a trick had been completed, both Calypso and Dead Betty would reappear together and take a bow. She gazed upon Dead Betty's shivering headless frame as it crawled about in a dying disoriented manner.

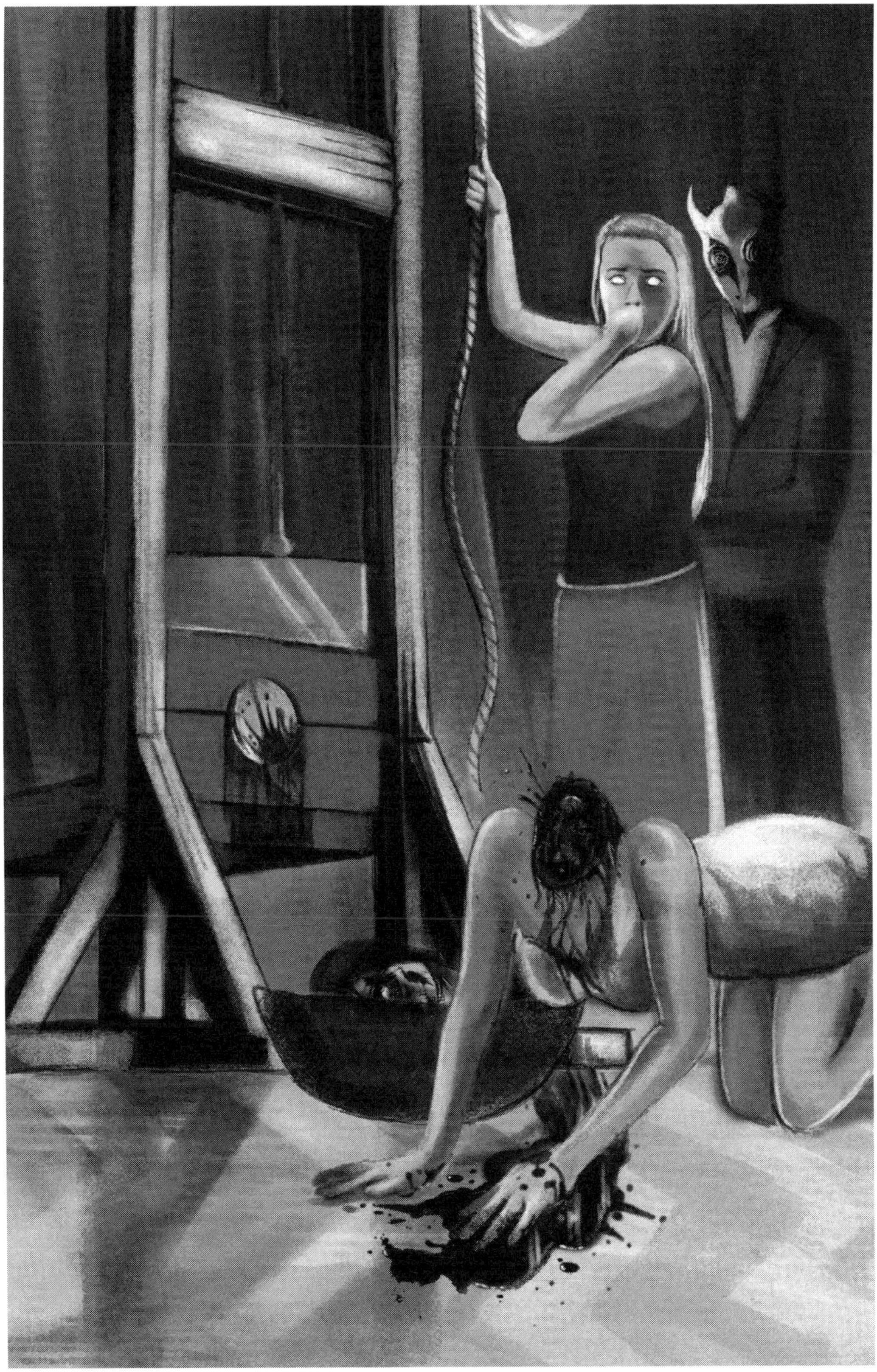

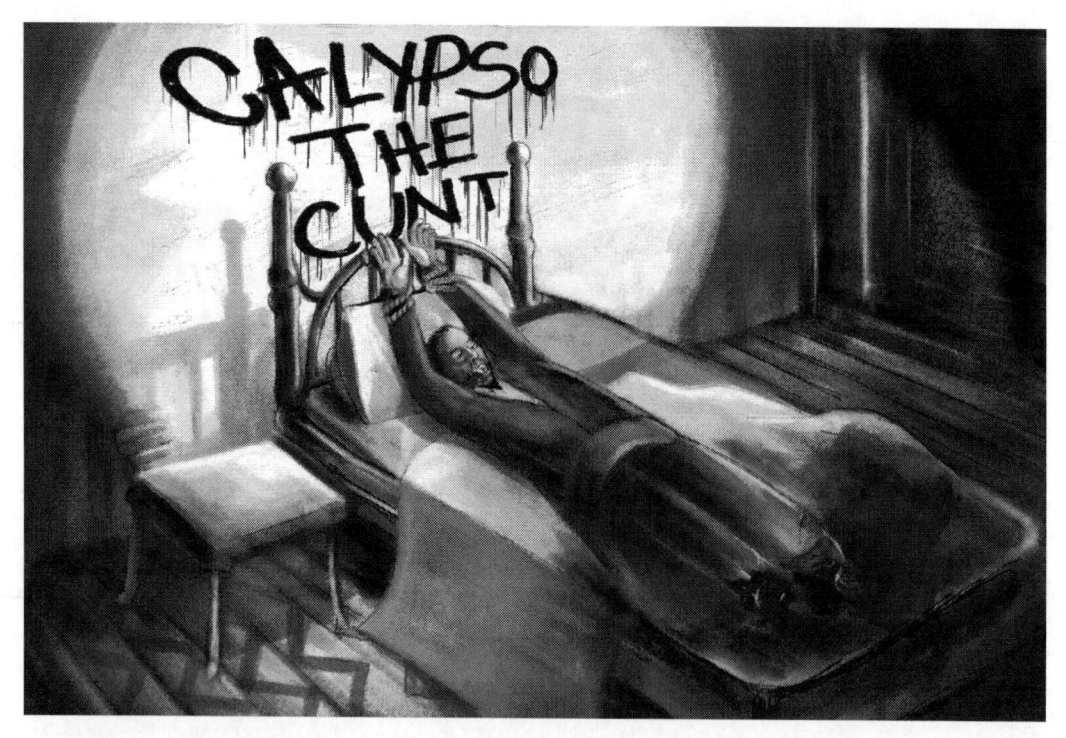

The confused woman continued to hold the bleeding skull up by the hair, waiting, watching as the snowy eyes rolled up, and the wobbly tongue slipped out like an animated house dog. After a minute or two passed, a confused uncertainty came over the crowd and they began to grumble and wonder what exactly was happening.

The realization started with a man in the front row who had gotten sprayed with the blood quite generously. The room had quieted down as a disturbing vibe now permeated in the air. He put his hand on his saturated sternum and spoke with a muddled nature to his tone. "It's… it's warm… this blood is warm…"

The crowd erupted in horror, unsure what to do. Was this the most realistic trick they'd ever seen, or a traumatic instance that would linger inside them for eternity? Once the police arrived and the hysteria in the crowd simmered down, they realized that the corpse slumped over in the execution device was, in fact, that of Dead Betty. But was this a trick gone wrong or something far worse? None of it explained why Calypso had vanished from the stage during the performance. His absence reeked of guilt and pointed to his involvement.

A short time later, the authorities arrived at Calypso's hotel room and burst inside. They found the magician unmasked with his arms tied to the bedposts and a ball-gag lodged in his mouth.

The lower half of the mattress was drenched in his wine-colored emissions—both of his feet had been sawed off. The words "CALYPSO THE CUNT" were smeared in his fluid above his static remains. What laid before them was no illusion, the hack had been hacked. The deceased performer had never been part of the show.

HOT CAR

I couldn't believe anyone would leave their baby in the car during such a sweltering heatwave. There had been a slew of cases earlier in the year that circulated in the news about this exact subject.

Even if it was just a few minutes, it was far from safe. Running in for milk and bread (or most likely cigarettes and whisky, judging by the degree of negligence in this situation) was just selfish. Even more than that, it was criminal and idiotic.

That particular summer was giving the argument for global warming more credence than ever. I was only a few cars away when I started recording. My vantage point was perfect, I could see everything that was going on, the tiring baby's every stressed motion. All of my followers began to comment immediately. What had started with ten or so responses quickly grew into hundreds, and they were all saying the exact same thing.

As the baby's face reddened and it struggled to breathe, they all agreed that the parent of the child was an absolute monster.

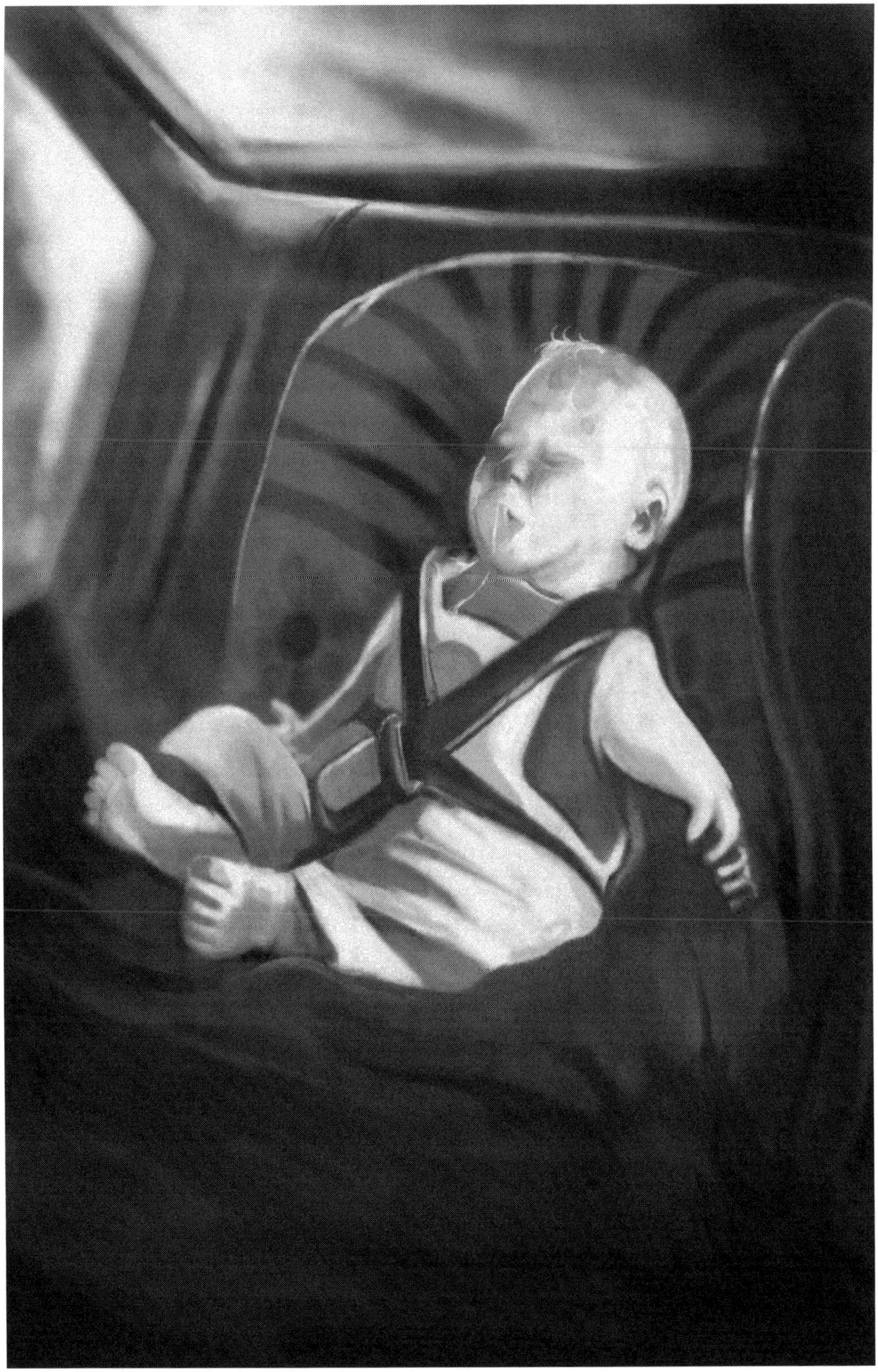

CAPTAIN HUNT

Floyd sat slumped behind the wheel of his big rig blinking his heavy eyes repeatedly. *Stay awake, just keep your peepers open for a few more miles,* he rattled over and over in his exhausted mind. The career box truck driver was becoming weary. His head slumped down every few minutes before snapping back up in a flash, like he was a boy bored in class all over again.

Most nights, he would've just pulled over for a few minutes and caught some shuteye, but he had to make the haul by morning. It was a rare hard deadline, something that didn't come up too often on the schedule. Something he couldn't fuck up or it might very well mean his ass was out of a job.

Floyd had never been one to plan properly, the dozen drinks and snaggle-toothed hooker he'd brought back to his motel room the prior evening made that clear. The blow-party and sexual marathon had taken it out of him. He wasn't the same young buck that did that every other route any longer.

The graying trucker struggled to stay awake during the midnight pull, as the sandman continued to beckon him. The long drives across state lines at unreasonable hours were taking their toll—it was all catching up to him.

Floyd strained his fat pupils with the little energy he had left to keep conscious. He'd heard the bizarre stories of other drivers being up for so long that they'd start to see things on the asphalt. He imagined much of it was embellished, despite the fact that sleep depravity *could* cause hallucinations.

They used creepy tall tales as a means to motivate their overworked minds. The verbally illustrated fear was a powerful tool, and some of the stories that got passed around at the stops preyed on it.

They were tricking their bodies and minds into releasing an extra shot of adrenaline. That self-brewed drug, at times, could be the only difference between making it a few more miles or passing out behind the wheel. He saw the stories as a good thing.

One such story had been circulating amongst the community of truckers for decades. It was one of the first that he'd ever heard when he was still green to the business, before the harsh realities and depression that came with life on the highway grabbed hold. It was also the tale that he thought of most often because it was the creepiest one…

The tale threatened that if a trucker drove for too long between rest stops, a car would eventually appear in their rearview off in the distance. The car of Captain Hunt. He would race up to the trucker in a blink and run him off the road. It wasn't really that part of the story that bothered Floyd so much; it was *why* people said he was doing it.

Captain Hunt was the picture of success, a well-respected and beloved fire captain. The version of the story he'd heard went that, years ago, Captain Hunt was driving down the highway on an evening similar to the one that Floyd faced that night. Dark and dry, a lonely black highway that was dead all but for the hum of the engine. Until he cruised over a hill and saw a great big semi-truck ahead of him.

After a few more minutes, Captain Hunt wasn't too far behind the trucker, close enough that he'd already flicked his turn signal to try and pass him when the eighteen-wheeler's tire blew out. Both he and the truck were going fast enough that when the blowout occurred, the massive chunk of ragged rubber tore through the windshield and ripped the top of the captain's car off completely… along with his head…

His car had somehow come to a stop without wrecking completely, and the police found his decapitated body still sitting upright in the driver's seat. Ever since the horrific accident, farewells like "Keep awake, the captain ain't far behind" were a dependable parting gift at most truck stops. Most said it in jest, but there were others who truly believed it. If they didn't keep their eyes on the road, before long, Captain Hunt would appear in their rearview and come and wake them himself.

That was the thought that got Floyd's eyes wide when he saw the pair of headlights appear off in the distance. They descended upon him almost as quickly as they came into view.

When the car pulled up beside him, he could see that it looked like a convertible. It soon became evident by the deformed metal and shattered windshield that the current model was not that of the car's original factory design. In his heart, Floyd knew there was something terribly wrong about this particular car.

It couldn't be… the vehicle was just as they'd described it. Just like in the stories, the borders of the frame were wrecked and the whole roof was missing. But far more spine-chilling than the car's exterior was that of its driver—a headless carcass that still exuded a fowl freshness. Its reddened spine bone splintered at the Adam's apple, pumping a fountain of hot liquid into the air. Defying all logic, the body was somehow still animated and able to keep steering the crimson-caked wheel.

Suddenly, the ghoulish rendition twisted its arms violently and drove directly into the spinning dual wheels of Floyd's rig. He instantly lost control of the wide load as it tipped onto its side and sparks flew while it scraped down the roadway still at breakneck pace.

When the mass of metal finally came to a standstill, all that could be heard on the deserted stretch of highway was Floyd's panic-stricken screams echoing throughout the nearby canyons. Until, all of a sudden, they stopped abruptly…

***

The next morning, the sun rose to reveal a detective crouched on the side of the wreckage. He peered into the cab of the semi with his brow wrinkled in discomfort. Another officer on the scene approached him from behind somberly, "It doesn't make any sense, how could that happen? He's still completely buckled in…"

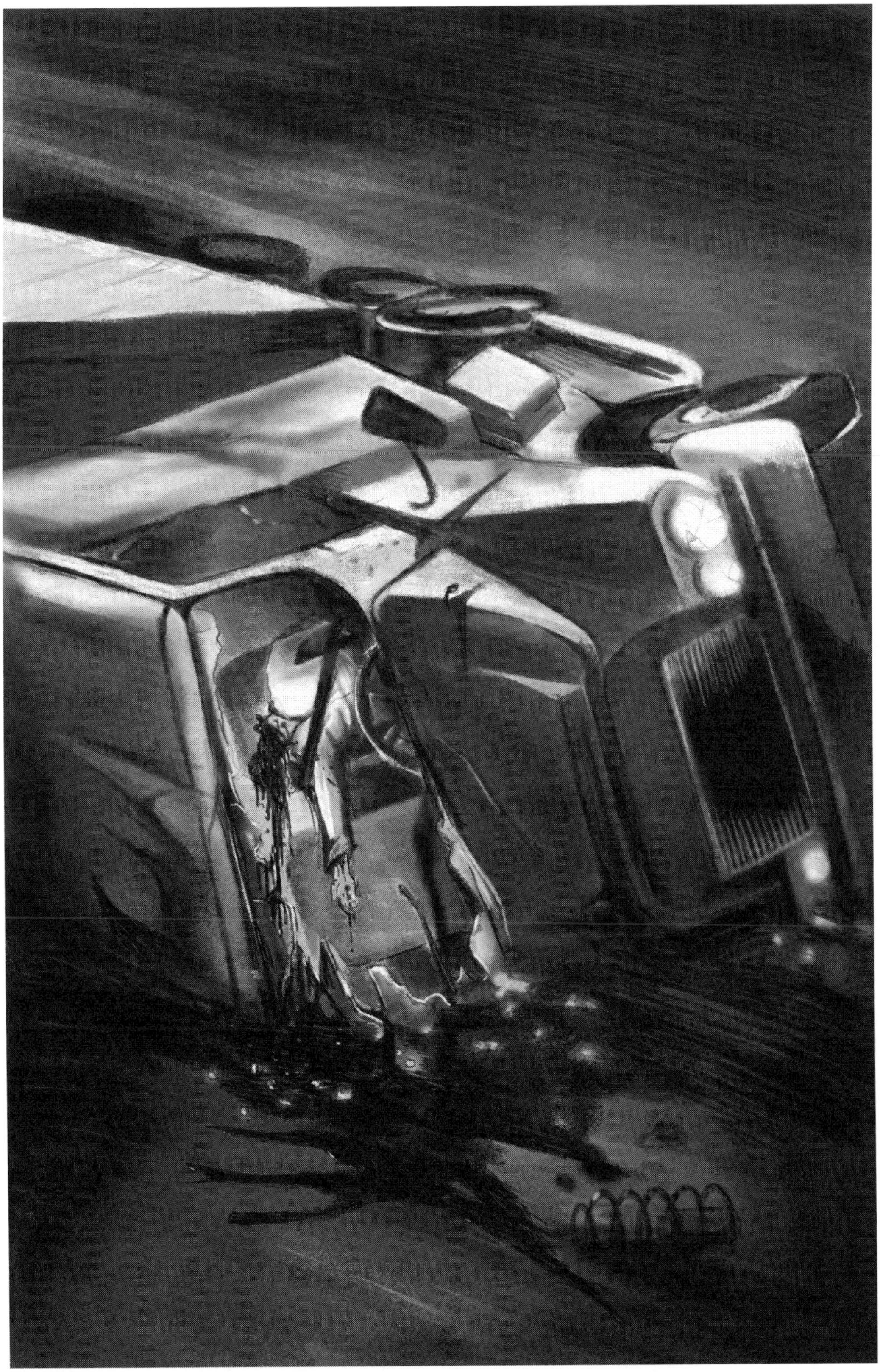

The detective looked back at him for a moment, then glanced over toward the gut-churning sight once more. Floyd's cold corpse was still firmly buckled into the driver's seat just like he was prior to the crash. He would have been in perfect condition, without a scratch on him, except that he was missing his head.

TIMMY'S TEETH

Timmy never really felt at ease around his Pop anymore. Ever since his mom died choking on a baloney sandwich with extra mayo, things were much different. He was able to take a small amount of comfort knowing that she left the family doing something she loved. Eating that deli meat with excessive amounts of smeared egg gel had made her happiest.

But Pop didn't see it that way. He just walked around with this gaping hollowness, like his heart had been ripped out of his chest and hammered into a stringy heap. He had always been so upbeat and positive before, but now things had become much different. Pop had lost the pep in his step, and it seemed like there wasn't much that Timmy could do to change that.

Until, one day, the atmosphere seemed to shift drastically. Instead of puttering around aimlessly, he'd gotten an idea. Pop was a dentist who was disgusted by the filth and deterioration that crept up in almost any mouth. His passions were only for oral hygiene and his wife, but now with the rot having found his woman, his growing obsession was aligned exclusively to his business.

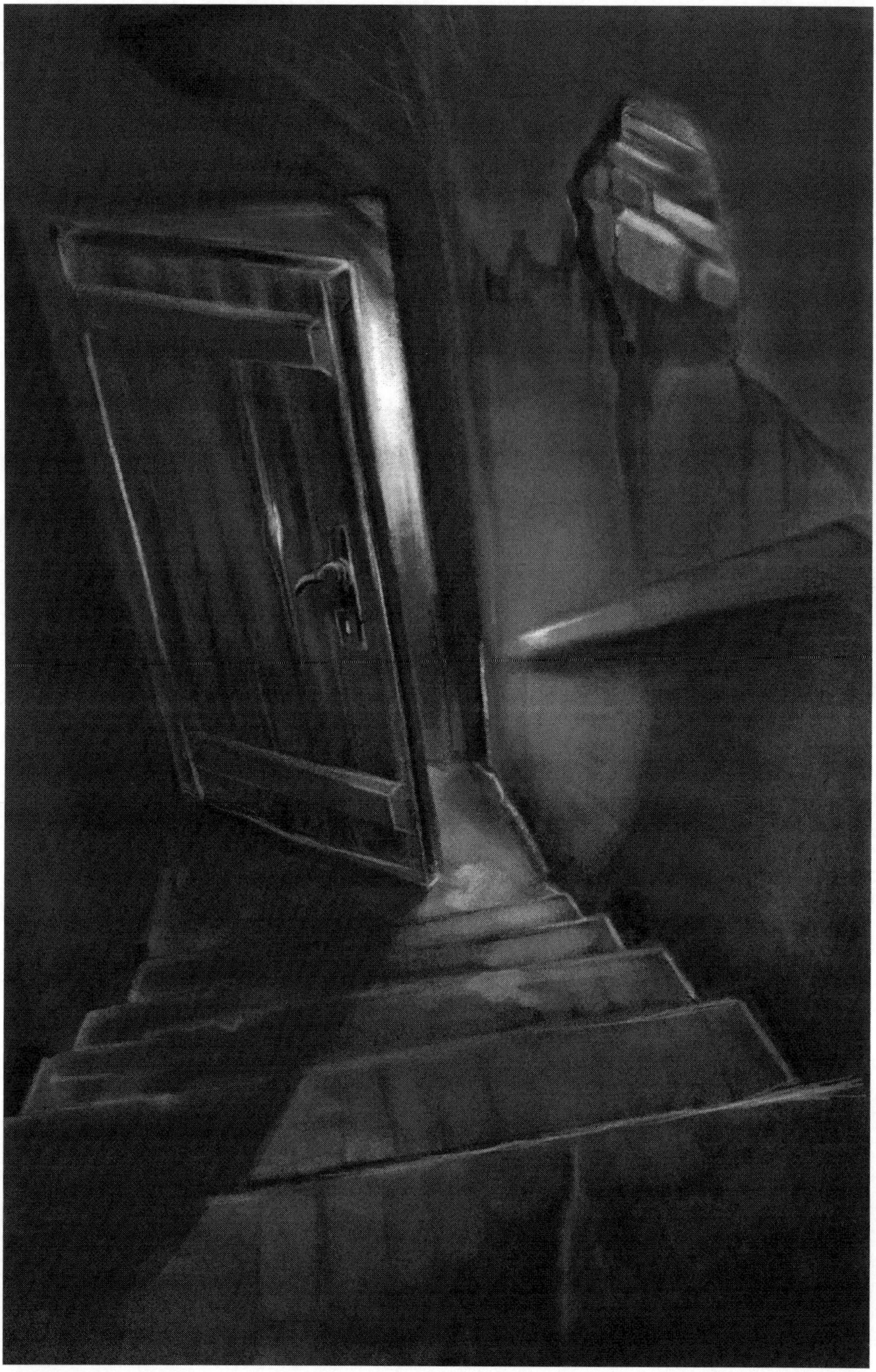

Timmy would sometimes go days without seeing him. Pop spent a lot of time in the basement working on preventing decay. Timmy didn't know exactly what he was doing down there, but on a few occasions, he'd caught glimpses of the "equipment" he was using. It all seemed very technical, foreign to any of the tools or research you would think a normal dentist would be involved with.

With his birthday around the corner, Timmy wondered if his Pop would even remember. He felt almost like he lived alone; every night when he returned home from school, Pop was already in the cellar, and there was a cold order of fast food in a grease-stained bag on the counter.

Timmy could stay up as late as he wanted to and leave the house whenever he pleased, but he never actually did. He noticed the sloppy meals and overall lack of boundaries to be an odd thing in comparison to how his friends lived.

It seemed like it had taken forever, due to the absurd repetitive nature of his routine, but finally, Timmy's birthday had arrived. He didn't expect that Pop would remember it; he knew he'd most likely be busy downstairs.

Timmy was taken aback when he arrived home to see Pop sitting in the living room with his legs crossed, patiently awaiting his arrival. His odd father sat with a single balloon in the shape of a cake that said "HAPPY BIRTHDAY TIMMY!" in colorful font. There was a big wrapped box on the coffee table.

"Go ahead, open it, son," Pop offered, flaunting the whitest smile.

"Thanks, Pop!" Timmy's excitement and surprise drove him toward the package. He tore it open like an animal and retrieved a small note from the inside.

"Your REAL gift is downstairs," the note read. Timmy looked at Pop, his enthusiasm stunted a bit by the notion of going into the basement. It was an uncomfortable area he preferred to stay away from. He associated a certain level of responsibility to the space with the unhealthy changes that had cropped up in his father.

"Let's go check it out!" Pop replied while Timmy reluctantly followed behind him.

When they reached the bottom of the steps, Timmy noticed the area looked a lot different than the last time he'd been down there. A big chair came into sight with a giant table beside it. Many vials filled with liquid, unknown masses floating in jars, and various scientific equipment was present. The one thing that stuck out like a sore thumb though, was the bulky cooler that had an array of tubes exiting it and was draining droplets of brown liquid into a pan.

"Will you have a seat up here, Timbo?" Pop sounded like he was asking but he really wasn't.

"Why, Pop? What is all of that stuff anyway? I thought you had a present for me?" Timmy's heart was beginning to jump out a little more with each pump.

"Oh, I've got a present for you, son. It's so special that you're going to be the first one EVER to get it."

"But, Pop, I don't—" he was cut short as Pop physically lifted him up and tossed him into the chair.

"Now, just stay in the fucking chair, alright?!" The edge in his shouting was enough to play with a psychopath's emotion.

Timmy started to cry; he'd never seen Pop act in that manner before. He was coming unglued, there was an evil twinkle at his gates. He produced a long glass syringe and filled it with the unappealing brown fluid. Once it had reached capacity, he pushed a little out of the tip. "Just smile a minute for me, okay, pal? This really shouldn't hurt that much."

"But I'm scared, I don't want to smile. What are you going to do to me?" Timmy's tender voice shook and more tears purged with each syllable he spoke.

"Oh, Jesus, that's right! I haven't even told you yet! No wonder you're so frightened. What I have here is something that's going to give you teeth for life. That's what I've been working on down here for so long. Once I inject this into your gums, if you ever have a tooth that goes rotten or gets knocked out, it will be automatically replaced with a new one! They'll just keep growing back!"

"Pop, please, I really don't want it," Timmy begged.

"Don't you understand what this could mean, not just for you, but for everyone? This could change the whole practice of dentistry forever!" The horrified look in his pupils did not exude confidence.

Pop knew he would need to restrain his boy, otherwise, he might miss his mark. He set the needle down for a moment and proceeded to strong-arm Timmy. Eventually, he was able to tie both of his wrists to the chair. Pop's gloved fingers then applied pressure, pulling up his chattering lips to expose Timmy's gums. He squealed as his disturbed father drove the thin spike into his pink meat and pressed the plunger until all the fluid had been forced out.

When he woke up the next day, Timmy's teeth were almost twice the size they were before he'd fallen under. Their form had altered too; now they were much pointier and more triangular. He learned of the evolved razor edging accidentally… as he was feeling around with his tongue, it gashed the slimy muscle open, but not before he felt the second row of teeth that was creeping in behind the first.

Over the next few hours, he spat out blood every minute or so since the accumulation was relentless. Finally, Pop made his way down the stairs to inspect the progress.

He looked at Timmy with an even deeper adoration for him than when he was fresh out of the womb. While Timmy choked from the bleeding pool in his mouth, Pop marveled at the overnight magic that had transpired. It was evolving into something even better than he could have dreamed. To Pop, he looked fantastic.

"I'm afraid these are getting dangerously long, son. We don't want them growing too quickly…" Pop realized aloud while grabbing hold of the dental forceps. "Not to worry though, we'll get these out for you. The babies behind should come in less aggressively. This is exactly what I was expecting." Timmy pleaded with him to no avail, but Pop set a firm grip around the elongated razor tooth and pulled mightily. The enamel and dentin cracked as he ripped it from the nerve root.

The fresh cavern quickly filled with scarlet as he dropped the tooth on the table behind him. The pain was extreme, a tier of torture that would easily drive anyone to take their own life to avoid feeling such agony for an extended duration. Pop pinched the gory forceps together a few more times excitedly. "Only thirty-one more to go."

Timmy passed out from the mind-numbing pain just before Pop latched onto the fourth tooth. Pop continued the purge even while he was out cold. His mouth overflowed with warm red, pouring out the sides and all over his chest. Before long, there was a heaping pile of the bizarre stained teeth on the table, and Timmy's mouth was all but barren except for the babies sprouting in the following row.

The next time Timmy saw the light, his ever-emergent enamel had ascended to a new degree of outlandishness. They were butted up right against the roof of his mouth, piercing and prodding the top of his drool slicked orifice. He wasn't sure what time it was or when Pop would return, but he knew he needed to get out of the chair if he intended to avoid any further blackout-inducing torment.

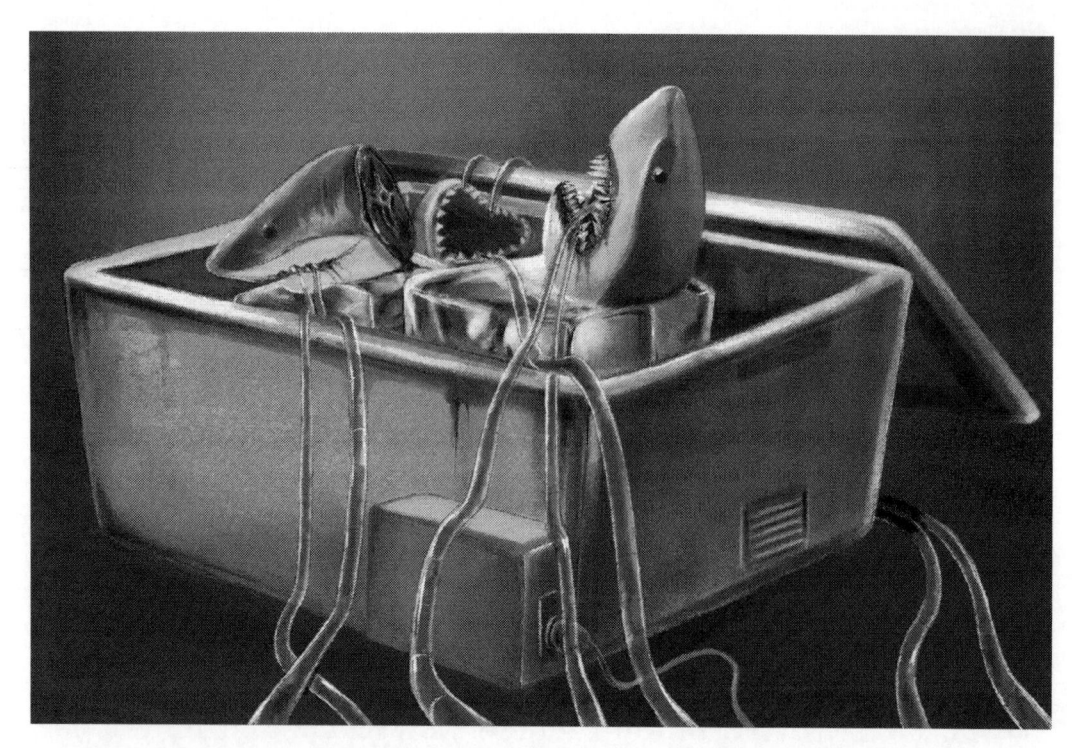

He aimed his stretching and wild razor fangs toward the rope that restricted him. The giant teeth shredded the coarse twine, fraying it before severing it completely.

After freeing both arms, he hopped out of the maniacal chair and looked to the staircase. Timmy's jaw felt like it was cracking open. Each moment that passed seemed to force it to unhinge wider. He looked back to the cooler with the dripping brown liquid—he had to know what Pop put inside him.

When he opened it up, he saw three shark heads. Each had a handful of the tubing inserted deep into different sections of their gums, which guided the secreted auburn river out.

His teeth were beginning to hurt again, they were growing so fast that he could feel them pressing into his tissue. He couldn't break them himself; it was too painful and demanding to extract each one like his sadistic father had.

Timmy needed to find Pop quickly, or it wouldn't be long before the sword-like enamel grew through the roof of his mouth and stabbed right into his brain.

Timmy made his way upstairs and through the door, "Pop? Are you there?" he called out.

There was no answer.

"Pop?" he tried again. The words exited slurred since he could barely move his jaws.

He received no response, just the eerie silence of their home that had grown so quiet that it bordered on discomforting.

Timmy looked almost everywhere in the house. He looked in the bathroom, outside, upstairs, in the kitchen, but his sick father was nowhere in sight.

"Where could he be?" As Timmy murmured through his barely usable jaws, he winced and grabbed them in pain. Just the slightest enunciation created a stabbing pain the likes of which he'd never felt before.

Then a thought found its way into his mind. He hadn't considered checking the spare den. It was a seldom-used room. The same room, in fact, that his mom had been playing crossword puzzles in when she died. When she inhaled her baloney sandwich far too quickly. When an inordinate amount of mayonnaise failed to provide enough grease to slide the oversized mouthful down her eager esophagus.

Neither of them really felt comfortable in the room. They never talked about it, probably because, in their own minds, they had erased the memory of her place of death altogether. Blocking out the memory made it easier for them to be in the house. It allowed them to accept the ridiculous and almost comedic demise.

When Timmy entered the den, he saw the outline of his father. Pop was sitting in his mother's favorite rocking chair, as still as dropped dust and facing the window.

"Pop, would you please take my new teeth out?" Timmy asked in agony, but yet again, gaining no response.

"Pop?" Timmy repeated, taking a few more slow steps toward the chair. When he made his way to his father's front side, he could see why Pop hadn't answered him. He sat motionless and stiff. The same syringe he'd spiked Timmy with was death-gripped by his rigor mortis, and unoccupied by the gross shark extract. Multiple empty syringes also rested beside the picture of his mother on the small table to his right, some of the brown dribblings had congealed below the various needle tips.

His eyes started from the bottom but he already knew what was at the top. Pop was clearly dead, his lower teeth had gored into and forced his head back, leaving it looking almost boomerang-shaped. The mass of jagged enamel, blood, and sliced meat looked atrocious. He was unrecognizable. He was an abomination. He was a god.

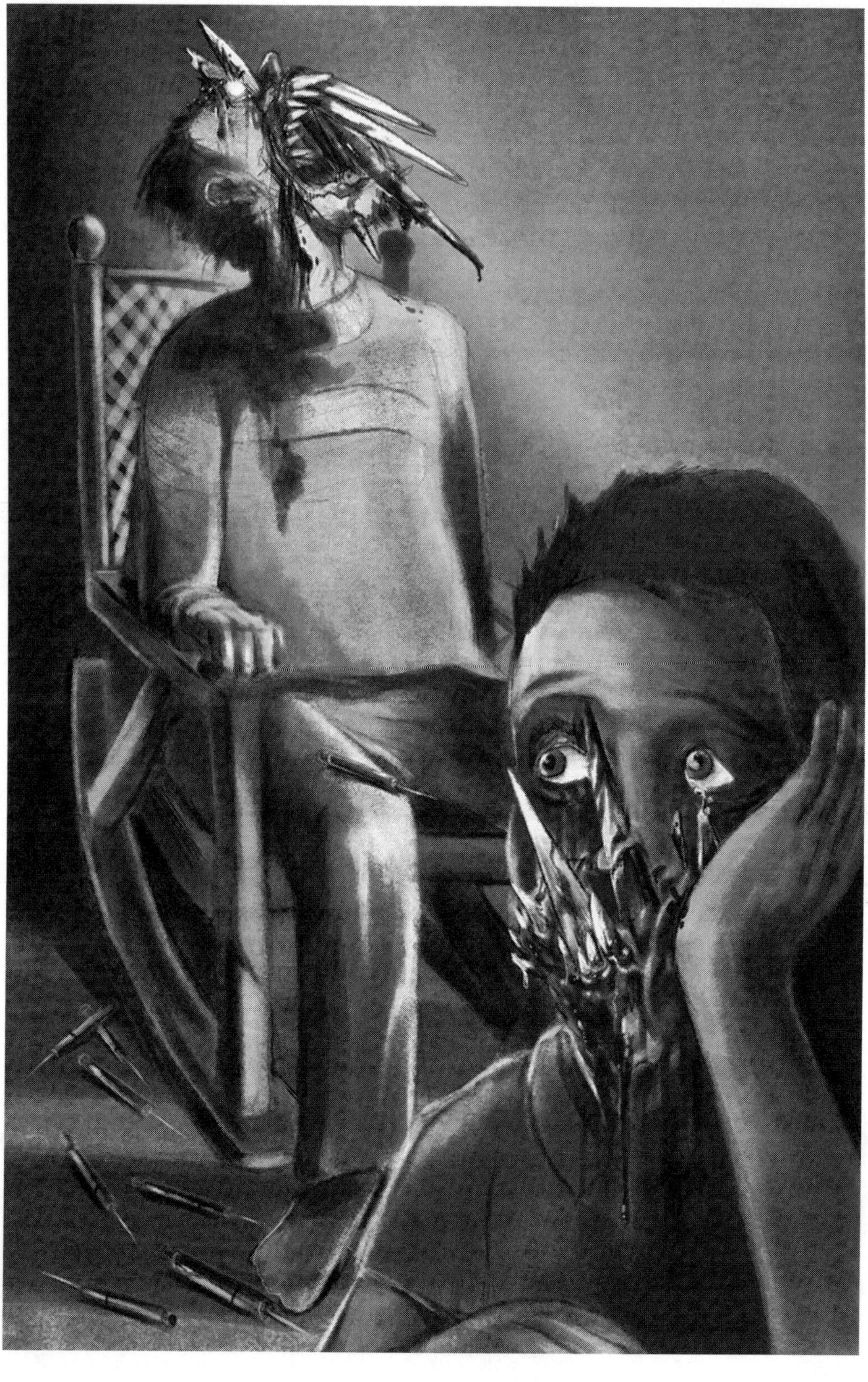

Timmy didn't know how to feel now, but at least there was no more uncertainty. He knew the information in Pop's destroyed mind was what he'd needed to solve his problem. A solution was no longer an option. He quietly marched over and pulled the other rocking chair beside his Pop. It was only a matter of time now.

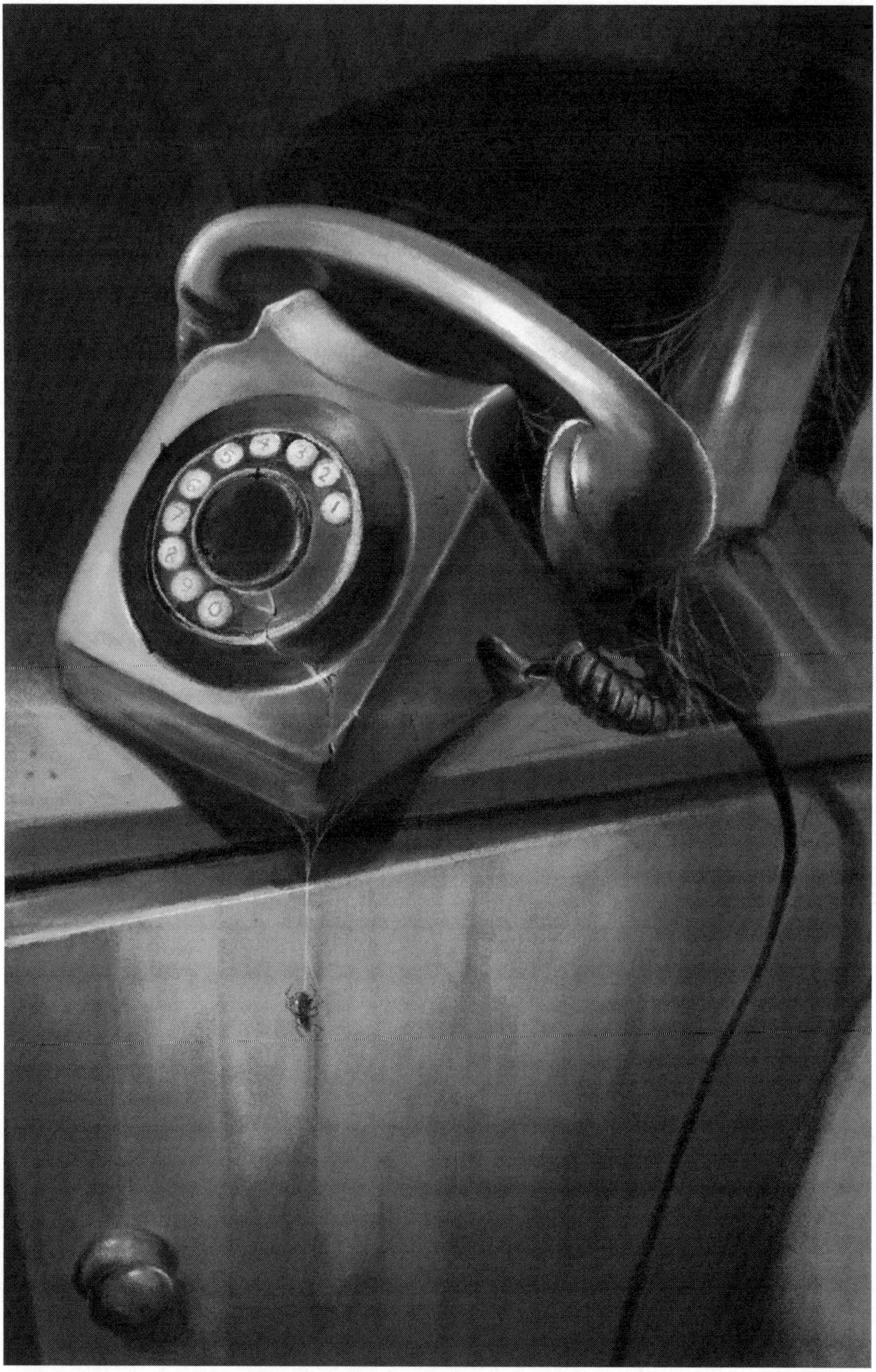

WHEN THE PHONE RINGS

Melanie couldn't help but stare at her shiny new prized possessions. After years of persistent hunting through various bazaars, yard sales, and antique malls, she'd finally found them.

Thankfully, she'd been able to find the classic black and white Kit-Cat wall clock months ago. It was buried within a bottomless stack of retro kitchen appliances and dusty yellowed cookbooks. More than likely, it had been cleared out of some dead person's kitchen with the rest of the crap. Regardless of the item's journey, the treasure was finally hers.

She'd already fixed it to the beige wall above the transparent honey-toned ashtray stand and a square end table. She watched Kit-Cat's eyes bounce left to right endlessly, while its tail wagged in unison. Something about the nostalgia it emitted felt almost drug-like.

The same old perfect feeling of absolute peace and relaxation came over her body, mind, and soul. The same feeling spawned ages ago when she was an ordinary, responsibility-free kid coming inside to relax after playing outside on a hot summer's day. Just like back then, she'd sit in the living room watching the silly Kit-Cat clock's all too predictable antics. It never got old, even though she had.

While she was fond of the vintage clock, in her mind, she knew the picture was still incomplete, until that moment…

As she watched the gentleman from the phone company finish wiring the nearly identical black rotary phone from her childhood, she exhaled relief. It was just like the one she'd spent infinite hours on as a kid growing up, chatting endlessly about the latest school gossip and many things that had evolved into utter irrelevance since then.

If I could only go back… maybe that's not possible but this is about as close as I can get, she thought with a melancholic excitement stirring inside.

The idea had come to her a few months prior—she'd dreamt about the old house and suddenly awoken on a mission. The tedious odyssey that had brought her many unexpected places was over. Finally, she'd recreated the small slice of the home she grew up in.

"You know, you're lucky this is an older house. A lot of the newer ones don't support the switches to run these rotaries anymore," the installation man said, inserting a wire.

"I guess it was just meant to be," Melanie replied.

"You could say that," the man concurred, brandishing a cheesy smile. "Landlines are pretty low on request in residential homes. When I saw the order, I was a little surprised, but I was also intrigued. Why'd you decide to dial up the nostalgia?" He snickered at his own silly pun.

"My dad used to call me from a phone just like this when I was a kid. He worked the night shift, so I didn't get to see him much at the time."

"Well, maybe he can call you on it again now."

"I doubt that," Melanie replied somberly. The pain and heartache in her response was all too glaring.

"Oh… I'm sorry, I didn't mean to—"

"It's okay, you didn't know, I just miss him a lot. This stuff, everything in this little area, is just to help me remember him."

"I think that's really cool. Reminds me of my grandfather's living room." He stood up from the floor and set the phone down on the end table. The dark glass ashtray caught his eye and he ran his fingers over the almost flawless dish. "I take it he was a smoker too?"

"Yeah, that's kinda what did him in."

"I see. Well, I've picked enough scabs for one day I guess," he said with a tint of embarrassment caressing his cheeks.

"Really, you don't have to feel bad, it's okay. I arranged this area to remember him, not because I wanted to forget."

"Right on. I figured you wouldn't want to forget him." He lifted up the phone and checked the dial tone. "Well, you're good to go now."

She thanked the man as he exited her apartment, grateful to be done with the conversation. It wasn't the worst talk, just an awkward one. The install had taken a bit longer than she expected it to. The sun had dropped below her third-story apartment and almost fallen out of sight completely.

Melanie moseyed over to the kitchen and uncorked a bottle of wine. With her glass nearing overflow, she slurped up a mouthful before slumping into her cushy armchair. It was time for her to unwind and relax beside the tribute she'd arranged.

As Kit-Cat looked on, she felt comfort, the small desk lamp beside the phone was a nice touch. Aesthetically, the quaint setup looked like something out of a detective novel—those were her favorite kind of stories. The ones that didn't give themselves up too quickly.

Melanie finished off her wine faster than she'd anticipated and found her eyes drifting away from the new setup to the bulbous orange vegetable that sat on the floor near the apartment door.

Halloween was her favorite time of year. The decorations, costumes, and chilly autumn air left her something to always look forward to. Despite never having known her mother, dressing up and going trick-or-treating with Dad was another reason she earmarked the holiday.

I miss you so much, she thought, getting up out of the fluffy chair.

After he'd left, she'd found herself isolated. Her extended family was non-existent, and making new friends wasn't exactly an easy task. She was just nineteen at the time. After figuring out how to arrange a funeral by herself, she didn't much feel like rushing into any relationship.

She hoisted the heavy pumpkin onto the countertop and then extracted a knife from the carving block. As she plunged the knife's chrome exterior into the orange shell, she couldn't help but think about the times that they'd enjoyed the activity together.

"I wish we could do this just once more," she whispered to herself.

Melanie was grateful that he'd prepared enough to leave her with some money. It was enough that she didn't have to stress about the future. She could've stayed at the house, but it would have been scary living in the same place where she'd found his corpse.

The intermittent chatter in the other apartment helped calm her and convince her of a fictitious sense of community. She wasn't involved in any of it, but it made her feel less alone. Her anti-social disorder had only amplified since she'd returned from Ireland a few years prior.

She had encountered so many new experiences that she was anxious to share with her father. Explain the culture and the food and countless wonderful sights that she'd been fortunate enough to gaze upon.

But instead of sharing her life-changing experience for hours with him, she was confronted by his slimy decomposing carcass. He laid on the couch motionless, coated with a grim expression and covered in a moving maggot marmalade. The flies feasted before being spooked by her and forced to rumble away like cars drag-racing each other down the strip.

As Melanie finished carving the pumpkin, she reached down into the cabinet below and extracted a tealight candle and matchbook. She scratched the match-head against the coarse strip and ignited the flame, then shared it with the tealight's wick. She dropped it carefully inside the ghoulish face, illuminating the Halloween tradition.

She stepped back for a moment and marveled at the creepy rendition. A big cheesy grin came over her face while watching the creepy glow flicker in different directions and bounce off the walls and ceiling.

RING! RING! RING!

Melanie's eyes widened and a befuddled look manifested on her face. She stared at the phone by the gloomy lamp again, still not quite believing that there was any reason it should be ringing. Less than an hour after being installed, somehow, she was being contacted.

RING! RING! RING!

She jumped a second time even though she expected the jarring noise would most likely resurface. The abrasive ring continued as she slowly crept toward the outdated device, holding her breath. She wasn't quite prepared to talk to whoever was on the line.

"Telemarketers sure don't waste any time," she whispered, trying to somehow help it make sense.

RING! RING! RIN—

Melanie pulled the surprisingly heavy phone up and slowly pulled it to her ear. "Hello?"

There was no answer. Just strange noises on the other end of the line that sounded like sobbing and heavy breathing.

"Who is this? Is everything alright?" she asked, unsure of what else was appropriate to say.

The weeping continued for only a few more moments before the line went dead. She slowly set the phone back down and drifted back to her chair. She couldn't help but keep one eye fixed on the rotary, even though it didn't ring for the rest of the evening.

***

It was just a few days before Halloween when Melanie returned home from work in need of a relaxing night. Customer service in retail was a crapshoot. Most days were fine, but others were a nightmare.

When she took a load off in the chair, she couldn't help but glance back toward the phone. Ever since it had rung the prior week, she couldn't help but let her mind wander.

Who was so upset, and why? the question remained echoing in her head every evening now. *Maybe a crank call? Is that still a thing?*

Melanie's social life, or lack thereof, left too much time to ponder. An incident that most would have brushed off moments later was still the top headline for her. To the point where she wished whoever had called would just ring her again so she could put the mystery to rest.

RING! RING! RING!

Before the redundant thought could complete in her mind, the blaring noise once again filled her living room. Her body trembled at the thought of confronting the call, even though it was what she had asked for.

RING! RING! RING!

She summoned a typically evasive courage and raced out of her seat and snatched up the receiver. She was ready to talk, but before her words could be presented, the voice pushed itself into her ear canal.

Between sobs, he spoke to her with an impossible tone, one that had been ripped from her life in grim fashion years prior. "Melanie, pumpkin, is that you, darling?"

Her mind was blown. The final pest-infested, grotesque images of her father invaded her psyche: *It sounds just like him, how can it be?*

"D-Daddy?" Melanie cried quietly as the breath left her lungs almost entirely. "Daddy, is that you?" she asked as tears flooded out of her eyes.

"Baby, I miss you so much, I needed to tell you," he said, pushing on through the sounds of a runny nose and tears.

"I miss you too, Daddy, how did you... how is this possible? Where are you, Daddy?"

"I'm right where you left me. It gets lonely here without you. I know that you've got a life of your own now, and I know you still think about me all the time, but... but..." his voice started to let up.

"But what, Daddy?" Melanie cried.

"But I just wish you'd still come and visit me sometimes," he wept, making the words barely audible.

"I'm sorry. If I'd have known you were still here, I would've... I just... I get so sad. I don't know what to do with myself."

"I understand, pumpkin... I know it's hard. It's hard for me too. When I called you last time, I couldn't even speak," he continued, finding a way to hold it together.

"I don't understand."

"Don't understand what?"

"How is this even possible, Daddy? What happened to you? Are you dead?"

"Yes, darling. I don't know if I understand it either. For the longest time, I kept trying to talk to you. Every moment of every night I tried to call you, just like I used to do on the night shift. You remember that, don't you, sweetie?"

"I remember."

"I just kept wishing for it. I kept wishing I could talk to you. Then one night it just happened."

Melanie stared down at the old creepy phone and a shiver ran down her spine. She wondered how it could be. It had to be the phone, that was the only rational explanation to such an irrational instance.

"I love you more than anything, Dad. I'm glad you're not gone. I'm sorry I went on that trip and left you alone. I hope you forgive me."

"There's nothing to be sorry about, darling. You didn't do anything wrong. You were just exploring and being a kid. I'm sorry I couldn't hang on a little longer for you."

"Daddy?"

"Yes, pumpkin?"

"Can I see you?"

"Of course you can, you can see me whenever you want. Like I said, I'm right here where you left me."

"But how? I mean, what are you?"

"Well, the best I can figure it is, I'm a spirit. But I'm conscious at least. When I died, I remained awake in my body. I wasn't sure what was supposed to happen. I saw a really bright light; it was blinding. Part of me wanted to follow it, the other part didn't wanna leave you. I've just been with my body since then."

"So, there is life after death then? Jesus, this just sounds so crazy," she said, rattling off three back-to-back sniffles.

"I know, it's a lot to accept. But millions of people all over the world believe it without seeing it. They have faith. Is it really that crazy to you when you think of it like that?"

She pondered it for a moment. He was right, but still, the supernatural connection was anything but easy to grasp. There was so much to digest with the unbelievable facts coming to light. It wasn't just specifically pertaining to Melanie's father's mortality and afterlife, but also the solid principles surrounding her own. They were crumbling.

Everything was different, and as spine-tingling as the entire exchange was, it was most certainly a dream come true. A seemingly unachievable dream that she had been kicking around in her head in the form of pure fantasy had suddenly become her reality.

"I suppose it isn't," she finally responded.

"I'm glad you understand. So, when do you wanna come and see me?" he asked, finally regaining hold of his emotions.

"I wanna see you tonight, Daddy."

"Tonight? Really? But isn't it kind of late for you?"

"Time doesn't matter anymore. I never thought I'd get to see you again, I need to see you now."

"Alright then, darling, you can see me tonight. As long as it doesn't cause you any trouble. It's not like I'm going anywhere," he said with a chuckle.

"Okay, Daddy. I love you. See you soon."

"See you soon, I love you too."

Part of her was afraid to hang up the receiver. Would it be the last time they ever spoke? What if she arrived at the cemetery and wasn't able to speak with him? There was still so much uncertainty stewing.

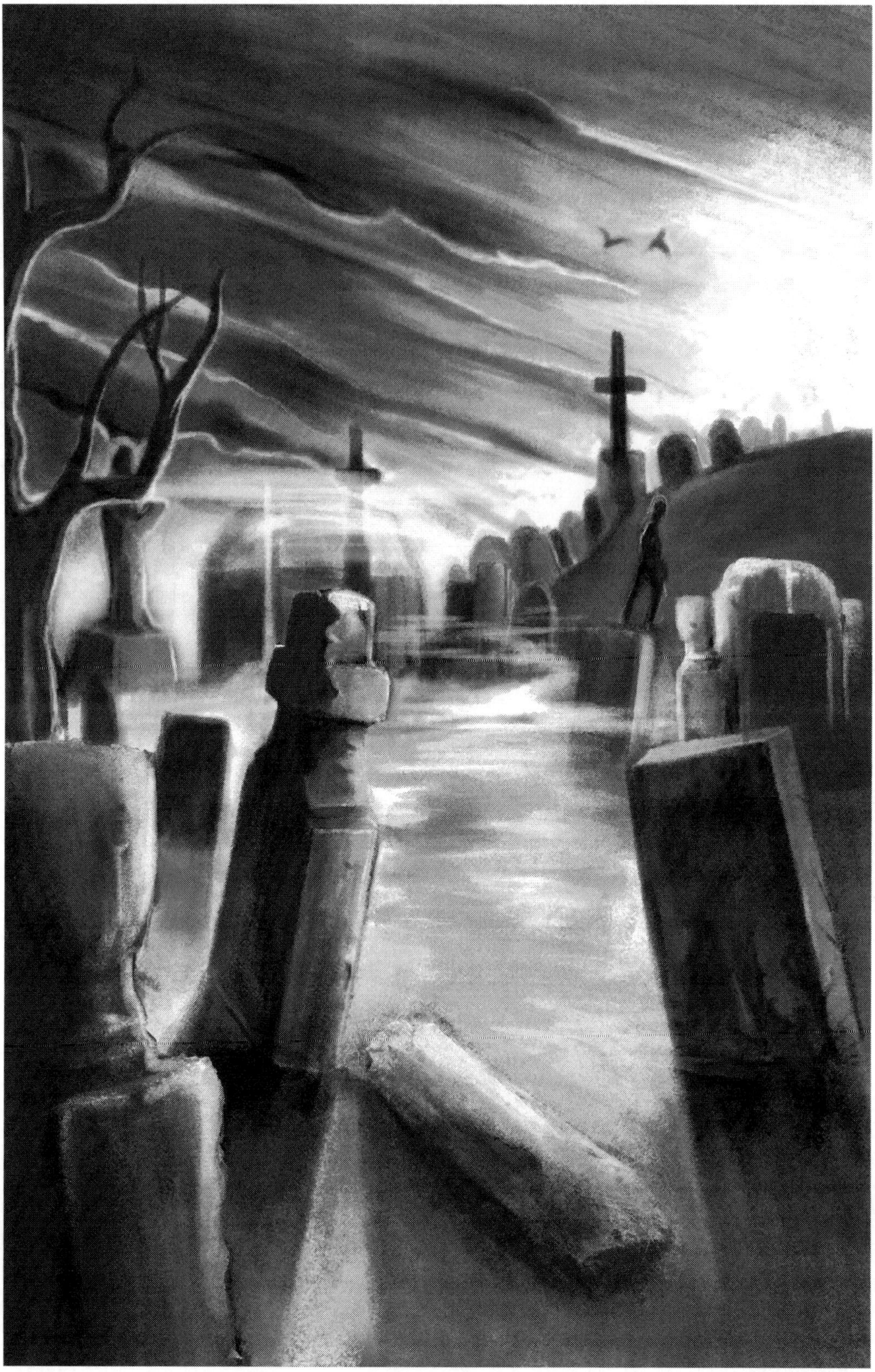

***

The fall air was frigid and painful when Melanie exited her vehicle. Breaking into a gated cemetery in the dead of night wasn't something she ever envisioned herself doing. Yet there she was, amid the oddest of circumstances, ready to do something else she never thought she'd have the chance to do—see her father.

She parked a short distance away from the necropolis in an effort to remain as inconspicuous as possible. She looked both ways down the deserted country road before taking hold of the spiky fence and carefully scaling it.

Melanie landed on the hard ground with each heel square and flat. She was able to maintain her footing and took off weaving her way through countless gravestones. She tore through the darkness and fog, heart pounding but fearless—she needn't worry knowing that there was a light at the end of every tunnel.

The massive oak that was plotted to the left of her father's grave acted as an easy landmark from what she remembered. The last time she was there leaving flowers, the tree offered her escape from the beaming sun. Tonight, it would only chill her bones further and block out the shimmer and glare of the full moon above.

When she came upon his plot, she didn't know what to expect. Amid the excitement, she hadn't really had a chance to think about it much. But she knew what she didn't expect. She didn't expect to see the soil upturned and his rotten corpse riddled with bugs and rodents sitting there for the taking.

"Daddy?!" Melanie couldn't help but shriek.

"Not quite," a voice said over by the oak tree.

Stepping out from the shadows of the dark nature was a face that was familiar to her. A face she'd seen before and thought nothing of. The same face that had been in her apartment installing her landline just a week before. The installation man held a shovel in one hand that was slung over his shoulder, and a sawed-off shotgun in the other.

"You really don't remember me, do you?" he asked just before pulling the trigger.

The hot lead erupted from the barrel and tore through Melanie's thigh, causing the femur to shatter and her leg to cave in awkwardly.

Melanie hit the ground hard, and her upper body fell into the lap of her decomposing father. The shock on her face let the teardrop fall, but the screams that would typically accompany such a violent activity were strangled by dread. All that could be heard was her struggle to inhale and the fidgeting of the meaty maggots and wiggling worms below.

"Gary Cooper's the name. You probably don't remember a nobody like me, but I used to live down the street from you," he explained, taking a few steps closer to her.

Finally, the screams were able to erupt from her chest. Melanie peeked back at her destroyed leg, her blood was flowing generously, and her bone and muscle ejecting in various directions.

"It's okay! Scream as loud as you want! We're lucky that your daddy is buried in the middle of nowhere! And the groundskeeper… let's just say he's not capable of helping you right now," Gary laughed.

"What are you doing! I don't even fucking know you! You've got the wrong person!"

"Oh no, I know exactly who I've got. I worked with your daddy. He was a special man. I listened to him call you every night, the sweet things he would say to make you feel better about being home alone." Gary changed his vocal cadence. "Don't worry, pumpkin, you don't gotta be scared anymore." His voice sounded exactly like her father's.

"How was that?" he asked, allowing his tone to transfer back to his normal speech. "You see, when you ain't got a family of your own, there's a lot of free time on your hands. I can't tell you how long it took me to be able to talk like that. I talked to you most of my life, but you just never heard me."

"You sick fuck! Leave me alone! Just leave me alone!" Melanie yelled, wishing it was all just a nightmare.

"I watched the two of you together while you grew up. You both were just perfect together. I wanted that so bad, but the group home didn't exactly have the same warm and fuzzies. The idea of us being together seemed far-fetched. I prayed to God every night for a sign, but nothing ever came."

Gary angled the shovel down toward Melanie's father's rotten cock, and used it to toy with the maggot rife sausage. The Swiss-cheese-like flesh had gaping holes that were mostly occupied.

"There wasn't no sense in me working overnights anymore once he was gone. I forgot about being a part of your lives and got a job installing cable boxes and phone lines of all things. And then came the sign… God brought me back to you. He wanted us to be together."

"Please, I'm dying, don't rape me. I need help!" Melanie cried.

"Oh, please, don't flatter yourself. It's not about that, it's about something that the two of you could never seem to see. But I saw it, and that's why this is all happening. That's why the two of you needed to be reunited by any means necessary."

Gary aimed the shotgun at Melanie's shaking head, and dropped the shovel in the dirt beside him. Then he used his free hand to unbutton his jeans and unzip his fly.

"All I ever wanted was to watch the two of you. To be a part of your love and everything you share," he explained, beginning to stroke his solidifying cock.

"You're a monster, you sick bastard…" Melanie trailed off, knowing that she was getting weaker from the rapid blood loss.

"Do it for your daddy now, and do it good. If you listen, I'll let you live. If you don't, well, I think you know what comes next. And remember all that shit about the afterlife? That was pretty good, the light at the end of the tunnel and all that?"

Gary's voice snapped over and his face crinkled awkwardly as he shifted back to the dead man's tone. "Well, there ain't no light at the end of the tunnel, it's just dread. There ain't nothing but the insects for you to look forward to, darling."

Hearing the words sickened Melanie and made her stomach rumble in revolt. But there was little that she could do to get out of the horrific situation. It was either take the plunge into the uncertainty of death, or obey and tarnish her psyche forever.

The decision was instinctual. Her survival was of paramount priority that she had no way of subduing. Melanie used her fading strength and extended her arm toward her father's mauled manhood. As she took what was left of his soft pipe in her hand, she felt Mother Nature's minions gyrate and frolic.

As she jerked the wilted member up and down, overfed maggots got bumped off like hearty kernels on an ear of corn being shucked. They fell into her shimmering mane and twisted about, upset at being antagonized.

"That's a good fuckin' girl. Just do as you're told and everything will be alright," Gary continued breathing harder as more blood filled his enormous erection.

Melanie tried to maintain her composure as tears continued to run down her eyes. She tried to forget that her desecrated father sat in front of her and that she was beating the bugs off of his shriveled shaft.

"Now, put it in your fuckin' mouth, bitch. I wanna see you suck him. Suck your daddy dry."

Melanie looked down at the many pests that still peppered the hollowed interior of her father's member. The level of disgust was something she couldn't have fathomed, never mind have participated in. Yet, somehow, the fear of the unknown pushed her further off the plank.

As she suckled on the sloppy pile of vermin and dead tissue, she could feel movement in her mouth.

"Deeper!" Gary screamed, trying to motivate her with the firearm.

She pushed it further and felt the eaters of the dead climb into the back of her throat and tickle her uvula on the way down. She gagged and began to puke a lumpy mash all over her father's lap.

The tears and explosion of acidic barf flowed freely as Gary appeared to be reaching his ecstasy. The veins in his cock were as bulging and furious as the worms in Melanie's throat.

"Fuckin' take all of it! Ugggghhhhh! Keep going… keep going, Melanie, I'm so close. I'm almost there!" he cried as his knees began to shake and buckle.

As the seven roper Peter North caliber cumshot launched out of his dickhole, his hand accidentally tugged on the trigger. The blast unmade Melanie's mug, removing the exterior tissue and the top of her skull.

The gun fell to Gary's side and he focused on the remainder of his orgasm. It was one for the ages that saw the hot milky substance shoot off five more times, leaving Melanie's exposed brain coated in his babies.

When Gary finally finished draining his demons, he felt an incredible weight lift off of his shoulders. Like his life had finally begun. Everything felt so much better than every other day he'd spent moping around the planet. He'd finally achieved his goal.

Gary spent a few more hours lying beside Melanie and her father. They were his only family in the world. Once he'd reveled in the activity enough, he pushed both of their bodies back into the same upturned grave and started to bury them. After filling the grave, he left and never thought about killing anyone ever again.

***

When Melanie realized that there was life after death, she was excited. It was highly limited, but the dead were able to communicate with each other. And she was in the only place she ever would have wanted to be without knowing the circumstance.

It was a little awkward at first talking to her father after the incestuous episode of forced necrophilia. But he understood all too well that she had no choice in the matter. After a few weird and painful discussions, they put it to bed and things felt back to normal.

Aside from Gary coming back to visit them and masturbating on the gravestone every once in a while, things were quite peaceful. They were perfect really. Sure, Gary was evil and Melanie still hated him, but in the end, he'd inadvertently given her everything she could've wanted.

Melanie and her father discussed everything their souls could recall. All the great Halloween costumes, the movies they'd watched together, and the special moments that they'd shared.

Melanie also spent a sizable amount of time telling her father how society had evolved since his passing, which he found quite interesting. While a perverse tragedy had helped them reunite, to Melanie's surprise, death was everything that she could've hoped for.

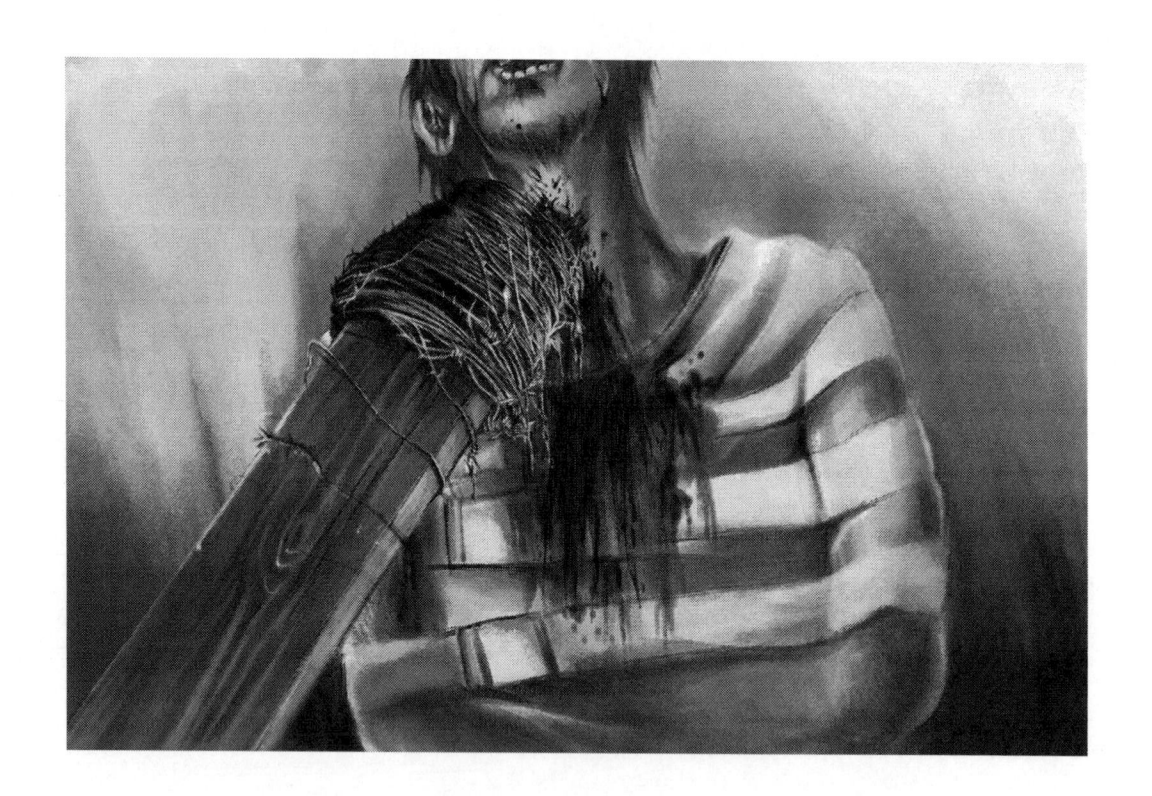

THE RETIREMENT MATCH

Madman Moses was the last person Earl expected to be on the other end of the phone when he lifted it off the receiver. It was two in the morning and he'd awoken still half in the bag on a night he really needed to concentrate on sleeping it off.

Morning was fast on its way and someone had to drive that school bus. Most any bastard that would've contacted Earl at that hour would have promptly received a dial tone in response, but not Madman, not the legend.

They hadn't spoken in years, but Madman's raspy, tortured voice was unmistakable. He'd always had a rugged tinge to it since he'd been smoking cowboy killers before he felt curls sprouting from his nuts. It had become drastically worse after taking a shot from a 2x4 wrapped in barbwire.

As the referee of the match, Earl witnessed the bloodshed firsthand. The particularly prickly steel buried into his Adam's apple and ripped right into his esophagus mid-match. It almost killed the son-of-a-bitch, but he still found a way to finish.

The canvas was covered in every hot juice and pulp his sweaty ass could produce, but that didn't matter to Madman. There was a fucking hole in his throat, but Madman wound a roll of duct tape around the leaky rip and finished up. He was a pro's pro.

The knowledgeable wrestling observer might ask themselves what in God's name is wrestling royalty such as Madman Moses doing in some gimmick blood and guts match? The man was a generational talent, one of the greatest in-ring technicians to ever grace the squared circle.

Hardcore matches, as they're still labeled, are typically when wrestlers with an inferior talent level face-off using a plethora of weapons to destroy and maim each other.

Nothing was off-limits. You'd see everything—garbage cans, barbwire, glass light tubes, staple guns, chairs, tables, thumbtacks, and chains. Anything goes during the indoor street fights for the entertainment of the bloodthirsty crowd.

The cuts, gore, and gashes were usually carefully placed, but that didn't make them any less painful. You still have to get stabbed or sliced to juice. Filthy steel still had to find its way under the skin of the fighter and open the floodgates.

But how could one of America's most popular wrestlers devolve their position to such a freakshow, carny breed of abhorrence? It didn't exactly happen overnight, but it all came quickly and unexpectedly.

Madman's career had taken a dark turn in the late 80s. They say professional wrestling's fake, but anyone who's been in the business for a cup of coffee realizes the ignorance of that statement. Choreographed? Of course. Pre-determined? Definitely. Fake? As David Schultz screamed in his legendary interview after slapping the spunk out of John Stossel so hard that he lost his hearing, "Does that feel fake to you?!"

The years of relentless punishment, savage bumps, and agonizing recoveries had left his body unable to reach its potential any longer. The craft had become a sacrifice. Each match he wrestled was a trade-off with pain, and the devil that drummed it up.

Performing sometimes five days a week for over three decades had taken its toll—he was at a stage where executing a standard suplex sent shockwaves of hurt jolting down his spinal cord. Like so many others that had taken their stab at the business, it was time to pay the piper. Madman's passion had finally robbed him of his well-being.

It's a miserable moment when it dawns on a professional wrestler that his body has gone to shit. The lone tool in their box, their only means to support themselves, and their only shot at being a contributing member of society has been stripped. It's like cutting off a painter's hands, or pulling out a photographer's eyes. When the crowd stops cheering and you're suddenly all alone with nothing but the cost, it's the most stinging of all suffering.

So, there Madman was, at the pinnacle of his career—World Wrestling Division Champion. He could go no higher having attained the most prestigious honor in the entire crooked industry, despite the politics. He was getting the push and given the rub. He was so hot that it was a given… anyone that stepped through the ropes while he was in the ring was doing the job.

His disturbingly fun straitjacket gimmick and the manic expression always gripping his hairy face was everywhere—magazine covers, late night shows, shitty B-movies, action figures, he was *the* guy.

When you're the best in the world, then, suddenly, a piledriver later, you're waking up in a mechanical bed searching for feeling in your extremities, it's safe to say there's going to be some changes. At the time, it was hard to tell just how it would play out, but in the theater of violence, there is no way to predict one's trajectory.

The World Championship belt was vacated due to the severity of Madman's injury, and it was months before he learned to walk again. This is a bridge that almost everyone who steps inside the squared circle is forced to cross, and on the other side of that bridge lies self-medication.

Whether it's pills and needles, or alcohol and powder, you become a sponge for change, a fiend for distraction. As the addiction grows, so does the intensification. If you can't continue to create that rip in reality, there's nothing left, you're mere seconds from madness. It was no different for Madman. He was a few steps from becoming the character he'd created.

Once you've lost the ability or opportunity to compete as a professional for a respectable company, you're exiled to what's called the independents, or the "indies" to enthusiasts. Independents are smaller companies that put on shows with a few hundred people if they're lucky, which usually go down at bingo halls or VFWs.

While the indies can be an exciting springboard for up-and-coming talent, there is nothing so somber as watching one of your all-time favorites trot out to a disinterested crowd at fifty-three years old.

The drastic change in appeal screams out at the audience—the tan skin faded, the bulging muscles shrunken, the flowing mullet thinned out, and a smile erased. The disheartened grumblings of fans filling the venue, replacing the cheers as they realized that the "legend" they'd paid their hard-earned ten bucks to see, is now a distorted shadow of their youth.

A caricature of a caricature. Their charisma having bled out, too inebriated to even work the mic anymore let alone an opponent. They try to talk to the onlookers but their disappointed faces say it all. They find themselves unable to connect with the viewers any longer. They are no longer influenced organically, they are just influenced by the gamut of substances lapping through their rickety system.

This fate that had befallen Madman became so distressing that it sent him into hiding. He'd been floundering on the indies infrequently for a substantial stretch after his tragic fall from grace, before disappearing altogether. Yet now, there he was, randomly resurfacing for unknown reasons. He didn't sound well to Earl at all, not one bit.

"Earl?" he asked, but knew who he was calling.

"Madman, shit it feels like it's been forever."

"Referee Earl Holly?"

"I said yeah, it's me."

"I need a favor, kid."

"I can't wait to hear this, a 2 AM favor huh? What are you calling me from the station or something?" It wouldn't have been the first time he'd called Earl looking for bail money.

He'd seen him burn a lot of bridges with plenty of others. He'd heard horror stories about Madman's out-of-control behavior, but the guy had never been anything but respectful to him. They'd always had this special kind of relationship. Even though they hadn't talked in some time, it felt just like it always had.

"Not tonight, Earl, but it's soon. I promise, it's the last time I'll ever ask you for anything."

Earl considered it for a moment but not really; there was no way he could say no to the guy. The short lingering silence was only for dramatic effect. No matter how crazy the ask, Madman was a close friend that had gone to bat for him. He'd never asked him for shit in the grand scheme of things. Plus, Earl needed to be there for him, mostly because he knew there was no one else willing to take on the task.

"You know you can count on me, old-timer, what's the occasion?"

"I want you to referee my retirement match."

"Retirement match? Wait, didn't you submit to Ricky Star in a loser leaves town match back in '96? I figured that was your retirement being that you ain't wrestled since."

"I did, but that match was the drizzling shits. I'm not going out to a yawning crowd, fuck that. And those World Wrestling Division cocksuckers overshadowed me last time. They just happened to book Wrestlepalooza on the same fuckin' day I choose MY RETIREMENT MATCH? It's a goddamn conspiracy!"

"Madman, Wrestlepalooza is on the same day every year… I don't think they were trying to put you out—"

"Bullshit, they had heat with me since that wrongful injury suit in '87. Imagine that, multimillionaires getting pissy over a few grand getting dealt out to the son-of-a-bitch that literally broke his back for the fuckin' business!? They ain't gonna get the last laugh, I'll tell you that much! I'm gonna have one last classic for the ages, something that peoplc are going to talk about forever. And I'm turning the tables. *I'm* gonna steal the show from them this time. But I need your help."

"Madman, what are you like fifty-five? You haven't wrestled in years, I don't mean to sound like a non-believer, but how could you possibly pull something like that off?"

"There was a time in my life when people wouldn't have questioned me. I understand things change, but the pain don't change. The pain's in my body. This is a roadmap of horror and violence, but now, I'm at the end of that road. I'm closing in on my final destination. So, in case you and the rest of the world forgot, I'M MADMAN MOSES, MOTHER FUCKER, and two weeks from Sunday, I guarantee everyone's going to remember that again. I've already got the venue. You just get the goddamn word out, okay?"

Chills ran through Earl's jittery frame. He couldn't believe that Madman just cut a promo on him. Madman mother fucking Moses just cut a promo on him! As the phone hung up, Earl didn't know much about what he'd agreed to participate in, but he knew one thing—Madman wasn't messing around. He was set to do something special, or at least that's what he believed.

***

The venue smelled of sweat, body odor, and stale popcorn. It was packed; there had to be at least sixty, maybe seventy people. Earl had gotten the word out as best as he could, but he was a referee, not a promoter… what did Madman expect?

The audience was a solid mix of variety that included both adults and children who had sat through a mainly boring affair to that point. Typical squash matches and lightweight bouts jampacked with far too many high spots had been the extent of the card.

Certain members of the docile crowd clapped, trying to hype shit up as best as they could. It was a miracle they had as many people in attendance as they did, considering the biggest show in the industry was transpiring parallel at that exact moment.

Earl stood in the ring stoic with a slight annoyance clawing at him. He knew that the main event of Wrestlepalooza was unfolding on Pay-Per-View as he stood tall on the worn ring apron.

As a fan himself, he felt slightly bitter. *This better be good, I'm missing goddamn Randy Savage to call this shit,* he thought. He was a bit concerned that Madman's opponent hadn't even been announced for the match. *How can you book or promote a match without knowing the freakin' opponent?*

Normally, he liked to hunch over the rope and relax before a match, but the ropes had been replaced with unforgiving rows of barbwire. A variety of instruments that would undoubtedly be used for violence littered the entire ring.

A toolbox, steel chairs, several light bulb tubes that sat atop a small, wooden table, a barbwire bat, computer and keyboard, and an oversized television were just a few of the items that would be in play during his final match.

When Madman's music hit, it still got a pop out of the crowd, and riled up some butterflies in Earl's stomach. "Holy fucking shit, here we go," he mumbled under his breath. Madman came running down the aisle with the same crazed look in his eyes.

He looked bizarre, old, and disturbed. Regardless of if you loved him or hated him, you still didn't want to fuck with him. A handful of creeps that stood by the rails near the stone stairwell in the decaying hall hurled insults at him and spat in his direction.

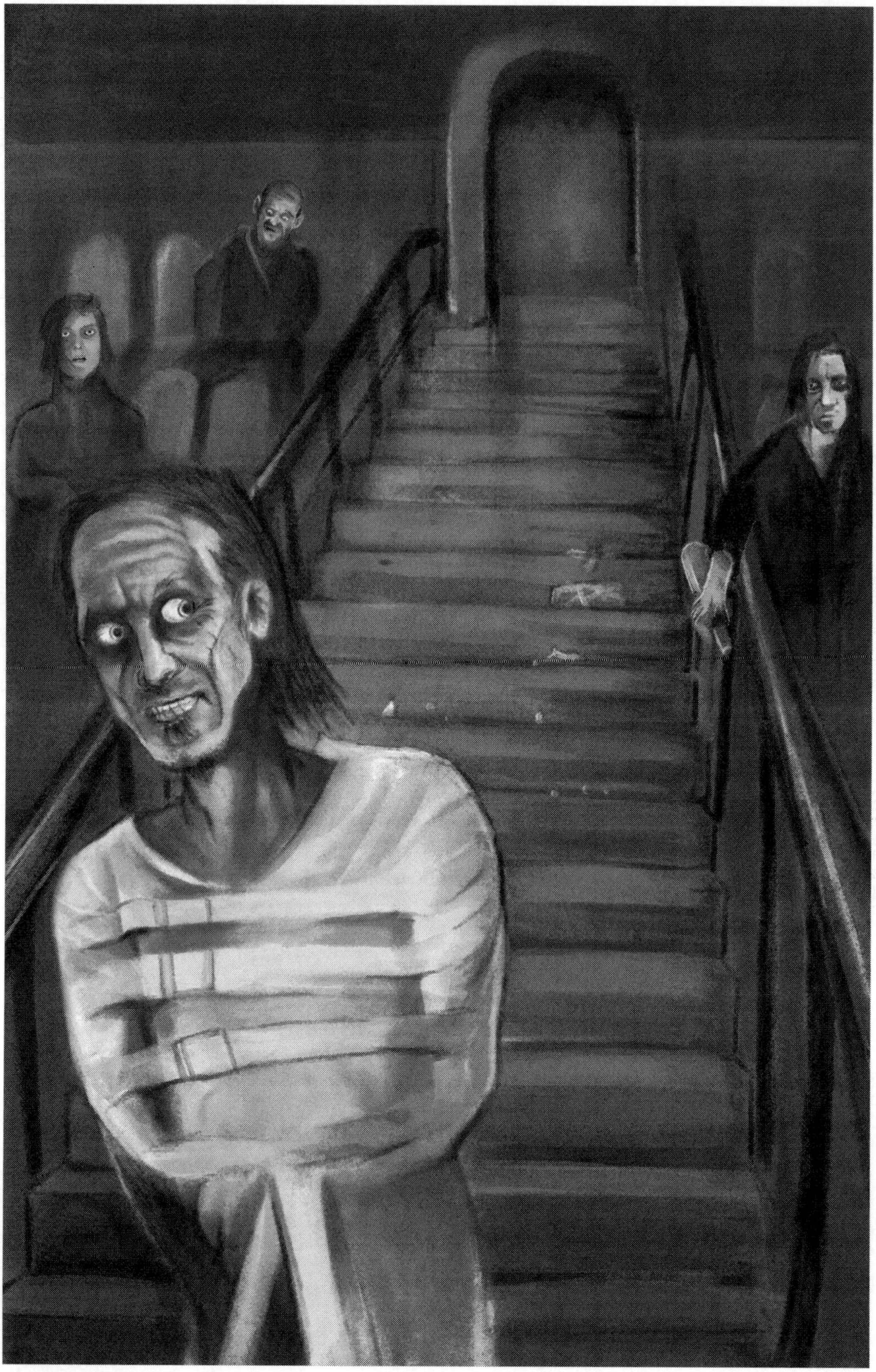

Madman paid them no mind and continued to make his way into the prickly ring, bopping his head in an unhinged fashion to the sound of the heavily distorted guitar in the background. He let some of the frothing Alka-Seltzer tablets he had stowed in his mouth leak out. He looked just as rabid and deranged as he did during his glory days.

When he found his feet in the center of the ring, he immediately began grinding the side of his straitjacket against the barbwire in an attempt to free himself. As the cheap fabric quickly ripped open and burrowed deep into his arm, the crowd cheered.

He didn't have time to start working the other arm. When the entrance music transitioned to the morbid funeral-style track, the audience couldn't believe it. The boredom that had been trapped in their eyes for the majority of the event evaporated. Their jaws slacked in awe, and their asses left the seats.

"That's the fuckin' Gravedigger, man! I can't believe it!" one man shouted at his friend.

Another man's face turned pale as a ghost as he muttered, "I thought he w-was dead…"

"To the wrestling world maybe, but it looks like he's risen again," an obese woman replied, finishing off the last of her hotdog.

His towering frame stepped through the ratty curtain dressed just like the salivating fanatics remembered him. He held the squared-off shovel in one hand, and the dark top hat hid most of his face aside from the rotten smile and chapped lips that surrounded it.

The painful plain shirt and slacks that were held up by suspenders looked difficult to wrestle in. His attire didn't seem to matter though. Nothing could hinder the stoic veteran, not the rumors of his passing and certainly not the fucking outfit he'd chosen to square off in.

As Gravedigger slithered as slow as the walking dead toward the ring, he looked like a horror movie monster that had slipped through the projector at a drive-in double feature. He stared Madman Moses down like their bout had been a long time coming.

Earl was blown away. The match really was going to be something special. Gravedigger had been off the circuit for an even longer span of time than Madman, and he was far more decorated.

He was a twelve-time World Wrestling Division champion that had seen a similar melancholic spiral to the one that befell Madman Moses. When Gravedigger tilted his hat slightly and glared up at the ramp toward

Madman, it was like looking into a mirror. The same faded glory saturated each of their diverse personas. The same desperation thudded inside their chests, and the same conclusive glimmer raged in each of their pupils.

The duo had so much in common and the crowd could sense it. There was a certain level of fright and uneasiness that paraded around the room. No one in the crowd could quite put their finger on it, but they knew what they were about to witness was historic and different than anything they'd ever seen before.

Earl wiped his sweaty palms against his black and white striped shirt, feeling one with the audience. Their emotion and unease connected to him like an electromagnetic wave. As the moderator of the match, he had no idea what the hell was going to happen. Like the rest of them, he would just have to find out.

"No matter what, promise me you won't stop it, kid," Madman said through sudsy gritted teeth.

Earl could tell he was being dead serious, but still not trying to break character. *What in God's name does he mean? I know it's a hardcore match but why would I need to stop it?* he wondered.

"Fuckin' promise me, dammit!" he screamed.

Earl nodded his head slowly, not even knowing what he'd actually agreed to. The sense of terror and dread was suddenly overwhelming. It was the bad feeling that people got randomly, and didn't know why it had gripped them. There was no way he could've.

Earl looked at Madman and he returned his nod, which was also a signal for the bell. The jittery referee signaled over to the teenage nerd that was manning the time keeper's table. The acne-riddled scrawny bag of bones lifted the hammer and tapped it against the bell three times.

Before anyone could blink, Gravedigger cocked back the metal shovel and lunged at the still one-armed Madman Moses. The tip of the burial tool connected with the top of Madman's skull, creating a beefy gash and sending the old bastard off his feet.

Earl was a bit taken aback by the hit. It was stiff as the dead. While guys in the ring that knew each other as well as the Gravedigger and Madman Moses tended to be snug and let the potatoes fly, the kind of reckless abandon that he'd just seen was still shocking.

A crimson mask began to form over Madman's face as he toppled over near the corner of the ring where the red toolbox laid. He wiped the blood out of his eyes and flipped open the lid.

As Madman palmed the flathead screwdriver in his red hand, he truly embodied insanity—he was no longer playing the gimmick. He spat what remained of the fake foam out of his mouth, along with a wad of yellowed phlegm, and used the small table beside him to regain his footing.

He looked at the variety of fluorescent tube lights that were laying in front of him, before deciding that he'd rather stab deep into Gravedigger's body than merely slice the exterior. But when he turned around, the shovel was rising up from the floor and connecting with his chin in an uppercut-like fashion.

The swiftness of the blow sent Madman reeling. He levitated a few feet off the ground and went crashing through the sharp glass, easily destroying the cheap wood.

The crowd cheered rabidly, not really understanding that the blow had broken Madman's jaw and cracked a pair of his molars. The severity was lost in them still, even when they watched the glass cut deep into his exposed arm. The generous flow of blood in a hardcore match was not something that was surprising to see.

Gravedigger looked away from the broken heap that was Madman Moses, and turned to the modest but energetic crowd. He raised the blood-spattered shovel into the air and they cheered with amazement.

Suddenly, Madman shot up off the canvas full of shattered glass and his juice. He'd never lost his grip on the long rusty flathead—he held it so tight that his hand started to shake.

The audience gasped, watching the corroded tip of the tool tear through Gravedigger's side, fitting in between a pair of ribs and running so deep that it lacerated his liver.

Gravedigger hit the ground hard with his hands wrapped around the handle of the screwdriver embedded all the way inside him. The veteran was doing something that he had never done in the ring before—sell. He laid on the mat, twitching in pain and screaming out, praying that the anguish would subside.

Earl watched Gravedigger break character, something that he hadn't done for his entire thirty-four-year storied career. It was obvious why... it was because it was real. There was no way to fake five inches of steel spiking through your abdominal cavity.

The audience still couldn't seem to settle on the reality of it. They weren't as intimately entangled with the sport as Earl was, but it seemed by their pigment-drained expressions that some knew what the deal was.

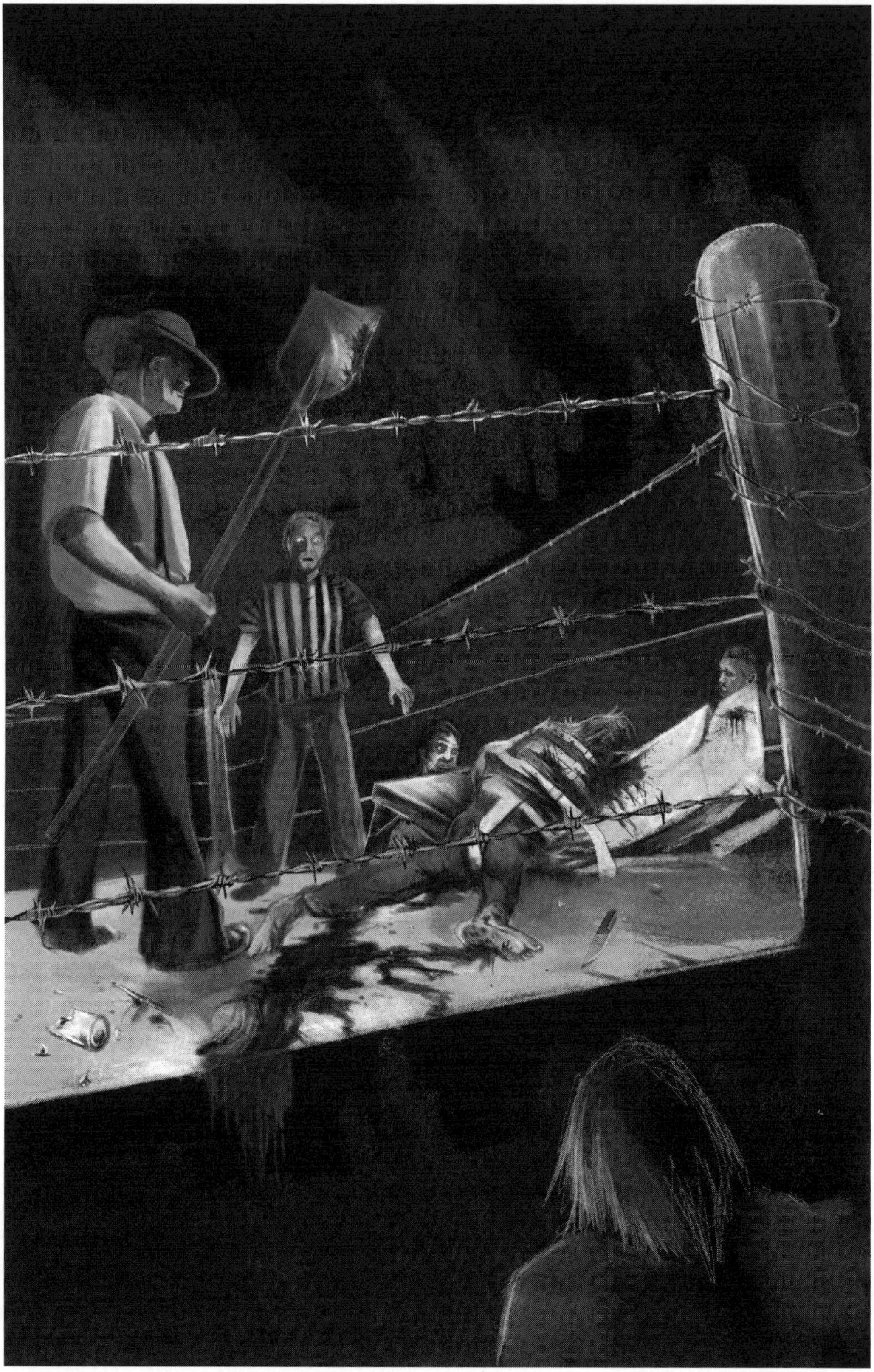

Madman Moses was biting down on the barbwire like a junkyard dog on a fresh steak. He seemed to relish in the gory gouging of his mangled orifice as the crude metal tore into his tongue, gashed his gums, and split his wrinkled cheeks.

He was still peddling his gimmick to the crowd and giving a good show when he eyed the computer keyboard. He picked it up with his bloody free arm as he watched Gravedigger pull the nasty screwdriver out of his mid-section.

Before he could get to his feet, the keyboard came down on top of his head. It knocked off his top hat and exposed the forest of gray hair hidden beneath. The ferocity of the strike sent a couple of dozen keys shooting out of the board and spraying all over the ring.

The more traditional and safer spot in the match seemed to put the crowd at ease. Maybe the screwdriver stunt was just that. It seemed like the wrestling match had reverted back to things that they were accustomed to seeing until Madman went back to the toolbox…

He extracted a pair of needle-nose pliers and held them up to the crowd. Madman dove, wrapping both of his legs around Gravedigger's neck, using the head-scissors to restrict his airflow.

As Gravedigger's mouth opened up to gasp for air, Madman used his shredded arm to clamp down with the pliers on one of his exposed teeth. The ends of the hard metal pressed down and applied the kind of pressure most only felt at the dentist's office. He twisted heartlessly and snapped the enamel at the midpoint.

The sickening crack could be heard by the disgusted crowd as he lifted the fragmented tooth up for all to see. The woozy grumbles resurfaced again. Was what they were seeing just part of the show? The horrified moans emanating from Gravedigger made things even more uncertain than before.

Earl slid down beside the two, forgetting about the glass. Deep slices ripped into his arm flesh and his own blood was now part of the perverse theatrical sacrifice.

"Madman! What the fuck are you doing?!" he barked just low enough to keep the exchange between them.

"I told you, just call the fuckin' match, kid!" he responded, yanking another yellowed chomper from Gravedigger's gushing pie hole.

"This isn't wrestling, th-this isn't you, man!" Earl retorted.

"This is the end, kid. This is going out on top," he smiled sadistically.

As another raw and pink stubby hole was uncovered, the hot blood overflowed from Gravedigger's mouth. He searched blindly behind him for the screwdriver that he'd just tugged out of his side. He needed to act quickly. His face was turning purple and Madman's head-scissors were about to leave him unconscious.

Gravedigger's fingers finally felt the hard plastic handle and curled around it. The cagey wrestler jammed the gore-caked length of steel directly up Madman's rectal cavity. The psycho's asshole aligned to his strike zone perfectly, and upon the tearing penetration, his once tense and crushing legs went completely limp.

Earl's eyes shut momentarily in unison with the disturbed onlookers. The few parents in the crowd shrieked and covered the eyes of their young. Some appeared on the verge of regurgitation, yet still, they watched, fascinated by the display of violence before them.

Gravedigger staggered out to the edge of the apron and looked down at him. The mesh of fecal matter and anal bleeding glued together like a microwaved plate of refried beans and donut jelly. As Madman Moses tremored in agony, he knew he had to set up his next offensive strike.

When Gravedigger could block out the pain flaring in his mouth and pulsating throughout his insides enough, he focused on the tube television that sat a few yards away. If he could lift the son-of-a-bitch, he could do some serious damage.

Just as Gravedigger hoisted up the TV and used the barbwire barrier to balance it, a voice came over the crackly PA speakers.

"Stop the fuckin' match. Stop this goddamn abortion of a wrestling match!" Loudmouth Louie Falcone yelled, trotting down to the ring.

The obese promoter could hardly even walk on his own anymore. The rolls of fat sagging off his face and the balding combover that sat atop his scalp made him look more like a cheap used car salesman than a wrestling personality (although many in the industry would argue that they were one and the same).

As the pudgy penguin-like promoter approached the barbwire ropes in front of Gravedigger, Louie continued his rant. "I said you could have a hardcore match, not fuckin' kill each other. You must be getting simple in your old age. Do you retards wanna get me sued?"

Gravedigger's grip on the TV intensified and a rage boiled inside him. He gritted his teeth and did something that had only been done by his character a handful of times before—he cut a promo.

"It's pieces of garbage like you that live off the scraps of the dying men that gave their lives for this business. Parasitic carny scumbags like you don't deserve the money. In fact, you don't deserve to live. Didn't you always say that you wanted to be on TV, Louie?" Gravedigger asked, hoisting the weighty television above his head.

He used every ounce of his strength to send the appliance flying glass-first into the cheapskate's liver-spotting scalp. The glass broke through and covered his head, forcing his beefy neck sideways and letting another sickening crack erupt out into the stupified audience.

Louie Falcone's last day had arrived—he fell over sideways and all the blood that he'd sucked from the withering legends that had come through his doors, was now being released from his bloated, lard-insulated frame.

Earl knew they weren't fucking around, and he knew that he needed to keep his mouth shut and soldier on through the match if he didn't want to end up like Loudmouth Louie.

He watched many of the people in the crowd scurry toward the exits like cockroaches when the lights came on. Yet there were still a dozen or so who remained glued to their seats, watching the historical bout with a profound morbid curiosity.

By the time Gravedigger got his leaking head turned back toward the competition, Madman had fished the flathead out of his rectum and got hold of a rubber mallet that was calling to him from the still open toolbox.

The shot hit Gravedigger like a ton of soft bricks. He bounced off the barbwire ropes and plopped down on the canvas. There was a tiny brown bag that looked filled to capacity a few feet away. Madman picked it up and ripped it open with his teeth like an animal.

The thumbtacks spilled all over the mat into a pool of hot blood and watery shit that had exited his still tender anus just moments ago. Madman gently rolled Gravedigger over until his mutilated mouth was filled with tacs and red excrement.

Earl watched Madman pounce on his back raising the mallet. He shot down to one knee immediately, "Do you quit?! Just fucking say I quit, Gravedigger!" he screamed.

He wasn't conscious enough to quit. Normally, that was the point in most matches where it was the referee's duty to step in. Protect the fighter from themselves, and allow them to still have a future. But the look in Madman's eyes said there was no future.

"What do ya think we're both doing?" he responded.

Madman wiped the blood off of his face and drove the mallet into the back of his head with everything he had. Gravedigger's mug mashed into the pointed steel, shit-smeared tacs as they embedded in his facial flesh. He hit him half a dozen more times until the back of Gravedigger's skull had a lump for every decade he'd spent in the ring.

He dropped the mallet by his side as the onlookers started to become physically ill. Screams mixed with tears were stunted by gagging and projectile vomiting. No one was having fun anymore. The sick display was no longer a wrestling match. It had turned into something much darker than they could have ever imagined.

Madman seemed to fancy the toolbox still, and removed the box cutter harboring a maniacal grin on his face. He hovered over Gravedigger's backside and grabbed a fistful of his aging follicles. He kicked out the blade on the utility knife and whispered, "I always wondered what it'd be like to be a babyface."

He jammed the blade around the edges of his face and traced the cut around the jawline all the way up to the top of his forehead. Once he'd cut around his entire expression, he buried his rough fingers under the skin flap below his chin, and set a death-grip on his facial shell.

Madman used all of the might in his puny arms to tear the skin off his head. The ripping sound was gut-rumbling. As a few of the vomiting fans got their bearings back from the prior violence, they saw his ruby undertones exposed to the world.

The extreme agony must have somehow awoken Gravedigger from his death slumber again. As the remaining skin of his forehead dislodged, his cries ripped through the ears of the weeping fans. He fell forward and then onto his side. Gravedigger watched Madman don his excrement-stained and tac-punctured persona and yell at the crowd barbarically.

"This is what you paid to see, right?!"

Earl watched in disbelief as he flailed about wildly without a care in the world. As Madman freed his other hand and finally loosened the other strap from his straitjacket to embellish his taunt, a small revolver fell out of the blood-smeared jacket.

Gravedigger, nearly senseless, still noticed the gun hit the mat and brush against his partially numb hand. "Dirty son-of-a-bitch. We agreed no guns," he muttered, palming the revolver tight.

He aligned the barrel to the back of the crazy bastard's greasy head and smiled, "I'm gonna miss you, buddy."

When he pulled the trigger, it was almost poetic, the bullet went in through the back of Madman's skull and launched his brains out of the top of his head. The muddle that was his final thoughts of glory and euphoria splattered all over the face of a twenty-four-year-old virgin boy that was still crying in the front row.

The young man wiped the gore off his face and mouth in horror. He spat out a few hunks and shrieked like a child might. Then he thought about everything that had gone on for a moment, and there was a slight change in his demeanor—a morbid appreciation took hold of him.

The men in the ring had given the crowd everything over the years. There was nothing left to offer… it was the end of an era. While they would all most likely be mentally scarred for life, they were also given something that almost no other fan could claim they'd seen—a true deathmatch.

As Madman's hollow-headed body fell down, it landed on top of Gravedigger, whose breathing had slowed to a standstill. Earl slid into the shit and tacs next to the still-smoking gun, and did what he promised Madman he would do—he called the fuckin' match.

Earl's hand came down and the pain surged into his palm. The sharp tacs stuck into and penetrated his skin. "ONE!" he screamed. He reeled back and smashed it down even harder the second time, "TWO!" he bellowed out.

Earl cocked his arm back, tears in the corner of his eyes, and hammered it down as hard as he possibly could. He wanted to bleed. He wanted to hurt. He wanted to pay tribute to the tough bastards that he'd always idolized. The bloody steel stabbed into and prodded the bones in his fingers. "THREE!"

***

The next morning, the entire world of professional wrestling mourned the loss of two greats, and that piece of shit Loudmouth Louie Falcone. The story of the match made front-page headlines for weeks. The bizarre conspiracy that would push two men to go to such an extreme, just to entertain the fans, was the stuff of legends.

It was so unique and impactful that, moving forward, no one ever recalled the bouts that had occurred during World Wrestling Divisions granddaddy of them all, Pay-Per-View Wrestlepalooza. That year was remembered for "The Retirement Match." Both Madman Moses and Gravedigger had finally reclaimed the spotlight that had died on them decades ago.